REVERT TO TYPE

Colin Mardell

APS BOOKS

Yorkshire

Also by Colin Mardell

Keep Her Safe
Fetch Them Home
Revenge Ain't Sweet
Wolf In The Hen House
Into Africa

APS Books,
The Stables Field Lane,
Aberford,
West Yorkshire,
LS25 3AE

APS Books is a subsidiary of the APS Publications imprint

www.andrewsparke.com

First published worldwide by APS Books in 2024

This is a work of fiction. Names, characters, places and incidents either are products of the author's imagination or are used fictitiously. Any resemblance to actual events or locales or persons, living or dead, is entirely coincidental.

A catalogue record for this book is available from the British Library

GLOSSARY

APB	All-Points Bulletin
ATF	Bureau of Alcohol, Tobacco, Firearms and Explosives
ATV	All-Terrain Vehicle (quad bike)
AWD	All-Wheel Drive
CPS	Child Protective Services
CSI	Crime Scene Investigation
CT	Connecticut
DDI	Deputy Director (Intelligence)
DDO	Deputy Director (Operations)
DEA	Drug Enforcement Administration
DHS	Department for Homeland Security
FYI	For Your Information
GED	General Educational Development test
GPS	Global Positioning System (satnav)
GTA	Grand Theft Auto
ICE	U.S. Immigration and Customs Enforcement
MD	Maryland
PD	Police Department
PFQ	Pretty F**king Quick
PS	Professional Standards (Internal Affairs)
RFID	Radio-frequency identification
SOO	Senior Operations Officer
SUV	Sports Utility Vehicle
UVA	University of Virginia
VA	Virginia
WV	West Virginia

REVERT TO TYPE

Prologue
June 1991

Highly regarded as a CIA field operative for almost ten years, Patryk Wilkanowicz had been deeply involved in the war against the cartels of South and Central America. Then, for his own safety, after his cover identity – Alfredo Gonzalez - was burned with the Latino drug barons, he was reported killed, and transferred to the Russian Section, something he begrudged.

Moving his field of operations halfway across the world made him feel like a rookie, in spite of his seniority. He had no contacts, his relevant language skills were rusty, and his value in the field was thought to be limited. Therefore, he was initially forced to work predominantly as a home-based analyst. Many in his position would have taken that as a signal it was time to move on - there were plenty of opportunities in the private sector for someone with his expertise and skills - but Patryk was, by his own assessment, a stubborn bastard, and he felt he still had a lot to offer the agency he'd dreamed of joining since high school. It wasn't in his nature to take patronizing treatment by peers and immediate superiors lying down. He continued to argue, even with his obvious lack of recent geographically-appropriate experience, that he could still be a useful asset. Eventually, the head of Russian Section agreed to use him as a low-level undercover field agent with responsibilities for gathering simple information.

With Patryk's faultless Spanish, he was a shoo-in to pose as a sales rep for a Spanish agricultural company. They posted him to Moscow, and his cover gave him good reasons to be in or near government buildings, where he could surreptitiously take photographs or make video recordings of people entering or leaving. In the early days, those menial tasks were the only ones allotted to him, but as the first year wore on, his superiors came to recognize that his work product was becoming more and more valuable. The thing was Patryk was rarely a guy who'd stick religiously to his brief, he was someone who would use his initiative. He wasn't just a regular new kid on the block, he'd been an agent for a decade and knew how things worked, an agent who could join dots to reveal a picture long before analysts in Langley even got out of bed.

There came a day when he had an early 9.15 am appointment at the Spanish Embassy with an attaché to discuss importing olive oil to Russia from Ceuta, the Spanish Enclave on the North Coast of Africa. Not his first visit to the building, in fact just the latest of many. On this occasion, the purpose of his visit was purely what it appeared to be. Thus far, none had yielded any outstandingly useful information for anyone in Langley. Nonetheless, as he left the official's office on that day, a small thing happened which would be pivotal to his career and have far-reaching consequences for the agency as a whole.

The brief meeting had gone well, and he came away congratulating himself for finally gaining approval for his attempts to establish a new trade route between the Spanish territory and Russia. It would be a small yet valuable contribution to the economy of the tiny autonomous city. Making his way out of the building, Patryk decided to make use of the men's washroom. If he hadn't, he might have entirely missed it - or worse, come face to face with someone he really wouldn't have wanted to. However, timing is everything, and as he left the restroom, a man he hadn't seen for more than two years, crossed the foyer in front of him. The man was someone he would never have expected to have seen in Russia, let alone in the Spanish Embassy, someone who knew his true identity.

Intrigued by what the man could be doing there, he held back, and watched. Following someone inside a building without being spotted is normally problematic, but on this occasion, it was simplified because the man climbed the stairs, turned left and entered the very same office suite he had himself left only a few minutes earlier.

The man's name was Wilson Perry and he was a junior staffer at Blair House, 1651 Pennsylvania Avenue, Washington DC, the State Department HQ. His job title was Senior Technical Specialist (Transport), which Patryk translated as Carpool Manager. His job was to ensure provision of the correct transportation for senior officials and visiting dignitaries where and whenever required. The only reason for Patryk to have any awareness of Wilson at all, was because they'd been neighbors. Three years earlier, their houses had been across the street from each other, and occasionally they'd pass the time of day on those rare occasions when Patryk was in the country. Soon after his appointment, Wilson had boasted about his new employment being *at the heart of government* and Patryk had congratulated him and told him that his own job was as a travelling salesman in bitumen products.

Having established who his old neighbor had been to see in the embassy, Patryk left the building but instead of returning to his apartment as he'd planned, he waited in his car. He was already over the limited parking time, and it was important not to draw attention to himself by getting a fine, so he cursed when he saw a parking inspector enter the street. He had a pre-paid annual ticket, but it didn't exempt him from time restrictions.

He started the engine and pulled away from the curb, hoping that he'd be able to park nearby again then run back to watch Perry leave the building. He dumped that idea straightaway, because if he returned on foot, and his prey was in a car or a cab, as was most likely, he'd lose him immediately. His only other option was to drive around the block and hope he didn't miss him.

On his third lap he found himself behind a cab that stopped outside the embassy, blocking the narrow one-way street. Moments later Wilson Perry emerged and furtively looked each way before stepping into the waiting vehicle.

From Patryk's point of view, even with his years of experience, he couldn't have timed it better. The cab moved away, and he followed behind, allowing two cars to get between them when they turned into the next road. When they crossed the Moskva River, he was expecting a long journey, but that idea was discarded when the cab pulled up outside the Hotel Ukraina, a five-star luxury hotel in the Radisson Group which would be expensive, even with exchange rates as they were. There was no way it was legitimately coming out of Uncle Sam's pocket. Neither would a low-ranked public servant normally be able to afford it.

He drove past, turned and parked up. Even if Perry was only visiting a guest or attending a meeting, his presence there was suspicious. Patryk knew that he should report his sightings to his controllers, and then do no more without authority, but instinct told him that waiting for a response from those up the line might cause him to miss something important. Walking back to the hotel, he approached the reception desk and using broken English with the Latino accent he'd perfected in his previous existence he asked, "I believe you have a package for me from Senor Perry. I believe he's a guest here."

The clerk smiled and said, "Let me look, sir. What is your name?"

"Senor Alfredo Gonzalez."

The clerk tapped at the computer terminal in front of her. "I'm sorry, sir, we don't have any packages for you, nor a guest registered under the name Perry."

"That's strange, I was sure he said he was staying at the Radisson."

"Is it possible he's staying at the Olympiyskiy or Belorusskaya hotels? They're both in the Radisson Group."

He knew then that if Perry was staying there, he was using a different name. "That must be it. I'll call him. May I use your bar while I'm here?"

"Yes of course, sir."

There was no need for directions, the entrance to the huge lobby restaurant-bar was obvious. As he stood at the entrance, a greeter offered to find him a table, but he indicated he was searching for a friend. It didn't take long to spot Perry seated at a small table with another man whose face was obstructed by a nearby column.

Taking a table by a window about twenty feet away, he sat so he was sideways on to the men he was observing. Making a video would have been far too obvious, and possibly not allowed in the exclusive building. So, making great play of taking still photos of the view from the window, but with the camera set to front-facing, he managed to get some good shots of both men over his shoulder.

"What can I get you, sir?" a waitress asked in English, before he could examine the pictures.

"Oh, yes thank you. I'll have a white coffee, and two blinis with honey please." He paid with cash, so he could leave whenever he was ready.

Once she'd gone, he took a closer look at his snaps. Zooming in on the face of the man at Perry's table, he got his second surprise of the day. It was someone he knew almost as well as the members of his own family, even though they'd never met. The man was Juan Esteban, and the last time they'd crossed paths he'd been a senior tenientes, or lieutenant, in the Colombian drug cartel La Familia Rojo. Following the death of its leader, and the arrest of most of its lieutenants, the ultra-violent gang had been broken up, in a successful operation in which Patryk himself had been instrumental. Esteban had slipped the net.

In Patryk's view any link between these two people had to be bad news in and of itself, but when you added in a Russian connection, it was potentially a major discovery that deserved an urgent and serious response.

While he waited for the waitress to return he sent a message to his Langley handler via an opaque circuitous chain of international servers:

> *Look who I spotted living the high life at the Hotel Ukraina this morning. Two good friends of ours. You remember John Stevens of the red company, and our very own transport manager at the country division. Looks like they've been doing business locally too.*

He attached the photograph and sent it. It was 4 am in Washington, only the night agent would see it. He'd given it Level 3 priority, which meant that it wouldn't be looked at for another four hours. There were five priority levels: *1. Urgent, immediate attention/action required. 2. High, attention/action required within 24 hours. 3. Medium, advice required. 4. Low, consider action. 5. Information only.* Patryk knew that if he'd given it any higher priority, he'd be accused of overreaction. He suspected that might yet be the case.

The waitress brought his order, and he took his time with it. They were talking Spanish, but as hard as he tried, he couldn't hear much of what they were saying, but enough to know that the subject involved olive oil, cocaine, armaments, and, interestingly, *Ceuta*. Were they going to attempt to use the supply route that he'd just established, to transport contraband?

He ate the blinis, and drank half his coffee when, reflected in the window, he saw Perry stand up and offer his hand to Esteban, who waved it away. Leaving the rest of his drink, Patryk rose casually to follow, hoping to get Perry's cab number, and once again luck was with him; he overheard Perry ask the driver to take him to the Olympiyskiy.

Driving to the hotel at his own pace, made it impossible for Perry to spot the tail, although Patryk doubted that he would have anyway. Leaving his car in the underground hotel car park, he took the elevator to the entrance lobby, and waited near the desk for a quiet moment.

"I'm sorry to bother you," he said to the clerk, "Was that Jonathon Woodgate I saw come in just now. I'm a huge soccer fan, and I was sure it was him. Used to play center-back for Real Madrid. I saw him score a fantastic goal against Barca - amazing."

"I'm sorry, sir I can't give you information about our guests."

"Absolutely, I understand. I shouldn't have asked. I didn't want to speak to him, I just wanted to tell my wife that I'd seen him. She once had the biggest crush on him."

"If it helps, sir, we have nobody of that name staying at the hotel at the moment."

"That's a shame, thank you. He's probably staying under a different name."

"Unlikely, sir, we're obliged to register our guests under their passport names."

"I understand. I know he sometimes used to travel under his birth name, Wilson Perry. He's probably using that."

The clerk's momentary change of expression told Patryk he'd been right. "I couldn't say, sir."

He returned to his car and called the night desk at Langley, "I need someone to look at the guest list of the Radisson Blu Hotel Olympiyskiy and tell me what room Wilson Perry is using. Also, if he has anyone staying with him."

"What, now?"

"Yes, now."

"I thought your message said this was a Level 3 Priority."

"It is for you lot in Langley, but for me this is a definite Level 2. Are you going to get the information for me or not?"

"I'll ask someone in intelligence to do it. How soon do you need it?"

"Eleven hundred your time."

"Do you need any hardware?"

"Not at the moment, I'm fully kitted out."

Patryk returned to his apartment and adopted one of the disguises he used from time to time. It was nothing elaborate, just some pale theatrical cosmetic foundation to make him look older, a wig, and a change of clothes. Ignoring the online booking sites, he phoned the hotel direct, hoping they'd have a room free for the night. It wouldn't be the end of the deal if they didn't, but it would simplify things. As it happened, they did have two rooms free, an executive suite and a family room. He chose the family room because it was the cheapest, knowing that he'd still have to fight to be repaid in full. 'Fuck it,' he thought, convinced he was onto something significant. If needs be, he'd cover the cost himself.

He drove to Raikin Plaza, a large mall in the city, parked and caught a cab to the hotel, checking in using his new persona, Roger Parkinson, an aging Australian with greying ginger hair, an Akubra hat and a walking cane. When the desk clerk offered to provide help with his case, he accepted while he went for a drink in the bar.

After a cold beer and a sandwich, he returned to the lobby. He took a seat where he could watch people coming and going, whilst pretending to read a newspaper.

It was ten past five when the text message arrived.

Your friend is in Room 406, and travelling alone.

By seven-forty Patryk had begun to suspect that Perry was in for the night but then his quarry appeared from the elevator lobby and headed for the door. That was the signal for him to go to his room, where he took off his jacket and took a glass of water. He lay down on the bed and poured the liquid all over his pants making sure to get plenty on the bed sheets, picked up the internal phone and called the desk to explain that he'd fallen asleep with a glass of water in his hand and spilled it over the bed linen. They told him they'd send a maid to change the sheets. He knew they'd think he'd pissed the bed but he didn't care.

It was over an hour before two housemaids arrived. They knocked on the door and he let them in. They didn't speak any English, so when he attempted to make an embarrassed explanation, they just smiled. On the pretext that he was waiting outside for them to finish, he stepped outside and found exactly what he'd been hoping for, a master key attached to the handle of their trolley on a spiral keychain.

There were cameras in the corridors, so he needed to disguise his actions. He gripped the trolley's handle as if he were unsteady on his feet and faced the wall, knowing that he wouldn't have long to complete his task. He quickly inserted the card into a device he'd been hiding behind his back, to create a cloned copy, completing the task only moments before the maids re-emerged and signaled that he could go back inside.

Waiting long enough for the two domestics to leave the floor, Patryk left his room, and summoned an elevator. Descending only one floor, and maintaining his appearance as an elderly man, he made his way to room 406. Then, after checking there was no outward sign that Perry had employed a simple ruse to see if anyone had been in the room, he let himself in.

He didn't credit Perry with any level of tradecraft, but he was taking no chances as he quickly searched the room and travel bags. He photographed everything of potential evidential value and replaced it all in exactly the position it had been in before. The speedy yet painstaking process only uncovered one piece of evidence to confirm his suspicions, but that one thing alone justified his actions. It was a printout of a statement from the Cay Heritage Bank Ltd, based in Belize. The account was in the name of Perry Wilson, and there had been a deposit of $20,000 two days earlier. He grinned at the pathetic attempt to disguise the account's ownership by reversing his first and last names, photographed it and put it back it in the envelope with the Radisson Hotel Ukraina logo on the outside and replaced it.

After searching for a suitable position, he placed a tiny microphone on the underside of the table that held the coffee maker. An opened bottle of Macallan 15-Year-Old Single Malt Scotch and a used glass were already there. Reaching into his pocket he took out a small sachet of powder and emptied it into the bottle. Unless he had a rare allergy, the Rohypnol would be unlikely to cause harm, but coupled with the alcohol, it would put him to sleep for a few hours, enabling Patryk's final chore later in the night.

After taking one last look around, he took his walking cane from where he'd left it and opened the door. As he heard the lock click behind him, he heard a quiet ding and the whisper of elevator doors sliding open. Wilson Perry and an extremely beautiful woman in her mid-twenties, wearing a cocktail dress and tall heels stepped into view ahead of him. He ignored them as they passed, and he doubted they even registered his existence.

Back in his room, after dispensing with the wig, he opened an app on his phone and began listening to the chat he'd been recording between Perry and the woman, clearly a high-priced prostitute. He was congratulating her for bringing him luck at the roulette wheel, and in her heavily accented English she was asking him how much he'd won.

Perry boasted that he was a responsible gambler, who never bet more than he could afford and knew when to quit. He told her that he'd bought a thousand dollars' worth of chips and come away when he was $8,000 ahead and in the company of the best-looking girl in the room.

She responded by telling him that she was pleased to have helped, and asked if his wife would be happy with his success. He told her that he was divorced so spending the night with her would be an entirely guilt free way to use his last night in Russia.

"How much is tonight going to set me back sweetheart?"

"Three thousand United States Dollars for one whole night," she told him. "It's good bargain, yes? I give you discount because you already give big tip."

"You come with great references, so I think it's a good deal. You want another drink baby?"

"Maybe very small one. I have two tonight already. You want little blue pill; help give Anya good time too?"

"Why not. Make it two."

'What a dumb bastard,' Patryk thought, 'Alcohol and Viagra? It's like taking uppers and downers at the same time.' He continued listening to their activities and couldn't help laughing at Perry's pathetic attempt at romancing the girl into doing what she'd already agreed to do in exchange for money.

An hour later, Anya had given up her attempts to raise an erection from him, and Patryk fully expected her to get dressed and go home. However, it seemed that Anya had either succumbed to the Rohypnol herself or was a hooker with a conscience who had decided to stay and fulfill her side of the bargain.

By twelve-thirty he decided it was time to complete what he'd set out to do. He refreshed the makeup, and re-donned the wig, before making his way back to Perry's room and letting himself in as quietly as possible.

Once inside the room he put on a medical face mask. Thankfully, the pair had left one of the bedside lamps switched on so he could see straightaway that both were asleep. Perry was snoring and the naked Anya lay beside him. There was no way to tell how either might be affected by the drugs, but he gambled that the man was at the very least in a deep drug and alcohol induced sleep.

When he clamped a hand over the girl's mouth, she became instantly awake, her eyes wide with fear. Patryk held his index finger against his mask indicating silence and when she nodded, he handed her two €200 notes and pointed to her clothes on the floor. She nodded again, took the money and hurried to the bathroom, picking up her clothes on the way. While she was in there, he found Perry's wallet by the bed, removed all the notes and handed them to Anya as he let her out of the room. She grinned like the Cheshire cat and hurried away.

Patryk knew that even if she decided to report him, he'd be long gone before anyone came. Lifting his victim's cellphone from beside the bed, he plugged in a flash drive and waited until the small light on the end had stopped flashing. After slipping the little device back in his pocket, he used a different flash drive and did the same thing with the unconscious man's laptop. Then he returned to his room and listened out for anyone coming to Perry's aid. There was nothing.

Making use of the room that he'd paid for, he slept well, undisturbed by any alerts from the bugs he'd planted in Perry's room or phone. Worryingly he'd had no contacts from his controller in Langley either. He had no intention of spending another night in the outrageously expensive hotel, even if a room had been available, but thought he'd avail himself of the inclusive breakfast before he left. It was gone nine when he got the first alert on his phone that Perry was awake.

He was making a call to someone speaking Spanish, Patryk assumed it was Esteban, but wouldn't be certain until someone analyzed the call data.

> *Esteban: What the fuck do you want.*
> *Perry: That bitch you put me onto last night has ripped me off.*
> *Esteban: What the fuck do you want me to do about it?*
> *Perry: She drugged me and cleaned me out.*
> *Esteban: She take your cash, anything else.*
> *Perry: No, I don't think so.*
> *Esteban: What she drug you with?*
> *Perry: She said it was Viagra.*
> *Esteban: Her drugs then?*
> *Perry: Yes.*
> *Esteban: (Laughing) You took somebody else's drugs, and you wonder why you got ripped off. Jesus you're a fucking dumb cunt.*
> *Perry: Tell me where to find her. I've missed my flight and I need to get my money back to get another ticket.*
> *Esteban: Listen to me you stupid asshole, that piece of ass is protected, if you went anywhere near her, you'd end up with your throat cut. Buy yourself another ticket.*
> *Perry: When will I get my next payment?*
> *Esteban: When you start producing something.*
> *Perry: But I'm out, can you give me enough to cover my flight?*
> *Esteban: I gave you five grand when you arrived. You got yourself into this mess. If you can't get yourself out of it you'll be no use to me. Now fuck off and don't call me again, I've given you the rules. You'll be contacted when you're back in the US.*

After finishing his breakfast, Patryk caught a cab back to Raikin Plaza, paid the parking fee, drove home, showered and changed. Before returning to his day job, cold-calling potential users of Spanish agricultural products, and patrolling the areas around the Moscow government buildings, he listened to the calls that Perry had been making.

Patryk didn't know how much cash there'd been in Perry's wallet, but it was well over the alleged $8,000 winnings, and from the desperation in his voice, it was obvious that without that money he was in a fix.

He couldn't tell how much time Perry had spent trawling the Internet for a cheap flight home, but he was now reduced to making phone calls, none so far been at a price he felt he could afford. He finally accepted a ticket with a cheap agent, but it wasn't for eight days, and Patryk heard him tell the agent that he'd lose his job if he weren't back in three days.

Then he overheard Perry call his Boss at Blair House and admit that he hadn't been attending his grandmother's funeral in Atlanta, like he'd claimed when applying for leave, but had actually taken a break to Italy, and been robbed. The fictional robbers had taken not only his wallet with all his cash, but they'd maxed out his cards.

"You're skating on thin ice Wilson. This isn't the first time you've done this, and I don't appreciate being lied to. I'll give you a few more days, but if you're not back at work by Monday, that's it."

"Thanks George, I'll do everything I possibly can to get back there."

Patryk smiled; this was music to his ears. He stopped listening and drove to a wheat exporter he'd been cultivating. His aim was to attempt to close a deal in providing 100 tonnes of wheat to European Union disaster relief efforts in the third world. The guy would be paid a small percentage above the market rate when the order was fulfilled. After fruitlessly activity-spotting around Moscow City Hall for an hour or two, his controller, Tony Bellusci, finally responded to his Level 3 alert with a text message.

Thanks for the update, we'll add it to his file, but we don't believe the garage manager is worth using too many resources, don't waste your time on it. Good work for spotting it though, and great news about the olive oil trade.'

Whatever response Patryk had been expecting, it certainly hadn't been that one. Intuition immediately made him suspect that something wasn't right. In accordance with protocol, everything he'd learnt and done since his first Level 3 alert had been reported in detail to his controller. But that response was worrying. He'd essentially told his supervisor that a State Department employee had flown himself to Moscow, consorted with a known high-level criminal and discussed the movement of arms. They now appeared to be saying it wasn't worthy of further investigation. Nothing in the message indicated that the matter was already under investigation. 'Fuck that,' he thought, 'there's no way I'm leaving this alone.'

He abandoned any further surveillance for the day, found his car and drove home. After taking a shower and with a change of clothes he returned to the Hotel Olympiyskiy, parking his car two streets away. Setting up shop in the lobby, once again making out he was reading a paper, he waited. From listening to Perry's phone calls, he knew that the man was deeply worried. Patryk had listened to the output from the microphone and overheard the man's desperate self-admonishments for allowing himself to be taken for a ride.

It was two hours before his quarry appeared walking from the elevator lobby toward the restaurant. Patryk waited for Perry to take a seat and settle, before following him through and taking a table directly in front of him. When a waiter came to ask to take his order, it was clear that Perry was searching for something cheap on the menu. In the end he settled for soup. That was when Patryk spoke up.

"Wilson?"

Perry looked up. "Patryk? What are you doing here?"

"I was about to ask you the same thing. Why don't you join me?"

"I don't know whether I should…"

"Come on, my treat, I haven't seen you for years."

"Okay, if you're sure."

"Definitely."

The waiter patiently stood by while they shared a few preliminary catch-up words, then took their orders.

"So, are you at the embassy here now?" Patryk asked. "That's a big step up."

"No, no, I'm on holiday. I kinda took advantage of a three-day break offer, which came through the door. How about you?"

"Me, I'm working. I changed jobs. I'm now in computer parts, RAM chips, hard drives, laptop batteries that kinda thing. Been doing okay too."

Their food arrived and they continued their conversation.

"I heard about you and Ella-May splitting up and her taking the boy. That must have been tough."

"Yeah. What about you? You ever thought about getting hitched?"

Since the last time they'd met, Patryk had in fact got married but he wasn't about to tell Perry. "Got close a couple of times but came to my senses before it was too late. My lifestyle doesn't lend itself to long-term relationships. I manage to get laid enough to keep my hand in if you know what I mean. Need to be careful about that in this part of the world though."

Perry winced, "Listen Patryk, I was wondering if I could ask you for a favor."

"I guess, what's your problem?"

"I feel terrible asking, but I'm in a bit of a jam. I got ripped off. One of those girls you were just referring to."

"No way. What she take you for, two hundred, three?"

"More than that, a lot more. She drugged me and took every penny I had."

"Shit. Did she take your cards as well?"

"Cards? Oh yeah she took them, and somehow maxed them out before I even knew they were gone."

"I can help you out, until you get home, what do you need, five hundred, a grand?"

"Thing is Patryk I missed my flight, and I've got to get home by Monday, or I'll lose my job. The only flights available are over five grand."

"Jesus Wilson, five grand, that's a lot of money. It's not that I don't trust you and all that, but it ain't as if we're close buddies, is it?"

"I don't know what else to do. I'm stuck here with no money and my visa runs out in a week."

Patryk could see the desperation in his face now.

"Okay, okay. But if I lend you the money, you ain't going to take it and blow it all in the casino are you?"

"No, no. I promise. I wouldn't do that."

"How about I book the flight for you on my card, then I can be sure that you don't get ripped off again?"

"That would be fantastic, Patryk. Thank you. Thank you so much."

"Write down your passport and visa number on that napkin, along with your date of birth that sort of thing."

Perry did as he asked.

"Wait there, I'll need to get my card out of the safe to do it. I won't be long."

Patryk went to the elevator lobby and called the duty officer in Langley. It was Rupert Golightly, a guy he knew well. Rupert had been aware of the operation Patryk was running without full authority but saw the potential and didn't object when Patryk asked him to arrange two flights. One for Perry, early the next day, and another one himself as soon as possible after that. It was a Saturday, and his controller wouldn't be around to refuse permission.

"Also, I need a team to go into Perry's place and give it the full treatment. Including electronics, we can sort out the warrants later."

"Bellusci will shit a brick when he sees this."

"Just tell him if I'm wrong, I'll cover the costs myself."

"He won't see it for a couple of weeks. He's on leave."

"First I've heard of it, when did this happen?"

"Arranged it late yesterday. Said he's got some personal problems."

"Who's standing in?"

"Bruce Psaki."

"Thank God for that, someone with half a brain at last."

"Not a fan of Bellusci then?"

"You could say that."

"So, this flight, does it mean that you're taking leave as well?"

"Call it my regular personal time, I haven't taken any for a couple of months."

"Gotcha."

When he returned to the table, Perry looked up wearing an anxious expression.

"Okay Wilson, you're on flight AC 5346 Air Canada, Sheremetyevo International to Dulles with a stopover at Toronto. Take off 08:20 tomorrow."

"That's fantastic Patryk, how did you manage that?"

"I called in a favor from an old buddy. Don't miss it this time, I can't do this again."

"How much do I owe you?"

"It's Business Class, so it was $3,600; best I could do. Have you got enough to settle your bill here?"

"I was going to skip."

"If they see you leave with your case, you'll be stopped before you board the flight. I'll lend you another grand, will that be enough?"

"Sure. Thank you Patryk, you've been a real good friend.

"When are you going to be able to pay me back?"

"I've got some money offshore; I'll be able to access it by Tuesday latest."

"That's great. Are you still in the same place?"

"That's right."

"I'll see you Tuesday evening then."

Patryk counted out ten hundred-dollar bills from his wallet.

He left his former neighbor with his groveling assertions of gratitude still echoing in his ears. What Perry didn't know was that when he tried to access that offshore money, he'd find it frozen pending the outcome of a money laundering investigation.

Contrary to what many people believe, hiding illegal money in offshore accounts, isn't quite as easy as it sounds. Many countries don't want to openly disregard efforts to control the illicit traffic in arms and drugs. They still do it of course, just more discreetly than before, but if directly requested to intervene by foreign governments, they usually comply.

*****

Patryk's British Airways flight was a great deal less luxurious than Perry's would have been, but his thirteen-hour direct flight to Baltimore/Washington International was five hours shorter. Even after stopping off at home for a shower, he'd be in the Langley headquarters talking to Psaki before Perry had even landed.

Bruce Psaki welcomed him back, in the way anybody would expect to be welcomed by any reasonably polite and competent manager, even though he'd had to come in from home late on a Saturday afternoon. But once the niceties were out of the way he was right down to business. "So, what's this all about Patryk, I saw the message about the meet-up between Esteban and Perry, but you didn't provide any details?"

"I typed a report while I was on the plane and forwarded it directly to you a few minutes ago. I didn't provide details on purpose, because if I did, the duty officer would have pulled Bellusci out of bed. He'd only have done what he normally does, and told me I was worrying over nothing, and chewed me out for going beyond my remit. Then he'd have put it to bed before I had chance to follow up."

"He wouldn't do that to you, would he?"

"That's exactly what he's been doing since they stationed me in Moscow. Seems to think my main function is to sell olive oil."

"I'm guessing from everything that you've put in motion that there's quite a bit more to it than a suspicious meeting between a junior State Department employee and a drug trafficker."

Patryk went ahead and described everything he'd seen, heard, and learnt.

"Jesus Patryk, this could be fucking huge. I've got to push this up the line. You won't have any trouble getting authorization for all you've done. The warrants are all in place for Internet and phone taps, as well as mikes. The Feebies are going to take over on Monday. The team did a full search, but they haven't got back with anything yet."

"I'm not expecting that there'll be much to find; I think we've been very lucky to get in on this right at the start.

"No luck involved Patryk; this was you being a top agent."

"Can you tell me more about Bellusci's sudden need to take leave?" Patryk asked.

"The first I heard of it was when they called me and asked me to step over."

"Did anyone know anything about it before he read my Level 3?"

"I don't know. Are you suggesting, what I think you're suggesting?"

"After the message I got from him telling me to leave it alone, yes that's exactly what I'm suggesting."

"I didn't know there was a message that said that."

"It was in a text - suspicious in itself."

"Do you want me to go ahead and freeze that Belizean bank account?"

"Oh yes. I want Perry to really sweat if I'm going to turn him."

"Don't you want to leave that to the FBI?"

"Definitely not, and I want my money back."

"You'll get it back in your expenses claim."

"Eventually, and only then after a fight."

*****

Tuesday evening at seven o'clock Patryk knocked on Perry's door. There was no immediate answer, even though he knew that he was home, his car on the drive. He called his debtor's cell phone and heard it ring and go to voice mail. 'Hi Wilson, I know you're in there, so are you going to continue hiding and leave me to call my pal to tow your car; or are you going to answer your fucking door?"

A couple of minutes later the door opened and the sheepish resident showed himself. "Oh, hi Patryk. Sorry; I was on the john."

"Yeah, and I'm the King of Sweden. Are we going to have a problem with you giving me my money back?"

"No, no. I'm good for it, but there's been some sort of issue with the bank. I just need to get that sorted out and you'll be the first to get paid."

"First? How many others do you owe money too?"

"I-I…"

"Let me come in, I need to know what's going on." They went inside. "Tell me how deep this shit you're in goes."

"It's not that bad really, and it's only temporary. Elli-May really took me to the cleaners with the divorce settlement and payments for the boy and I've been struggling a bit. I was just about keeping my head above water when I got pulled over by the cops for a broken taillight, and when they searched the car the cop said he smelt alcohol on my breath. He breathalyzed me and I was over the top, not by much but that doesn't matter right? I'd only had a couple of beers, so I don't understand how that happened."

"Yeah okay, carry on."

"I pleaded with him that if I got a DUI I'd lose my job and I asked if there was any way we could work it out. He went into one, accusing me of trying to bribe him. But after I told him that I was a public employee just like he was, he started paying attention and said he'd be taking a big risk to look the other way."

"Yeah, and…?"

"I told them I could only put about three grand more on my card, and that was all I could lay my hands on. Long story short, they followed me to the ATM I withdrew the money and handed it over."

So, when you decided to go off on your little holiday to Moscow, you were already pretty much tapped out?"

"I guess, but I'd already booked my flights."

"That was pretty dumb, wasn't it? So, tell me how you propose to give me my money, because this whole *issue with the bank* thing doesn't inspire me with a whole lot of confidence." Patryk was sure there'd be more to it than he'd said, but it didn't matter; the hook was in.

"I don't know what to tell you, the money's there but they said the account's been frozen."

"So where is it?"

"The Cay Heritage Bank in Belize."

"How much?"

"Twenty grand."

"So where did it come from? And don't tell me you won it on a horse."

"I agreed to do a favor for someone."

"And you don't have any other way to pay me back at the moment?"

"I'm real sorry, Patryk. I'll pay you back as soon as I can, I promise."

"Listen, Wilson. I need that money. I've got expenses of my own. I've got a pal - he's real clever with overseas banking and I know he's sorted things out for other people. Do you want me to give him a call?"

"That'd be great."

"I'll call him now; I don't know how soon he could get round to it. His name's Roy Sears."

"Okay."

Patryk picked a number from his call list, "Roy, it's Patryk Wilkanowicz. ... Yeah, I know, sorry about that. ... I was after a favor, and I heard what you did for Hugh Whitten, and I was wondering if you could help this old neighbor of mine. He's got himself in a bit of a fix, and all his money is tied up in Belize. ... I know but being the sort of guy I am, I kinda helped him out, and now he can't pay me back. It's left me struggling a bit. ... Wilson Perry. ... Yeah he's got a steady job. Just a minute, where are you working again, Wilson?"

Perry told him.

"Did you hear that Roy? ... The Cay Heritage Bank in Belize."

Perry interrupted to say that the account was in the name of Perry Wilson.

"Do you think so? ... I'll text you his address. ... What really? That'd be great, thanks pal."

"Roy says that swapping your names like that may have rung some alarm bells. He's going to make a few phone calls and he'll get back to you. It may be later this evening or tomorrow. He's going away himself at the weekend, so it will be two weeks if he can't get to it before then."

"Jesus Patryk, I don't know how to thank you."

"Yeah well, I'm still major league pissed off, and if I haven't got that money by Friday I'll get your car towed like I said. I don't like calling in favors like that."

Patryk left the guy practically wetting his pants and then went home to listen in to what happened next.

*****

At Nine thirty Patryk listened in and heard knocking on Perry's door.

Voice 1: Good evening, Mr. Perry?

Perry: Yes that's right.

Voice 1: My name is Roy Sears. I'm an agent with the US Treasury Department. This is Special Agent Mason Jones of the FBI.

Sears was in fact Rupert Golightly and one of Rupert's functions at Langley was to work closely with the FBI and help deal with domestic issues where there was a dual interest.

Perry: Oh God.

Roy: We'd better come in. I think you have one or two questions to answer.

Perry: Do I need a lawyer?

Jones: We don't know yet. Possibly not, if you can give us the right answers to our questions.

Perry: What do you want to know?

Jones: About an hour ago I had a phone call from Agent Sears here and he alerted me to something that may impinge on some investigations of ours. I insisted that we clear it up straightaway. Hence the reason for my presence here tonight.

Perry: I thought that Roy was just going to advise me how to free up some money that has been frozen in an offshore account.

Roy: And that's all I was going to do Wilson, until I saw where the money came from.

Perry: Wh-what do you mean?

Jones: That money originated from a Columbian drug cartel. I want to know what it is that you had to do for them that they were willing to pay $20,000 for.

Perry: I didn't know… I think I need a lawyer.

Jones: We could do it that way, it might lead to charges under the Espionage Act. But there might be another way to deal with the problem.

Perry: What do you mean?

Roy: You could start by explaining what the purpose of your recent visit to the Spanish Embassy in Moscow was.

Perry: How do you know about that?

Roy: How we know is of less importance than your ability to answer the question.

Perry: I was doing a favor for a friend.

Roy: Explain.

Perry: He asked me to tie up the final arrangements for his shipment of olive oil from Ceuta to St Petersburg, and the export of some timber to the United States.

Roy: Why you?

Perry: He said that he wanted me to prove that I was capable of the other jobs he might have for me.

Roy: Would you be interested to know that those shipments include a ton of marijuana into Russia and two tons of small arms into America?

Perry: I don't believe you.

Jones: Mr. Perry, you've been lured into a trap to turn you into becoming an asset of the Russian secret service, the FSB.

Perry: Oh God!

Roy: All is not yet lost. What we'd like to suggest is that you comply with their demands, keep us informed and pass on any information that we would like them to know.

Perry: Be a sort of double agent you mean?

Jones: There we are Roy; I knew he couldn't be quite as dumb as you said.

Perry: You-you haven't got any evidence.

Jones: You mean other than records of you trying to access the money. Or a photograph of you having lunch with a notorious drug dealer. Or a recording of you calling him and requesting help with money and asking when you're going to get the next lot. That's sort of evidence do you mean.

Perry: What have I got to do?

Jones: First of all, Roy here is going to arrange an extension of the credit limits on your cards. That way you can repay the money you owe your friend. If you're going to be working for us we don't want you being hassled by creditors do we? Then we're all going to take a little ride to Pennsylvania Avenue.

Perry: FBI Headquarters. I thought you said we could sort it out.

Jones: And we'll do just that, but there are a few formalities to complete first. Roy will you get your pal's bank details so Wilson can fulfil his obligations?

Patryk listened as Roy, AKA Rupert Golightly, talked Perry through transferring $5,000 into his account, before taking him out of the door. He knew it was wrong taking the money back from Perry, when he'd be claiming it on expenses, but he was always getting ripped off by accounts department, and a little bit of payback was well overdue.

At 7:15 am the following morning his phone buzzed with an incoming message, it read, *'Meeting with DDO 09:00'*

"Fuck," he thought, as he dragged himself out of bed, 'Have I fucked up an ongoing investigation? That shithead Bellusci would love it if that were the case.'

He showered, dressed and grabbed two slices of toast for breakfast, before jumping in the car. With the heavy early morning traffic, the drive to Langley from his home in Falls Church was painfully slow, and, when the security arrangements were thrown in, the ten-mile journey took over an hour. In the end he reached the DDO's outer office with five minutes to spare.

"Go straight in," the PA told him.

He knocked and heard the deep resonant voice of the incumbent CIA Deputy Director of Operations say, "Enter."

"Patryk, come in and take a seat."

"Thank you, sir."

"I've been speaking to Rupert Golightly, and he's brought me up to speed about the shenanigans with this Wilson Perry guy from the State Department."

"Yeah, I'm sorry if I went a bit over my pay grade on that, sir, but it looked like it was too important to let it slide."

"And we're glad you did. Another twenty-four hours and we'd have missed it."

"Glad to help, sir," he said, hoping his breath of relief went unnoticed.

"Tell me Patryk, do you like the Russian section?"

"I won't pretend that I wanted the move, but I appreciate why it had to happen."

"You didn't answer my question."

"It has its moments, but an undercover job as an agricultural rep isn't my favorite role."

"Yeah. That wouldn't have been my choice for you. What about the section overall?"

"I kinda like it. My PhD was in Russian studies; I never quite understood how I ended up in South America."

"Look Patryk, I think you're wasted doing what you're doing and I'm thinking of moving you again."

"Jesus, sir. Where to this time?"

"I was thinking here in Langley, as SSO."

"What of the Russian Section!? That's either the hottest ticket in town or a poisoned chalice. What about Tony Bellusci?"

"I think we all know he won't be coming back, don't we? It looks like he's on the run."

"What about Rupert?"

"Rupert has already been appointed Moscow Station Chief. Starts on Monday."

"And you want me to take over here?"

"Tom Alexander has been angling for the post, but I don't think he's a good fit, and I'm not ready to move him from the Caribbean Section."

"Does he have any history with Eastern Bloc countries?"

"No, that's what worries me. At least you have a masters in Russian studies, and now a year in the section. Do you want the job or not?"

"Are you kidding? When do I start?"

"You already did. You need to get over there right away, get your feet under the desk, and find out what the fuck else has been going on under Bellusci."

"Sure. Thank you, sir, thanks a lot."

'A home posting, and one where I can actually make a difference,' he thought, as he made his way back to his new desk. 'Caroline will be beside herself.'

His wife was desperate to start a family but had been adamant that they shouldn't until they could rely on him being around to help raise them.

Chapter One
May 2024 - Wednesday 1:30am - Mclean, Virginia.

After the death of his wife fifteen years earlier, and since his children had left home, Patryk had lived alone. Then six years ago he'd lost his right eye in a botched cataract operation, and he'd employed Hugo, as a personal aide. Some might have described him as a butler, but in fact Hugo was more like a paid companion.

The former CIA Deputy Director of Operations had taken early retirement three years earlier, although many would have said that he jumped before he was pushed. Without his knowledge, Patryk's personal assistant at Langley had been exposed as a Russian asset responsible for the deaths of three field agents, and his position had become untenable.

Under normal conditions, Hugo would have been driving, but tonight the circumstances were anything but normal, not even for him. In fact, very little about Patryk's life had ever been what most people would classify as normal.

Patryk drove the Mini Countryman into the garage at the side of his $4million home in Mclean, Virginia, relieved to have got home alive. The gunshot wound in his left arm had made the twenty-mile drive from Burke Lake Park seem like a hundred. He was losing blood, and he was praying he'd left none at the crime scene.

Hugo had waited up, and when he heard the garage door operate, he came to make them both a late-night drink. When his employer staggered into the kitchen with blood pouring down his arm, Hugo reached for his phone to call the paramedics.

"No, don't call anyone, I've got to deal with this on my own. It's a through and through; the exit wound is going to need some stitches or something, but we can probably glue the front one. Are you up to giving it a try?"

"I've never done anything like that before."

"Would you mind trying though? I can't think of anybody else nearby."

"Okay, but it looks like you've lost a lot of blood."

"I'll be alright, if we can stop it bleeding long enough for it to start healing. You know where the medical kit is, there's a tourniquet in there, and I need a couple of Vicodin."

Hugo had often questioned the need for such an elaborate medical kit, but before his wife died, she'd insisted that they be fully prepared after Patryk's last brush with death. Now weak with pain and loss of blood, Patryk succeeded in guiding Hugo through the business of closing the wounds and stemming the bleeding.

"Are you going to tell me what happened? You told me you were meeting someone to clear up a long-lasting misunderstanding."

"You don't need to know the details, but let's just say that out of the two of us at that meeting, I came away the better off. If anyone asks, you had the night off and spent it watching TV or something and you were in bed when I came home."

"Like anyone's going to believe that with a gunshot wound in your arm."

"I'm hoping that if anybody ever does need to ask, the wound will have healed enough for that not to be a problem. But there's probably a bit of blood in your car."

"Will your arm be okay when it's healed?"

"I doubt it. Help me up to bed, I feel like shit."

By 6 am the painkillers were already beginning to wear off, and Patryk had barely slept. He got up and after a failed attempt to put on his bathrobe, he settled for having just one arm sleeved and the garment draped over his other shoulder.

In the kitchen, he one-handedly succeeded in making himself a cup of coffee and a bowl of cereal, but it had been an awkward and painful exercise. The bullet had passed through the bicep, and he knew it was unlikely he'd regain full function. Indeed he might not even if he'd gone to hospital. He was ambidextrous but his left had been his dominant hand. His main concern was that there was a dead body lying out there at that picnic spot, and he didn't want to explain his involvement with it.

Disturbed by Patryk's clumsy movements in the kitchen, Hugo joined him with an admonishment for not waking him. "I'll cook, you need something substantial inside you after losing all that blood."

Patryk didn't argue, he was hungry, even after the cereal. The last full meal he'd eaten was breakfast the day before. He'd spent the day trying to unravel the puzzle behind an anonymous threatening and mysterious email he'd received. It had stirred up issues that he had believed were long since laid to rest. He'd thought that his days of secrecy and intrigue were behind him. He was unaware of anything substantial he might have been guilty of that could be used to blackmail him. Nevertheless, in the world of espionage and intelligence things could often be made to appear like something they're not and against his better judgment he had agreed to a clandestine midnight meeting with the email's author.

In the exchange of messages that followed, both had undertaken to go alone and unarmed; neither had fully complied. With his firsthand experience as a field agent now many years behind him, he'd foolishly allowed himself to be ambushed by amateurs. It transpired that neither of the people that turned up were even the author of the electronic blackmail demand, just low-level crooks he assumed had been employed to kidnap him.

As instructed, Patryk had gone alone, but nothing would have tempted him to arrive unarmed, nor without checking the scene beforehand. Therefore, he had arrived over an hour before the arranged time, initially parking some way off, approaching the site on foot, and clambering through the thick forestry undergrowth by torchlight. He'd seen the Mazda sedan drive into the parking area and continued to watch until a guy got out of the car and looked around for any sign of Patryk.

After allowing time for anybody else to turn up, Patryk returned to his car and drove back to the picnic site. As soon as he got out of his car, the guy walked toward him, pulled an automatic handgun with a suppressor, and pointed it at Patryk. Before the guy could speak, Patryk pulled his own gun with his right hand. No words were spoken before a gunshot from an unsuppressed weapon rang out. The shot hit Patrick in the left arm.

He staggered back, but managed to stay upright, lift his own weapon, and fire. His shot hit the guy close to him in the eye, probably killing him instantly. A second man came out from behind a tree and fired three more shots. Before he could empty the revolver, Patryk's second shot, hit the guy in a leg.

He didn't think there were any houses close enough to have heard the shots, but not wanting to chance it, he climbed back in his car and drove away, without bothering to collect his shell casings. Somewhere, there would be a bullet with his blood on it, he hoped not within a reasonable search area. But when they autopsied the dead guy, they'd know there were at least two others involved.

As things stood, there was one dead guy, another injured, and he was himself seriously wounded. Yet he'd learned nothing about who had sent the email or why.

In his former life he'd had access to every conceivable investigative tool, together with the physical ability, and a team of colleagues at hand. Now he had none of those things and was physically disabled with the loss of sight in one eye, and potentially permanent loss of functionality in his left arm. He needed help.

Two more Vicodin topped up with a couple of Tylenol, two strong coffees, and a bacon, egg and cheese sandwich provided by Hugo, and he felt he was as good as he was likely to for the immediate few hours. Hugo changed the dressings on his arm, and then disappeared into the garage to assess the damage to his car, finding the bullet that had passed through Patryk's arm embedded in the rear door next to the door handle.

By eight-thirty Patryk had summoned enough courage to call the one person who he thought could help him, although whether they would or not was an entirely different matter.

*****

Dunn Loring Virginia

"You've got one hour before your tutor arrives, and when she gets here, I expect you to be clean, respectably dressed, your books ready, and your prep finished."

"Yes, Mom," her two sons chorused.

"Are you going out later, Mom? If not, can we go and watch football training at George Mason again?"

"I guess so, if nothing turns up. It's been quiet lately, so you might be in luck."

As she spoke, her personal phone buzzed with an incoming call from her answering service.

"Hello?"

"Good morning Ma'am, we've got a call waiting, tells me it's urgent but doesn't want to leave a message. Says he's an old work colleague."

"Did he give a name?

"Says it's Patryk Wilkanowicz."

"Put him through."

"Saffie, it's Patryk."

"You're going to have to do better than that, Patrick who?"

"Patryk Wilkanowicz."

"Patryk it's been too long. Remind me when we last met."

This was a test, but he'd been expecting it, "About four years ago at Falls Church Police Station, when you told me that one day you might forgive me, but not right then. I was hoping that that day might have arrived."

"I might consider it. Depends on why you've called."

"I was kinda hoping you'd help me out."

"In what way?"

"In a PI kinda way."

"You were a field agent for decades, why do you need my help?"

"Two reasons, first because I've not been a field agent for thirty years, second because I'm kinda laid up at the moment."

"Does that mean you need me to make a house call?"

"I'd be grateful."

"Are you still in Waverly Way?"

"That's right."

"Okay, but I won't commit to anything until I've heard what it is that you want."

"Understood."

Saffron Price, herself a former agent with the CIA, had left the service at about the same time as Patryk, and for much the same reason. Her husband Brett, also an agent, left with her. They both acquired Private Investigator licenses and went into business together as Price Investigation Agency or PIA for short. The pair quickly developed a reputation and were making good money, which was welcome with the additional expense of a second son, and private tutoring.

Then, a year ago, Brett came down with Covid. Already with reduced lung capacity from a bullet wound early in his career, after catching a secondary infection, he succumbed and died. Saffie, a tough woman by anybody's measure, had been nearly broken by the loss, but Ben their son and his adoptive brother Josh, along with her lifelong friend Mary, pulled her through and she emerged the other side as tough as ever.

An hour after Patryk's call she was standing at his front door, surprised that it was Hugo who answered it. "Ms. Price, come in. Patryk's in the lounge, please go through."

The first sight of her former boss shocked her. He'd lost weight since she'd seen him last, but that wasn't what surprised her. His arm was bandaged and in a sling, there were signs of blood on the dressing, his skin was pale, and he was sweating.

"What the fuck Patryk? What happened?"

"Somebody decided I didn't have enough holes in my body and tried to remedy the situation."

"Gun, knife or what?"

"Gun."

"You need a doctor."

"Maybe but not yet. I was hoping that you could use one of your contacts to acquire some powerful antibiotics after we've had a chance for a chat. They wouldn't sell them to Hugo without a prescription."

"Fuck the chat, I'll sort that now."

She took her phone from her shoulder purse and selected a number from her contacts list. "Ajay? … Yes it's me. … Antibiotics and painkillers for a gunshot wound in the upper arm. … Adult male 180 pounds, about six foot two. … Yes please, and anything you think will be helpful. 1231 Waverly Way, Mclean. … Thanks Ajay, do you want to bill me, or would you prefer cash? … That's great thanks." She turned to Patryk, "They'll be here in about half an hour. Now tell me what the Hell's going on."

In between pulses of pain, Patryk described the events of the past twenty-four hours.

"So, let's get this straight. Someone puts a burner phone in your mailbox with a Post-It sticker saying, *'Turn me on when you get my email, or you'll regret it'*. Then, when you open your email app, there's a message from an unknown source telling you that if you don't agree to meet with them they're going to release some sort of damning information that will destroy your life. You turn the phone on, and receive a text, that says, *'Failure to follow the email instructions will have catastrophic implications for you, your family, and the country'*. Then for some unfathomable reason, you actually go. Is that about right?"

"Sounds pretty dumb when you say it like that, doesn't it?"

"Seems to me that the time to have called me would have been yesterday not this morning. Having said that, nothing you've told me so far tells me what they want from you, what they've got on you, or what you're supposed to do about it."

"As to what they've got on me, I've no idea. We've all got skeletons in our cupboards, including you, some of which I know about. None of mine would put me in the electric chair nor yours either I suspect."

"And yet you didn't just tell them to fuck off."

"No, because I was curious to find out what it's about. I don't want to get into this too deeply, but I've got pancreatic cancer, it's inoperable and I probably only have about six months. When I go. I'd like to leave a clean slate; I don't want anybody coming at me, my kids, or grandkids trying to screw anything out of them. If necessary, I was prepared to buy them off, but I wasn't going to do that without knowing who I was paying and for what."

"So, you want me to locate person or persons unknown. People who allegedly have some information about a crime you may or may not have committed at some unspecified time in the past, for which they proposed to extort an undisclosed sum of money from you. Is that about right?"

"I don't think they were there to extort money from me, at least not directly. I think they were there to abduct me, and not for money."

"Why? Why do you think that, and why would they want to?"

"If they were there purely to extort money from me that's a bloody stupid way of going about it, and if they were going to abduct me with that in mind, who do they imagine would have access to my money in order to pay out?"

"Which begs the question what other reasons could they have."

"Revenge?"

"You think this is some sort of vendetta?"

"Most of the confidential information I ever held on national security will be at best out of date, or more likely completely redundant."

"That isn't true, and you know it. You'd have been party to many operations and relationships over decades, some of them could still be active and even if they weren't, the revelation of their very existence could put people in danger."

"You're right, of course."

"If you want me to help you Patryk, then I need you to be completely honest with me. I don't expect you to sit here and reel off a diatribe of personal and professional secrets, but I can't have you withholding relevant information. I know that somewhere you'll have a cache that contains all the confidential material that you've amassed since you first joined the agency. I'm not asking for open unfettered access to it, but I'll be surprised if the answer to this isn't hidden somewhere in there."

"Does that mean you're prepared to help?"

"Up until I get the first sniff that you're holding something back."

They heard an electronic alert somewhere. "I expect that'll be your friend with the drugs," he said, but it was Hugo who put his head around the door.

"It's the police, but I haven't opened up yet."

"Is it just a patrol car then?"

"That's right."

"If they want to talk to Patryk, ask them what they want, but tell them that Mr. Wilkanowicz is too unwell to come to the door at the moment."

Patryk and Saffie waited quietly for the cops to leave. It didn't take long before Hugo came back in the room.

"Apparently I picked up a ticket on I-495 last night on my way home from visiting my brother in West Springfield."

"Shit, Hugo. I'm sorry."

"No problem. The kid from the drug store came just as they left. I paid him. Do you want this injection now?" Hugo efficiently administered the injection, said he'd change the dressings later, and left them to carry on.

"Hugo's been amazing since my diagnosis," Patryk told her.

"That's great, can we pick up where we left off?" she told him, anxious not to get sidetracked. "Am I or am I not going to get access to any appropriate material information that you've got squirreled away in lock boxes or digital warehouses?"

"Yes, of course. There was never a question of me withholding anything from you."

"If you say so," she said, her reply dripping with sarcasm. "All I've got to go on now is the email you received, which you still haven't shown me, the phone, and the ID of the dead guy, that I still need to establish?"

"That's about the size of it, yes."

"Right. I shouldn't have to ask this question, but how secure are your personal IT arrangements?"

"I use a company called Data-Fort Cybersecurity based in Arlington. They took over everything after I left the agency. They monitor my systems for any signs of hacking, viruses and malware. Any hardware changes or updates have to be approved by them as well as me, and they do regular hacking raids to test the system. They're in the top 25 rated companies for commercial security every year."

"As well as a printout, I'm going to need Data-Fort to provide a digital trail for that email, and I want you to hand over that phone."

"Can I just forward you the email?"

"I'd rather you didn't, at least not yet. I need to be digitally isolated from you for the time being." She handed him an unregistered cell phone, "From now on, I want you to use that to communicate with me. The phone number I'll be using is already programmed in, and so is the email address *layzeebones2@fastmail.com*, but don't forward anything from your network without speaking to me first. The phone's got about $100 on it at the moment; if you need to top it up it's using the AT&T network."

"You haven't changed, no stone unturned, no risk uncovered, and no quarter given. You always were one of the best agents I ever had."

Saffie ignored the compliments and asked, "Give me a brief history of your service. The first time we came across each other was Berlin, but before that and after."

"From recruitment until the late 1980s I was a field agent in South and Central America, but after my cover was blown I was transferred to Russian section at Langley. I served in Moscow for a year or so, before being promoted to SSO at Langley. It was a bit of a leap, and it upset a few people at the time. But I stayed there until I was appointed ADDO at Langley, and then to DDO."

"Who took over from you in Russian section?"

"At first it was Art Brunswick, until he was killed in that car accident, then after the Bannerman business, Dianne Abbotsfield stepped in temporarily. Tom Alexander took over from her. I think he's still there now, at least he was when I last asked. So, are you going to take the job?"

"We haven't talked about money."

"Whatever it costs, Saffie. This needs to be sorted."

"I'll charge the same rate for you as I do for everybody else, but I anticipate that I'll need to hire in specialist expertise over and above my associate Jan Wolski. So, I'm going to have to insist on a $500,000 deposit, if it's over the top you'll be refunded, but my gut feeling is that it won't be enough."

"I'm not concerned about the money, Saffie. How do I pay?"

"Cash, get Hugo to hand it over to Wolski. I'll send you the instructions."

"Cash?!"

"I do that with all my special risk clients. I declare it and you'll get a receipt, so there's nothing illegal about it. The IRS are familiar with the way I work now."

"I was real sorry to hear about Brett by the way; he was one of the best as well."

"Yeah, what is it they say, 'Life's shit then you die'?"

"I know you don't believe that. How's Ben and the new boy?"

"They're good. They support each other. Josh was a mess after his dad went inside and his mom was deported. He doesn't want anything to do with either of them now. Not that either of them have shown any interest in getting in touch, but Ben really came up trumps. Then after Brett died,

Josh did the same for him. Nowadays they're like Siamese twins, joined at the hip. They're home tutored and I've got live-in home help."

"Thank you for doing this, Saffie. I'm pretty well persona non grata at the George Bush Center these days, I don't know who else I could have turned to."

"Just so long as you don't screw me Patryk, because the first sign that I'm being fucked around, and I'm gone and so is your deposit. If you can just give me that printout, I'll be on my way and let you figure out how you're going to explain away a bullet wound that's gonna leave you disabled."

"The email should be in the printer out-tray, in the study. You know where that is."

Climbing back into her recently acquired BMW X7 SUV, she paused and wondered if she'd done the right thing by accepting the contract. Then, moving the shift into drive she drove away.

It was only a short drive to her home. Nonetheless, she was now so schooled in checking for a tail she did it without thinking. There were a number of routes she could have taken, and there was no particular reason for choosing the one she did. However, as she hit her left-hand signal to turn off the Georgetown Pike onto I-495, she glanced in the rearview, and spotted a grey F150, two cars back do the same thing. The lights were in her favor, but they changed as she began her turn. A further glance at her mirror watched the Ford turn as well. Whoever he was had almost certainly picked up a ticket.

There was no point in attempting evasion tactics, and anyway she wanted to know who it was. So, as she joined the Interstate traffic she maintained a steady speed that encouraged the three cars that now separated her from the F150, to pull out and overtake. Her rear-facing camera should now have taken a good shot of her follower's license plate, and hopefully the faces of the two people in the front seats.

At the very last moment, she signaled her turn off onto the Leesburg Pike, then immediately turned onto Towers Crescent Drive, sped up, and pulled into the parking lot of the Tysons Corner Marriott Hotel and waited to see if her fans had managed to keep up. After fifteen minutes without a sign, she assumed they'd lost her and casually completed her journey home. 'What the Hell's this all about?' she wondered.

As she reversed into her garage there was a loud beep. She recognized it immediately, even though it was the first time it had happened. Amongst the security devices she and Brett had had installed when going into business together, was a scanner that would detect a tracker on their cars as it entered the garage. Experience had taught them, if at all possible, to always garage their vehicles. A quick once over with a handheld scanner located the cheap device almost immediately. She left it where it was.

The tracker could only have been fitted while she was at Patryk's house, so she called him. "Patryk, do you have security cameras covering your front yard?"

"Yes, of course I do."

"While I was with you, someone fitted a tracker to my car. Will you or Hugo have a look and see if you can spot who it was. If it was the cops, then this business just ratcheted up a few notches."

He cursed, then promised to do what she'd wanted.

"Send me the footage via text if you can," she asked. She sat back and thought, 'Shit! I'd promised myself I was finished with all that secret agent bullshit.'

Chapter Two
Wednesday 12:30pm - Dunn Loring VA

When Saffron and Brett had received enhanced severance packages from the CIA, they'd used a lot of the money to build a two-story addition to the house that included a school room and gym on the first floor, and self-contained accommodation for live-in help on the second. With their planned future as independent private investigators, they knew that there could easily be times when they would both have to be away from home at short notice.

The lovely lady she'd described to Patryk as her home help was Cindy Bouchard, a sixty-four-year-old retired school teaching assistant from Canada. Cindy had been widowed only to find that her husband had gambled them into bankruptcy. Homeless and penniless, Cindy had been their third attempt at finding a suitable person for the post. Her support after Brett's death had been invaluable.

As she walked into the kitchen Cindy greeted her with her normal smile, "You're just in time for some lunch, if you're hungry."

"Starving, what are you making?"

"Just a snack platter with cold meatball subs."

"Sounds fantastic, give me a shout when it's ready. I'm taking the boys out after school so no need to prepare anything for us tonight."

In her study-cum-office, she sat at her desk and began making calls. Her first was to Jan Wolski, a former detective with the Fairfax County PD. Wolski was a good cop who'd found himself caught up in the fallout from the events surrounding her and Brett's departure from the CIA. Justifiably pissed off at the treatment he'd received, he handed in his badge and got himself a PI license. Since Brett's death, Saffie had been using him more and more as an associate, and was considering asking him to join her permanently.

"Jan, how busy are you at the moment?"

"At this precise minute, I'm busy trying to balance my books, because it looks like I've been stiffed for a big slice of an account."

Saffie wasn't going to get into another one of Jan's tales about unpaid accounts. She been telling him forever that he should ask for money up front. "What about work-wise? How busy are you?"

"Nothing that can't wait. You got something for me?"

"Jan, much as I enjoy our little chats about your clients' inability to pay their bills, why else would I call?"

"I could do with the work. What you got?"

"I've just picked up a new contract that needs working on straightaway. It could be a quick job, but I've a hunch it's going to be huge. Either way I'll start you off with a ten G non-returnable down payment. What do you say?"

"I say, do you want me to start right this minute, or can you wait until I've used the john? What's so big?"

"I don't want to talk about it over the phone. How soon can you get here? I'll see if I can get the boys to save enough lunch for you if you haven't eaten."

"I'm on my way. One thing though, can we cut the *Jan* thing, it don't feel right. Just keep to Wolski."

She smiled, "Okay then, Wolski. See you in a bit."

Her next call was to Linda Baker a former CIA technical expert who held a PhD in electronic engineering from MIT. Nowadays she owned a very successful business providing electronic and digital security services in the Northeastern states of America.

"Saffie. Haven't spoken to you for a while. How's things?"

"Not too bad, you?"

"Same. Pretty busy. Is this a social call?"

"Sorry no, professional."

"I thought you were doing a lot of this stuff yourself these days."

"I am but this has the smell of something a bit more international than my usual stuff. I need an email traced. Firstly, I want to be sure that I've reached its actual source; and secondly I need the originator not to know that I've been looking, if you catch my drift."

"Are you straying back into agency territory again?"

"Could be. The client is Patryk Wilkanowicz."

"I didn't think you'd ever want to speak to him again."

"On a personal level I've sort of got over that. He wasn't to blame for what happened, he just dropped his guard and got a bit sloppy."

"Okay, send it over through our back door channels, and I'll take a look, but his ISP should be able to do that.

Her next task was to actually read the email.

To: PatWilk1231WW@zoho.com

Tue May 7, 2024. 10:04

From: Nemesis666@hushmail.com

Subject: Paying your dues

Everybody has to pay their debts Wilkanowicz, now is your time. Failure to attend or comply with any part of your instructions will result in the immediate release of information that will expose you as the traitor you are. Furthermore, it could have devastating consequences for your family and America.

01:30 Picnic Area 2, Burke Lake Park. Come alone and unarmed, and you'll be given your next instructions.

Nemesis666

She wrote herself a list of questions:

1. How did Nemesis know Patryk's Email address?
2. What possible crime could Patryk have committed that would have *devastating* consequences if revealed after all this time?
3. Why is this only now coming to light?
4. What consequences, other than humiliation could there be for his family? Were they referring to a revelation being the threat,

or to how Nemesis would respond if their instructions weren't followed?

5. What family? As far as she knew, Patryk only had two children, and both were adult singletons.

6. Who could Nemesis be, foreign or domestic?

She was pondering the final point when the gate bell rang. A quick glance at the repeat panel on her desk confirmed that it was Wolski, so, she pressed *open*, and watched him drive through. Standing to get the door for him, she heard Cindy's call that lunch was ready when she was.

"Will there be enough for Jan?"

"No problem."

"Wolski. That was quick," she told him.

"The prospect of a ten grand check and one of Cindy's lunches encouraged me to move my ass."

"Hi Uncle Jan," the boys said in unison as they joined them in the kitchen for lunch.

He returned their greeting, secretly enjoying his status as an honorary uncle.

"Have you got a new case, Mom?" Josh asked. Saffie was also enjoying her promotion to Mom by Josh. He hadn't asked, or announced that he would stop calling her Saffie. He had just tried it out one day, and, after she hadn't commented, continued saying it.

"Yeah, I think this one will be a bit different. It may be unpredictable what's involved, and how much time it will take, so you boys will need to be patient with me if I'm not as available as you want me to be."

"Can we still go to watch the football training later?"

"Shouldn't be a problem. I don't think the case is really going to swing into action before tomorrow. I'll drop you off after, then go onto fight club."

"I wish you wouldn't do that Mom, you always come back with bruises," Josh told her.

Ben leapt to her defense. "Mom needs to be able to defend herself."

"Brett didn't used to go."

"He did before he was injured in Ukraine, before you came to live with us."

Saffie's fight club was once a month at the local karate dojo. It was attended by former special forces operators and a few agents from the FBI and CIA. What they practiced didn't have a name and didn't have a belt system. It incorporated some aspects of different recognized disciplines like *defendu*, *krav maga*, *MCMAP*, and some karate. It wasn't regulated because it was dangerous and not exclusively for self-defense. The only rules were that fights should always be one on one unless otherwise agreed, and combatants weren't to leave their opponents dead or with a permanent injury.

"I don't know what you do at that place, but it sounds downright dangerous," Wolski observed.

"We're less likely to kill our opponents than you would be with a gun," she told him.

Cindy shook her head, "Me, I'd rather stick to CS gas or a pepper spray."

The boys went back to the school room to do their prep unsupervised; their tutor having already departed for home. She was so proud of them for how diligent and mutually supportive they'd become. Before he died, after he'd passed the point that he'd recognized that death was a possibility, Brett had had a long talk with them both. Although he'd asked her to wait outside, she'd seen how deeply affected they were when they finally emerged from his hospital room. They never revealed what he'd said to them, and she'd never asked.

Saffie and Wolski went into the study, a large room that had been open plan until she and Brett had decided to have it partitioned off to separate home from business.

"So, what's the job then, boss?"

"If I agree to call you Wolski can you agree to call me Saffie?"

"If that's what you want."

"This job is going to be a bit different to anything we've been doing until now; no missing person, no industrial espionage. This on first glance is just an attempt at extortion. However, I'll bet my last pair of panties that there's a lot more to it than that."

"Okay, I'm listening. Who's the client?"

"Patryk Wilkanowicz."

"Fuck!" Wolski had been involved in the events that had been responsible for ending the careers of herself, Brett, and Patryk.

"Exactly that." She handed him the email printout.

"This is a cop job. It's straightforward blackmail, demanding money with menaces."

"There won't be anything straightforward about this, and I doubt it's money they're after." She spent the next twenty minutes bringing him up to speed, and explaining why calling in the police would not necessarily be the right idea. "If the cops get to learn about Patryk's involvement in the shooting last night then so be it. We weren't there, and the only people that know that we're involved in any way at the moment are Patryk and his personal aide Hugo Wayne."

"I don't understand why both the phone and the email. Surely the email would have been enough on its own."

"I'm guessing they thought the email might have gone into his spam folder."

"Okay," he said. "What do you want me to do?"

"To start with, I need to know the name of the dead guy from last night and everything you can tell me about him. Also, the name of the injured guy, if that's known. Next, I need to know who's the owner of the F150 that followed me, and whether or not he's the driver or passenger."

"No problem. You keep referring to Wilkanowicz by his first name. Does that imply you and he have some kind of personal connection?"

"He was my first Senior Operations Officer or controller when I first made field agent. We worked closely during that time, mostly 5,000 miles apart, but there was never anything romantic between us. He was partly responsible for what happened to Brett in Ukraine, but only by omission. I can't go into the detail of that."

"Why you?"

"He doesn't have many friends in the agency anymore, and even if he did, he wouldn't want them going through his dirty laundry."

"How dangerous is this likely to get?"

"Too early to say. The Burke Lake Park thing was so amateur, it's hard to believe that there's any serious opposition, but that may just have been a move to see how he'd react. There has to be more, or they wouldn't have fitted a tracker to my car and had me followed. That in itself doesn't make sense, why both?"

"What are you doing about that?"

"It's in hand."

Wolski didn't hang about. He left her to her work, so he could get on with his.

Her next job was to look at the messages from Patryk. Data-Fort had provided a trail for the email which was pretty short. In fact, according to them, there was no trail. It was posted from a few miles away - the Starbucks Internet Café in Fairfax - and that was it.

She sent a text message to Patryk via the burner she'd given him.

Please forward the email to the fastmail account asap.

Her next call was to someone she was only supposed to know as *Patsy Cline*, but since she'd first done some work for her, Saffie had made it her business to discover her true identity. She was Audrey Lancaster, a twenty-two-year-old literature graduate who now worked in an independent bookshop in Vienna VA. Her sideline was tracking down and tracing cell phone activity. As far as Saffie knew, outside the law enforcement community, there was nobody else with the skill level she had, although she had no idea how the girl had acquired the knowledge. The other extraordinary thing about her was that she was very selective who she worked for, and what she did for them. Patsy had to be convinced beforehand that the end client was worthy of her services. For that reason, Saffie rarely sought her help.

"Patsy, it's me, are you free to do some work."

"Spook, long time no speak. Who's the client?"

"A former colleague. He and his family are being threatened, I can't use my regular expert."

"I get it. Send me the details, I'll see what I can do. Normal rates."

"Are you asking me, or telling me?"

"Telling you. I still like staying under the radar."

Patsy charged ridiculously low rates because she didn't want to be seen to be acquiring large sums of money that were inconsistent with her day job. Saffie couldn't figure out the logic of that but lived with it.

"Okay, just remember, that if the time comes when you need my help, you get it free."

"I hope that never happens, Spook."

"Is that who I am now? Spook?"

"I think you know that I'm not really Patsy Cline, just like I've always known you weren't just Mad Mom."

Saffie laughed, Mad Mom was the pseudonym she'd adopted when they first did business. "If you ever need a job…"

"No way; just send me the message details. I'll get it done as soon as possible."

She opened the cheap burner phone, and in a few minutes had made a note of its number along with all the available metadata of the message. Then in a message of her own, using one of her own phones, she sent it to Patsy.

Thinking she'd done all she could for the day, she went to see how the boys were doing with their prep and found Josh helping Ben with his history essay. "How's it going boys?"

"Nearly done, Mom. Josh is just checking my spelling and punctuation."

"Do you still need him to do that?

"We check each other's."

To the boys' bewilderment, Saffie ordered them a cab to take them to the football.

"Is there something wrong with your new car, Mom?" Josh asked as they drove out of the gate.

"No, sweetheart, the car's fine. I just need to engage in a little subterfuge while we're out tonight."

When they got out at the football field, she sent the boys off to the bleachers. Then she waited and observed the other vehicles that arrived over the next few minutes. Several cars contained people there to do exactly what she and the boys were there to do. One was a cop car driven by the father of one of the players, someone she'd met on an investigation. Leaving it until the cop was out of sight, she quickly put the tracker she'd removed from her own car beneath his rear wheel arch.

Saffie waited out of sight to watch for other new arrivals, and it wasn't long before a two-year-old Kia Optima sedan, with two men in suits inside parked up. The driver stayed in the car while the other got out, presumably in search of her.

Making it appear as if she'd been in the restrooms, she crossed in front of the Kia and went in the same direction as the guy who had got out. She found him trying to spot her among the forty or so people, including her sons, watching the players go through their paces. Taking care to stay out of his direct line of sight, she continued to watch. When the guy made the move to start looking closer at the spectators, Saffie moved out of cover and crossed to where the cop was watching his boy practice tackling techniques.

"Hi, Officer Martinez isn't it?" she asked.

"That's right Ma'am, can I help you?"

"Is that your cruiser out there?"

"Sure, is there a problem?"

"Probably not but there were a couple of kids by it just now, and it looked as though one was messing with it. I couldn't see what he was doing though."

"Thank you Ma'am, I'll check it out. I know you don't I?"

"That's right, Saffron Price. I was the PI involved in that kidnapping in December."

"I remember now. What are you doing here?"

"My boys like to watch the practice sometimes. That's them over there. You got someone on the team?"

"Yeah, Jose. That's him wearing 37."

"He's good."

"Yeah, he is. I better go check the car. They've probably put gum under the wipers or something. Thanks for telling me."

When Officer Martinez had gone she went back to where she had been standing before and waited. It was fifteen minutes before the searcher gave up. Saffie followed him back to the car, succeeding in taking a good shot of his face as he passed. In the parking lot the cop car had already gone, and as soon as the searcher climbed in the Kia, it drove away, presumably blindly following the tracker.

Saffie joined the boys and watched for a few minutes, before Ben asked, "Where are we eating, Mom?"

"There's a Wendy's in walking distance. That okay for you two?"

They both agreed it would be okay. As Saffie expected, just the mention of food was enough to make the boys ready to leave.

"Did you manage to finish your business while we were at the football, Mom?" Josh asked.

"I think I did, yes."

When their cab dropped them home, she left Cindy to supervise the bedtime routine and set off for fight club in her car. The monthly sessions at the dojo were tough, and not something most would look forward to, but Saffie found the adrenalin rush addictive.

Chapter Three
Thursday 7:30am - Dunn Loring, VA

The Price household was up, about, and at the breakfast table. As usual Cindy had marshalled the boys out of bed, into the shower and into their clothes. Saffie had already completed half an hour in the gym to iron out the knots from the night before and showered.

"How was fight club, Mom?" Ben asked.

"Not too bad. I only had the one bout last night. I won though; and managed to come away unscathed."

"That's good."

Her statement had been something of an under-exaggeration. Right at the beginning of the fight, her opponent had caught her with a painful kick to her left thigh. He'd been hoping to dead-leg her but had been slightly off target. She'd probably still have some of the bruise by next month's session, but her opponent had left the mat with his nose broken for probably the third time.

In the office she looked at the pictures she'd shot of the men at the football stadium, and the footage of the guy planting the tracker on her car. The man at Patryk's house had made obvious efforts to prevent showing a clear shot of his face to the camera. From his build it was clear that he wasn't one of the other two. However, on the other side of the street, almost concealed by foliage, was another man whose face was just visible. Examining the picture from the stadium revealed that she hadn't got much of a shot of the driver, but the passenger's face was clear as day.

Running an Internet search alongside facial recognition software and using a photo that hadn't been posted before as a sample, took massive amounts of computing power and could take a very long time. It was something she rarely needed to do. As CIA agents, she or Brett would have been able to authorize something like that, but now, as a civilian, it was out of the question, and there was only one guy she knew that could do it discreetly, a Brit called Michael McGlover. She'd only used him once before, but he'd come with unimpeachable recommendations.

Knowing it was nearing the time when many Brits would be thinking of going home for the evening, she looked for a cell phone she'd used to call him before. Selecting his number, she hoped he'd pick up.

"Mrs. Price, this is a nice surprise, we haven't spoken for quite some time. What can I do for you."

"Mr. Glover, glad you're free to take my call."

"It's just Digits to my friends."

"As it's just Saffie to mine. Digits, I have a photograph I took last night, of someone I need identifying, and it's quite urgent. I was hoping that you might be able to help."

"It's certainly something we can do, but it's quite expensive as I'm sure you know."

"Yes, I know, but I think this case warrants that level of commitment."

"It's $8,000 for the first sweep; for any additional sweeps $500 per hour."

"I'll transfer the money right now and send the picture immediately."

"I won't wait for the money to arrive, but if you can send me a screenshot of the confirmation with the picture that'll be enough."

She sent the photo of the man from the football stadium, and hoped Digits would be successful.

Linda's report about her examination of the email, and the report provided by Patryk from Data-Fort didn't match. Linda's was much more detailed. The email had been made to appear as if it were initiated in the internet café, when in fact it was an edited version of one that had been halfway around the world beforehand.

Linda explained that it didn't mean that the Data-Fort report was wrong, only that they hadn't looked beyond what they first found. Linda had known that the enquiry from Saffie meant she would want more than basic metadata and went the extra mile, but what she hadn't been able to establish was the root source of the other email. That fact was worrying in itself.

Wolski arrived while she was still mulling over what all this meant.

"Hi, how did you get on?"

"The dead guy's name was Ricardo Morales, a low-level gangbanger with loose connections to the Latin Kings. From prints in the car, they suspect his buddy might be a guy called Guido Ruiz, but the injured guy left in a car of his own. They haven't found Ruiz yet, and they'll need a DNA match for a positive ID, but from the amount of blood they found at the scene, whoever it is might not live long without help."

"What else have they found? Any cellphones?"

"Not yet, no."

"Have they searched his home?"

"Found a lot of drug paraphernalia, but not much else."

"What are their thoughts so far?"

"They're working on the assumption that the dead guy arrived in the Mazda, then at least one other person turned up in a second unidentified car and fired at least two rounds from a .38, killing Morales and wounding a second - presumably the second guy would be your pal. There was a blood trail to where a third vehicle had been parked in the trees nearby."

"So, unless the guy that Patryk shot drove himself there and away again, there could have been a third unknown person present."

"That's possible."

"What do you know about this Guido Ruiz?"

"As far as I can tell, he's not a gangbanger; he's a hustler. Did two years in Augusta Correctional Center for Internet fraud, been picked up several times for various low-level scams, but they've never made them stick. Gets into debt playing poker in private games, but once again he's no high roller or Cincinnati Kid."

"Would it be worth digging a bit deeper?"

"I already did. Asking around some old CIs, I had to pay out a couple of grand, but I managed to find out that he's in the shit. Owes a lot of money, to some not very nice people. When the cops turned over his place in Alexandria, it looked as if he hadn't been there for weeks. But one of the CIs told me his mom lives in Danville."

"Do you think it would be worth a visit?"

"I was hoping you'd say that. Her name's Elizabeth Ridgely. She lives in Edgewood Drive."

"If we leave now, we might be able to get there before your former colleagues."

Using Saffie's car, they drove to Beth Ridgely's home. When they stopped outside there was no outward sign of activity, but they went to the door and knocked anyway. After a delay and knocking again, they heard and saw movement behind the opaque glass door.

"Mrs. Ridgely, my name is Saffron Price. I'm concerned about your son."

The door opened and the face of a woman about fifty-five years old appeared between the frame and the door, which was secured by a chain.

"What do you want?"

"We believe that Guido may be in trouble, and we might be able to help."

"Who are you?"

"My name's Saffron Price and I'm a private investigator. This is my associate Jan Wolski."

"What makes you think that Guido's in trouble?"

"Guido's fingerprints were discovered at a crime scene in the early hours of yesterday. A man died there Mrs. Ridgely, so I doubt the police will be far behind us."

"What makes you think you can help Guido?"

"We believe that your son has been caught up in something he didn't fully understand, something very dangerous. If Guido agrees to help us by answering a few questions, we'll give him money to help with his defense."

"Who's paying you?"

"I'm not at liberty to divulge that at present."

"How do I know I can trust you?"

"I guess you won't know until after I've spoken to Guido, but the police won't know about our visit here today unless you tell them."

"Wait there." The door closed, and stayed that way for about five minutes. When it opened again, the chain was off. "Come in, Guido's through there on the left."

When they entered the bedroom, they found Ruiz sitting up in bed in his underwear, one leg wrapped in bandages that looked as if they were just strips of sheet. His skin was gray, and he was clearly in a great deal of pain.

"Guido, before you say anything, I can see that you're suffering, would you like me to get you someone to help?"

"Are you going to get me a doctor?"

"Not a doctor, but someone with a lot of medical experience, who'll be able to treat that wound and give you some pain killers."

"Is this gonna cost me?"

"No, only some answers to a few questions while we wait for her to get here."

"They gonna be quick? I'm dying here."

"I'll see what I can do." She picked a number from her contacts list and called.

"You busy? ... Adult male, forty-one, about five ten, 170 pounds. Gunshot wound left leg, thirty hours ago. ... 720 Edgewood Drive, Danville. ... Usual terms."

"She'll be here in about twenty minutes."

"Thanks."

"Now's when you fulfill your part of the bargain. Tell me about your part in that nasty little tryst in Burke Lake Park last night."

"It weren't supposed to go like that. I was only there as a backup. Nobody was supposed to get hurt, but that asshole pulled a gun. He wasn't supposed to be armed."

"As I understand it, neither was your pal; and you weren't supposed to be there at all, but forget about that for a minute. Start at the beginning."

"Ricardo met me in a bar and told me he'd been given eight gees to grab this guy, hold him and cover his eyes until they came and took over. They told Ric that they were working for the CIA and the guy was a Russian spy or something. Ric's flat broke just like me, so he agreed. But Ric told me that he was too scared to go there on his own, so he gave me two grand to back him up. The spy story sounded like bullshit to me, but I needed the money, so I didn't argue. He brought me back here and told me where I had to go, and when to be there."

"Who was the guy?"

"I don't know. Neither did Ricardo. He was just supposed to grab him and tie him up. They told him that the guy would be alone and unarmed, but Ric said he didn't trust that he wouldn't have a gun, that's why he asked me to be there in case something went wrong."

"So, what did go wrong?"

"I went separately in case anyone was watching, like Ric told me, but I was late getting there and only got there just as the guy got out of his car. Ric pulled his gun to stop the guy doing anything stupid, but the guy pulled his own gun. I fired my gun to scare him, but I think I might have hit him. The other guy must have been like a sharpshooter or something, cos he shot Ric. I fired a few more shots at him, but I'd never fired a gun before, and I don't know if I hit him again or not, but he hit me in the leg as I was running away."

"Whose gun was it?"

"My mom's."

"So, you drove away in your own car then? That must have been hard with a gunshot wound."

"It's my mom's car, but it's my left leg and I managed."

"Where's the car now?"

"In Mom's garage."

"Who was it that paid Ric?"

"I've no idea. Ric didn't know either. They sent him the money in an envelope, and instructions on his phone."

"The cops didn't find a phone on him?"

"They told him not to take it with him, so he left it here. That's it over there, the gray one."

"Who else was there?"

"Nobody."

"Are you sure?"

"I didn't see anybody else."

There was a knock at the front door, and a few moments later Mrs. Ridgely showed a woman into the room. There were no greetings; Saffie and the woman just acknowledged each other with a nod before the newcomer got straight down to work stripping the dressings off the wound.

"We'll leave you now," she said, counting out twenty $100 bills onto the chest of drawers at the side of the room.

She picked up Ric's phone, and they were about to leave through the front door when a thought occurred to her, and she turned to Guido's mom, "I don't suppose your car has a dash cam, does it, Mrs. Ridgely?"

"Yes, why?"

"Well, if it recorded something that Guido didn't spot, it might help us find who got him into this mess in the first place."

"Won't the cops want that?"

"If the cops do actually wind up here, it will be to find evidence about how he might have been involved in that man's death. He didn't shoot the man, and I doubt they'll worry too much about who started it all. Might be best not to mention our visit here today though."

"We're not gonna say anything, not after you got him that medic. If you want the memory card though, you'll have to go in there and get it yourself, there's blood all over."

"I'll get it," Wolski offered.

Saffie handed the Ridgely woman another $200 for the card and to get the car cleaned when she was ready.

"I hope that Guido makes a good recovery," she said, and went to the car where she waited for Wolski.

The medic came out of the house, nodded to Saffie, climbed into her own car and sped away as Wolski climbed in beside her.

"Any problems?" she asked.

"No but the gun was in there on the floor, so I took that, in case they find the bullet with Wilkanowicz's blood on it and try to link the two together."

"Good thinking, but I think the bullet is still lodged in Patryk's car."

Back in Dunn Loring, the first thing they did was examine what the dash cam had recorded. The footage prior to the shooting provided very little information. Ruiz had driven straight there but stopped a hundred yards short and reversed in among the trees. The sounds that accompanied the video had until then been largely engine noises, accompanied by Ruiz cursing because he was late.

When the video restarted it showed his erratic journey back to Danville, as Ruiz attempted to control the vehicle whilst rapidly losing blood. His moans and groans of pain didn't make pleasant listening.

"Can you wind that back to just before he parks up?" Wolski asked.

Saffie did as he requested.

"There, stop," he pointed at the screen. There was a maroon Chevrolet Suburban stopped by a volleyball complex. "There, that car. It isn't there on his return journey."

They rewatched the relevant footage.

"You're right; well spotted. Why would anyone still be at the volleyball park at one-thirty in the morning?"

"Can you zoom in close enough to get the license plate?"

The zoom blurred the image slightly, but not enough to stop them reading the number. FN 9713 on a DC plate. Wolski quickly typed a text to his contact. "If it's not a fake plate, we'll know who it is in a few minutes."

True to his word, as Saffie returned to the office with two cups of coffee, Wolski's phone buzzed with the two-word response. *Access Restricted.*

"What the fuck does that mean?" she asked.

"Some sort of spook thing. Probably one of your old pals I guess, or the Feebies."

"If it's agency, they're operating out of bounds, unless it's someone from Professional Standards. In theory it could be the Feds, but it would be weird for them to drive away from a killing without at the very least making their presence known to the cops, wouldn't it?"

"Unheard of in my experience, especially in this area of the country. Normally the Feds can't poke their noses in fast enough," he told her.

"What would they have been doing there? They must have known about it in advance."

Wolski thought about it for a moment, "Perhaps they're the ones behind setting this up."

"Why though?"

"You're the spook. Are you going to get your secret cell phone girl to look at Morales' phone?"

"Not yet. She doesn't like me to keep going back or messing with hardware. I'll ask Linda Baker if she can give it the once over."

Patsy's report about the activity on the burner that Patryk had been sent, had come through while they'd been out, and it was interesting. She'd given IDs to all the phones involved. Patryk's burner was P1, the phone that messaged him was P2, and the originator of the text was P3. The incoming text message telling Patryk to go to Burke Lake Park had been sent from P2, located in or near 7811 Kincaid Avenue, Falls Church. But it had been forwarded from P3, another unregistered phone, located in the same area. It was P3 that Patsy had spent most time on, and judging from its call log, it wasn't a burner. It had made and received calls over the previous month to dozens of other numbers, and the same with texts.

Patsy had included lists of the numbers, dates, times, and duration of calls both made and received, as well as the date and time of texts sent and received over the same period. There were far too many calls and texts for her to have gone into more detail with all of them. One text exchange that had drawn Patsy's attention took place between P3 and a phone registered to Chester Boggs, a cop based at Fairfax County PD. It took place two days before the first contact with Patryk.

P3: If you want our help, this is your one-time opportunity.

Boggs: Yeah definitely want your help. What have I got to do and when?

P3: We'll send you a package with instructions. The first actions will be straightforward. How things develop will dictate what follow up actions need to be.

Boggs: I'm not going to be doing anything that's going to put me in jail.

P3: You won't be going inside, as long as you do what we tell you. But if you want Wilkanowicz locked up for the rest of his life, you need to do what you've agreed. If you let us down now you'll make some people very unhappy.

Boggs: I got you. Don't worry I'll do it. That asshole needs to learn that you can't treat people like shit and get away with it.

P3: Okay then. I'll be in touch after stage one is complete.

"Chester Boggs, does that mean anything to you?" Saffie asked Wolski.

"I know the name. He was a rookie who joined just before I put in my papers."

"I wonder what he's got against Patryk. I'm not going back to him just yet though. I need to get a handle on the bigger picture first. What did you find out about the F150?"

"It's registered to a guy called Clay Scott, forty-eight years old, done time for store robbery, released about four months ago. Rents a room in Samaga Drive, Oakton. It wasn't him driving though - too young. Could have been his son Clay Junior, nineteen years old lives with his mom in Fairfax, he's got a couple of minor misdemeanors."

"Maybe it was one of them that placed the tracker, but if so, why? Patryk wouldn't have told anyone that I was going there, and nobody else knew I was going."

"Maybe his phone's been hacked."

"It makes no sense that Patryk would use a phone that had been hacked. Like me, he'd have multiple safeguards against that sort of intrusion. I think I'll have to have another chat with Patryk after all. I'll drop this phone off to Linda while I'm out."

"I'll take a drive by Clay Scott's place then, and maybe have a chat with his neighbors. Then, if it's okay with you, I'll take the afternoon off."

"You're not on the clock Wolski."

Chapter Four
Thursday 1:30pm - Mclean, VA

She rang the doorbell of Patryk's huge luxurious home, and moments later Hugo opened the door.

"How is he?" she asked before he had time to greet her.

"A great deal better than yesterday, thanks to your friend's medications no doubt. Come in, he's anxious to see you."

Patryk was sitting in a rise and recline chair that hadn't been there the day before, his arm in a sling, but his color improved. He attempted to smile, but she could tell he was still in a lot of pain.

"You look like shit," she told him.

"Thanks, I love you too."

"When did you last take some painkillers?"

"Hugo gave me a couple of Oxycontin or Vicodin first thing."

"Then you're due some more."

"I don't want to get hooked."

"Brett was the same after Ukraine, but you won't be able to function at all without them at least for a week or so, and you're dying so I don't think addiction is your first priority at the moment." She called Hugo and asked him to provide Patryk with two more Oxycontin and a couple of Tylenol. "I need to have a sensible conversation with him, and I can't do that while he's writhing in agony."

Hugo smiled and fetched the drugs with a glass of water.

"Right let me bring you up to speed. Don't interrupt unless there's something that doesn't make sense." When she'd told him everything that she and Wolski had learnt in the last twenty-four hours, she asked him for his comments.

"I don't recognize any of those names, nor any of the faces you showed me. It's making less sense every time I think about it."

"Have you considered bringing in the Feds?"

"Only as a last resort. I don't want them rummaging around in my past, and you can be damn sure the agency doesn't want that either."

"Who's this Chester Boggs cop?"

"I've absolutely no idea. I've never crossed swords with the cops at any time in my life, other than a couple of traffic stops that went without incident."

"If he's got some sort of beef with you, it can't have anything to do with his cop life; he didn't sign up until after you left the agency. What about your personal life?"

"I don't really have a personal life. While I was at the agency, it was mostly a 24/7 work life, it didn't even leave a lot of time for my wife and kids. I never played around, not once. To be truthful, I don't recall having the opportunity more than twice in my whole life. I wasn't interested then, and there's been nothing since."

"Those cops that came here yesterday. Did you look at the video?"

"I did, after Hugo told me about the tracker. I didn't know either of them, but don't you think that's weird? How often do the cops deliver a speeding ticket personally?"

"How fast were you going?"

"According to the ticket, only 67; it's 65 on that section."

"The cops have got better things to do than make personal calls for minor traffic infringements. It must have been a cover for putting that tracker on your car.

"Can your friend Wolski look into that?"

"Maybe; I'll ask him. If your private life was as anodyne as you suggest, then this has to be something to do with your professional one."

"If it is, then it isn't domestic. The only domestic debacle I was ever involved in was the Bannerman business, and I've been informed that Congress is satisfied that that's all been dealt with."

"Whoever it is, didn't lure you there to kill you. If that's what they wanted to do, they'd have sent someone who knew what they were doing."

"He may have been an amateur, but that Ruiz guy got damn fucking close to putting me down."

"Except he wasn't there to do that either. He just panicked when you pulled your gun," she told him. "You need to go back through everything and look for any chink of weakness."

"It'll have to wait a day or two. I'm in too much pain at the moment, and Hugo won't be able to help. He isn't cleared to see most of what I've got."

"Have you got anyone who could help pin down the driver of that agency Chevrolet?" she asked.

"I doubt it. Haven't you?" he said as another pain shot through his arm.

"I'm not flavor of the month over there either. A lot of them thought that Felix got a tough deal because of me."

"He was a useless asshole."

"Yeah, well some didn't see it like that."

"While you're here, are you going to take your deposit? Hugo says he's uncomfortable with it sitting around unsecured."

"Sure."

She put the case with the money in the trunk, but before getting in and driving away, she swept the car for tracking devices. After a few moments of thought, she changed her mind about going straight home, deciding instead to have a little look at what went on around Falls Church, Kincaid Avenue in particular. Maybe she could identify who'd been luring a young cop into criminal activity.

Having driven round the block and passed the target house twice, she decided it was worth taking a risk, so she parked further down the road and walked. It was a quiet well-kept street with a variety of houses. Number 7811 was a small single-story house without a garage but with an ancient RV parked at the side, and there were no other vehicles out front.

One house that was about twenty yards further along and on the opposite side of the street had just what she'd been hoping to find, a camera pointing roughly in the right direction. She knocked on the door. It was answered by a woman carrying a toddler.

"Sorry to bother you ma'am, my name's Cissy Hanrahan. I'm a private investigator. I've been asked to look into an incident where a young child was knocked off her bicycle along this street the other day. I spotted your camera, and I wondered if it might have captured anything."

"That's awful, is she badly hurt?"

"She's got some nasty grazes, and a few bruises, but she'll be okay."

"When was this? I don't remember hearing about anything like that."

Saffie gave her a time and date and handed her one of her fake business cards. "The thing is, she isn't 100% certain it was in Kincaid or Jackson. I showed her on Google Street View, but she wasn't sure."

"Come in and we can have a look, I think the recordings will go back that far."

"That's real kind ma'am."

It took ten minutes for Saffie to confirm what she already knew; that there'd been no collision between a car and a kid on a bike in view of the camera during that time. However, on the footage from the previous day, she did manage to see a maroon Chevrolet Suburban parked on the front drive of number 7811, the same one she'd seen on Guido Ruiz's dashcam.

"That's a real nice car your neighbor across the road has. I was considering one of those when I bought my Beamer, but with my two boys and all their friends I decided the extra seating capacity took precedence."

"They're not real neighbors, I think they're just renting it. A couple of guys. They've only been there about two weeks, and we haven't spoken."

"You've been real helpful ma'am. Thank you for your time."

She hadn't expected her impromptu stop in Kincaid Avenue to bear any fruit, but in the end it had resulted in answering a very important question; where the Chevy's driver (and his pal) were basing themselves.

It was later than she'd intended and nearly sunset when Saffie, satisfied with her afternoon's work, drove home to Dunn Loring.

Still contemplating her next moves, she pressed the button on the remote control to the entrance to her drive. Then, when she quickly glanced in her rearview to confirm the gates were closing behind her, she almost missed a shadowy figure sneak through in her wake before the gates finally closed. It was still too light for the PIR-activated lighting to react to movement in the grounds.

Not bothering to garage the car as she would usually, Saffie locked it and went inside. Cindy was tidying the kitchen away after they'd eaten, and the boys were watching TV in the lounge. Before Cindy had the opportunity to speak, Saffie announced, "Operation Backstop. Not a drill."

Cindy's face went pale, she dropped the tea towel she was holding, rushed to gather the boys and hurry them to the gym that doubled as a panic room.

Saffie collected her gun and some zip ties from the office, and quietly let herself out the rear door, allowing it to lock behind her. She pressed herself against the wall, in the angle where the new gym addition protruded from the original building. Gambling that it wouldn't make sense for the intruder to attempt to make an entry at the front, she waited. Even above the sound of distant traffic, it wasn't long before she heard steps onto the eighteen-inch-wide pea-shingle border that surrounded most of the building. There was a brief pause before the feet began to shuffle. She figured that he was trying to open the window on the gym wall. His problem would be that even if he succeeded, all he'd find on the other side was a solid brick wall, the window purely there for aesthetic purposes.

She stepped out and pointed the gun at him, "Okay asshole, drop whatever you've got in your hands and turn to face me with your arms out to your side."

The startled teenage boy did what she'd told him.

"Right, now sit on the ground and secure your ankles with this," she handed him a pre-prepared zip tie. "and before you think about doing anything else, remember that I've got a gun aimed directly at your head."

Once she was satisfied that the boy was immobilized she moved toward him, but a man's voice behind her said, "Just drop the gun, bitch."

Her gun clattered on the stone paving, and the man came up behind her, pressed his own gun to the side of her neck and started to search her. As his hand slid toward her crotch, he spoke into her ear. "Nice tits bitch. Me and the boy are going to have some of this in a minute. Put your hands behind you and…"

That was when their movement triggered the passive infrared sensor, and the LED floodlights lit the grounds as if it were noon. Saffie used the distraction to spin and hit her attacker in the side of his neck with a karate blow that sent his left carotid artery into spasm, and he collapsed on the ground. After kicking the gun from his hand, she quickly knelt, and zip tied his hands behind his back.

Not yet satisfied, she stood between his legs. "I'm going to have some of that," she said, and kicked him in the balls as hard as she could. Swiftly, she then secured his ankles, as she had the boy's, and the boy's wrists as she had the man's.

"Don't go anywhere, I'll be right back," she told them, and pressing her hand against the palm reader, she let herself back into the house.

Using the entry code outside the gym, she opened the door, and told the occupants that the emergency was over, but not to go outside just yet.

"What was it, Mom?" Ben asked.

"Just a couple of uninvited guests. Seemed to think that we were anxious to make their acquaintance. I put them right. I'm just going to give them a little talk on the etiquette of visiting without an invitation. Then I'll be going out for a while again."

"You haven't eaten your dinner," Cindy redundantly announced.

"Thanks, Cindy, I'll eat it when I get back. Don't worry."

She grabbed a reel of duct tape from the office, and a bag of sugar from the kitchen, before returning to the rear yard and her two captives. It took seconds to quieten the man's groans of agony with the tape.

"That's Daddy Scott isn't it," she said, nudging the boy with her foot. He nodded sheepishly. "So, I'm guessing you must be Clay Scott Junior, is that right?" he nodded again.

Grabbing him by the back of his collar, she dragged him out of sight of his father. "Are you going to tell me what you're doing here, or do I have to give your crotch the same treatment as your pathetic old man's?"

"I dunno. My dad said he was paid to give you a hard time to scare you off from helping out the guy in Waverly Way. He said he'd give me a thousand bucks."

"Who paid him?"

"He didn't say."

"Did you come here in the Ford again, the one you followed me in the other day?"

"Yeah."

"Why did you put the tracker on my car if you were going to follow me?"

"In case we lost you."

"How did you happen to be there at the same time as the cops."

"Dad told me that one of the cops had said he would fix it so we wouldn't get caught."

"Why my car, I could have been anyone?"

"The cops were checking the plates of anyone that arrived."

She put a strip of duct tape across his mouth. Returning to the father, she ripped the tape from his head, pulling hunks of his beard with it.

"Okay then, Daddy. Let's get your version of events. What are you here for?"

"Fuck off bitch."

"One more uncooperative answer like that and I'll give you a repeat dose of the one I gave you earlier, and if that doesn't work I'll start on Junior. That would be a shame, because he's a bit young to have to start a lifetime of erectile dysfunction. If you think that's an idle threat, then you came to the wrong house. Start again."

"I got paid to get you to stay away from Waverly Way."

"Why me?

"I don't know, the cop pointed you out. He'd been watching the place."

"Who is it that lives in Waverly Way I'm to stay away from?"

"I don't remember his name; something Polish. It's the guy at 1231."

"Was it just me, or anybody else?"

"Whoever the cops pointed out."

"Tell me the sequence of events."

"I got an envelope the day before, with five grand in it. There were instructions to go to that street at five o'clock in the morning and wait until I was told by a cop to follow any car they told me to. They called me later in the day and told me that if I didn't follow the instructions, there'd be consequences."

"So, was the tracker your idea then?"

"No, theirs, after I told them I hadn't followed anyone before."

"But you decided to get your boy to put the tracker on."

"I got a busted knee from when I was beat up in prison. I can't kneel down."

"Carry on. Follow me; was that all?"

"We were to frighten you off but, I didn't know how to use the tracking software and we still lost you."

"That five thousand, was that going to be it?"

"No, I was supposed to get another five if I stopped you getting any more involved."

"Who was the cop, the one who gave you the instructions?"

"I don't know his name. I never seen him before, but the one who stayed in the car is called Blenkhorn. He was one of them that picked me up last time."

"Were you given any way of contacting the cop?"

"His number is in my phone."

She went through his pockets, took his phone, and car key, and emptied his wallet of everything except twenty dollars, and put it back again.

"I'm nearly done, then we can see about what I'm going to do with you."

"What do you…?"

The re-application of the tape over his mouth stopped him from finishing his question. Then returning to the boy, she stripped him of his belongings too.

A few minutes later she'd reversed their pickup up to the side of the garage. Then she cut the tie off junior's ankles, walked him to the car at gunpoint, and told him to get in the rear cab before securing his wrists to the head rest in front of him. After repeating the exercise with his dad, she got in the driving seat and drove. Halfway to Clay Senior's hometown of Oakton, she pulled over outside Vienna with the two captives mumbling their protestations from behind their duct-taped gags but with zip-tied hands, they were in no position to do anything.

"I want you to listen to what I have to say very, very carefully. You've got yourselves into something way more dangerous than anything you could imagine. The person that lives in that house in Waverly Way is a former head of the CIA, and the people that got you to mess with him, could be anything from an international drug cartel to the KGB. If you got caught being involved with any of that shit you could be charged with felonies under the Espionage Act, and that could mean thirty years. Nod your heads if you understand me."

Wide-eyed, they both nodded enthusiastically.

"Next, I need you to understand that if all you'd done was attach a tracker to my car, follow me, and invade my home, then this would have been the end of it, but Daddy here decided to take advantage of the situation to sexually assault me. That's why I crushed his balls, and why I confiscated all the money from your wallets. We'll call that compensation. Also, when I leave you shortly I'm going to leave you with another little surprise, that I shall call retribution. Are you keeping up?"

They nodded.

"You see there's one thing I didn't explain just now, and that is that you not only need to worry about the CIA, KGB, or drug cartels, you now also need to worry about me. The thing about me is that I'm just as dangerous as all the others, I'm vengeful, and I know who you are, what you look like, and where you live. So, if I see or hear of either of you ever again, what happened to Daddy's balls tonight will seem like a lover's caress. Capiche?"

They nodded again. She got out of the car, made a phone call, poured the contents of the sugar bag into the fuel tank, got back in the driving seat, and drove. By the time she stopped outside a taco restaurant in Vienna, the engine was already beginning to stutter, but she left it running, ensuring that the engine would soon stall. With crystallized sugar in the injectors and cylinders it would never run again.

"One last piece of advice, in case you're thinking of telling the cops that it was me who brought you here, I refer you to my earlier remark about hearing of you again. Night then boys, I expect someone will come along and release you soon."

The Uber she'd ordered was waiting where she'd told him to. She climbed in and gave him her home address.

It was gone ten-thirty when she let herself in the front door of her home.

"Is everything okay now?" Cindy asked.

"It's all fine, I just gave our guests a lift."

"Your dinner will be ruined; do you want me to get you something else?"

"I'm sorry, but no, it'll be fine, thanks."

Chapter Five
Friday 6:30 am - Dunn Loring, VA

Forcing herself out of bed, and into her training gear, Saffie began to sort through in her head all the things she'd learnt, all the things she had yet to find out, and everything she still had to do. Her mind had been so busy that the alarm on her fitness watch sounded her session over while she was still running full pelt on the treadmill.

"There's a gun on the ground in the backyard, Mom," Ben announced at the breakfast table.

"Oh shit," she swore. "You didn't touch it did you?"

"Of course not. Did it belong to one of those people who came here last night?"

"That's right sweetheart."

"How did you take it off him?"

"I persuaded him that, being a crook was probably not his best choice of career. He was underqualified by virtue of being as dumb as one of our gym weights."

"How did you do that?"

"I kicked him in his private parts. Probably not the subtlest of arguments, but it seemed to convince him."

The boys laughed and disappeared into the school room. Saffie was helping Cindy clear away the breakfast things when two things happened in quick succession. The first was the local radio station playing in the background, interrupted their broadcast for a breaking news announcement. They went on to describe a double murder in Edgewood Drive, Danville. The bodies of a woman, and her son who had been suspected of involvement in the death of another man the previous night, had been found when police called at her home. Both were believed to have died from gunshot wounds.

"Shit!" she cursed for the second time that day.

Then as she collected Clay Scott's gun from outside, her phone buzzed in her pocket, it was Digits.

"Saffie, just to apologize for not getting back to you earlier, but I had to do a second sweep to ID that guy for you, and it took a long time."

"Did you get a result?"

"Yes. I don't think you're going to like what I found though."

"Go on, let me have it."

"His name is Leonid Kozhukhov. Former FSB, if such a thing exists. He's now allegedly a political refugee living in Baltimore, under the name Mikhail Aristov. Do you want an address?"

"Can you stick it in an email."

"You don't sound surprised."

"I'm not, I've got another one for you, have you got capacity for that?"

"Sure, but this is getting very expensive. The first one went to $11,000."

"That's okay, the client can afford it, and judging from the results of the first one, he can't afford not to."

"If you send the photo now. I can start the search within the hour."

"Thanks, Digits."

Posting off the clip of the guy hiding in the hedge opposite Patryk's house, she wasn't confident that he'd be able to get a result. The picture quality was poor, and the face was partially obscured.

Wolski arrived shortly after, and she brought him up to speed with developments, starting with news about the killings.

"The bastards have killed Ruiz and his mom? Are you serious? Fucking animals. Who the fuck are we dealing with here?" That's when she told him about Kozhukhov. "This is some serious shit you got us involved with here, Saffie."

"Yeah, it is, but if you'd rather step back now, I won't hold it against you."

"Do you seriously think that if either of us walked away now they'd leave us alone? No, we gotta finish what we started now."

"I agree, I don't think this would be the Russian State doing this; or at least not directly. It's all too clumsy, and I can't see what they hope to gain from it."

"What's anyone got to gain from it? It doesn't look like they're after money."

"I keep thinking about the other car. What was it doing there?" she mused.

"And what's with the gun?" Wolski said, nodding at Clay Scott's weapon that she hadn't yet put safely away.

"That was the other thing I didn't mention." She was about to explain, when the gate bell rang.

Cindy knocked on the office door, "It's some detectives. I've opened the gate."

Saffie slipped the gun into a drawer, and a minute or two later, opened the door to two people who could have convincingly driven straight from central casting onto the set of a cop movie.

"Come in detectives. Can we get you a coffee?"

"No thanks, Ms. Price. I'm Detective Sergeant Martin. This is Detective Romero, Fairfax County PD. Are you Saffron Price?"

"For my sins, yes. Come through to the office. We can chat in there."

They were clearly taken aback to see Wolski who acknowledged them with a nod. "Martin, Romero."

"What are you doing here, Wolski?" Romero asked, with a sneer.

"That's Mr. Wolski to you Detective, and not that it's any of your business, but we work together," Saffie told him.

"Doing what exactly?"

"Like I say, it's not your concern," she replied, dismissing him. "Now Sergeant I expect you've come about Mrs. Ridgely."

"Why would you say that?"

"Just a wild guess Sergeant, based on the fact that I just heard on the radio about the murders in her street, and the fact that we were there yesterday."

"The radio didn't mention any names," Romero said.

"Like I said Detective, a wild guess. With Mrs. Ridgely's son suffering a gunshot wound, it doesn't seem such a big leap. Was I wrong Sergeant?"

"No Ma'am. Why were you there? And in case you were wondering, that is our business."

"Mrs. Ridgely called me."

"What about?"

"She didn't say until we got there. Her son, Guido, had been shot, he was refusing to call the police, and she wanted me to find out who was responsible."

"And what did you tell her?"

"I told her that investigating shooting incidents was the police's job not mine. I advised her to call 911 to get police and medical help. She told me that Guido didn't want that. So, I asked a friend of mine to give what medical assistance they could and paid for it myself."

"Why pay for it yourself?" Romero asked,

"Because, unlike some people, I'm not prepared to stand aside and do nothing while people die in agony for the want of a few dollars I can well afford."

"Did either of them tell you where and when he got shot?"

"Ruiz, didn't say much, he was too sick, but he said something about Burke Lake Park."

"Why didn't you call us?"

"I kind of wish I had now, but how long do you think I'd stay in business if word got out that I reported clients to the cops?"

"What do you think happened?"

"At the park, or in their house?"

"Either."

"It's my guess, that Ruiz got himself mixed up in whatever it was that went down in the Park when that other guy was shot. Then someone else who was also involved, found out where he was, went to the Ridgely house to silence him and the mom became collateral damage."

They asked a few more questions, before giving up attempting to implicate her in the shooting. She showed them out and returned to the office.

"That was taking a chance wasn't it?"

"What was?"

"Going out in front that we were there."

"They already knew that I'd been there at least at some time in the recent past. I left my card. Apart from that, it's not impossible that we were caught on a neighbor's doorbell cam."

"You were telling me about the gun."

After she'd recounted the events of the night before, Wolski laughed. "I'd like to have been there for that. Did you take their phones?"

"Yeah, but I'm not going to do anything with them just yet, especially Junior's. I've no doubt they'll just lead us up another blind alley of burner phones. Is there any way of finding out who was partnering Blenkhorn that day?"

"It shouldn't be too difficult, but Blenkhorn is about as straight as a nine-dollar note, so it wouldn't surprise me to find out if he's mixed up in it as well."

Her phone rang. She looked at the screen, "Digits. Is there a problem?"

"No, I just got a hit on that second photo."

"That was quick."

"I gambled and restricted the first search to known associates of Kozhukhov and got a hit within a few minutes. The new guy is Ivan Gradsky, Belorussian immigrant, also of Baltimore. Both of them are heavies for a nightclub owner called Sergei Lipov. Lipov is a second-generation Russian immigrant, who runs a prostitution and drug racket from his club called The Vault. Managed to stay one step ahead of the cops for years. No prizes for thinking that there's some payoffs being made. I'll only charge a nominal fee for the second sweep."

"Thanks, Digits. Send me your account and I'll transfer the money today."

"This is getting further and further into spook territory, or at least work for the Feebies," Wolski remarked.

"That's true I guess. I doubt that either Kozhukhov or Gradsky are working freelance so whatever their connection is to what's going on here, must link back through Lipov."

"Where does this connect to the Chevy or the Kia?" he asked.

"Maybe we can plant a bug or two inside the Kincaid Avenue place."

"That's not gonna help me if they're talking in Russian."

"We don't yet know if the Chevy driver is one of the Russians though, do we?"

"I guess that's true, but you aren't going there on your own. These assholes wouldn't think twice about wasting you and dumping your body in the Potomac."

"Just a minute, let me call Linda." She picked up her phone. "Hiya. I don't know if this is something you can do, or even if it's something you'd want to, but can you hack into someone's home outdoor camera system and look at what they're recording?"

"It's possible, but it's not something I'd want to get involved in. It's too open to abuse."

"I thought that's what you'd say. Do you know of anyone who might consider it. I'm not interested in viewing anything personal, only external shots to see who's going in and coming out of a nearby house."

"I didn't think you did divorce work."

Saffie laughed, "It's nothing like that; it's linked to the other stuff you did for me."

"There's a guy called Dexter McDowell. He used to work for me. One of my best engineers, but he left to set out on his own about a month ago. He might consider it; I'll send you his details."

"Thanks Linda."

"Are you gonna call him?" Wolski asked.

"Not yet, at least not to do the camera, not until I know more about him. Let's see if he can trace the cars. They're probably both rentals, but it would be good if he could find out who they're rented to."

The text with McDowell's details arrived, and she immediately called his number.

"Good morning, McDowell Digital Securities."

"Dexter McDowell?"

"Yes, how can I help?"

"My name is Saffron Price."

"Ms. Price. That was quick, I only just got the message from Linda saying you might call. What can I do for you?"

She gave him the license plates of the two cars and told him that all she needed for the time being were the details of their ownership, but it was possible there might be some sort of restrictions to the information.

"No problem. I'll get back to you ASAP."

"You didn't say anything about paying."

"Do you want me to send you a table of costs, because that's not how I work. I'm a one-man band, and I charge by the hour. Normally $300, but for a new client I can do it for two hundred."

"That's not what I meant. I was asking how you wanted to be paid; like do you want a deposit, or will you bill me?"

"Once again, normally I'd ask for a deposit of $300, but as I know I can trust you, that's not necessary."

"Do you know me?"

"You probably don't remember me, but I was part of the team that installed your alarm system, and again when you had it upgraded after your addition."

"That's great. I'll probably remember your face when we meet. What are you doing for dinner tonight?"

"Are you asking me on a date?"

Saffie laughed, "Not hardly, although I'm sure it would be fun. I'm suggesting you join my family for dinner, and we can get to know each other, to find out how good a fit we are for each other businesswise. I'm short of time at the moment, and I need to make use of every minute. Can we say seven o'clock?"

"Sure, looking forward to it."

"What are you like?" Wolski asked.

"A woman on a mission, that's what I'm like. I want this finished as soon as possible. I'm trying to think of ways to fuck these people up so badly that they won't have time to come after us, but without them knowing that we were responsible."

"How do you suggest we go about that?"

"I don't know yet, but for the time being, that car at the volleyball court is intriguing me."

"Yeah and…?"

"The only reason I can think of that it was there, would be to film Patryk in such a compromising situation that they can blackmail him into revealing something about an operation that started when he was in charge, but could still be active."

Wolski thought about it. "There's still the abduction thing. If it is a spook thing, they would want to keep one step away from it to avoid comebacks if it went wrong."

"That makes sense, because if they had a video of what went on at the picnic site, they would have used it, and the heavies would all have fucked off to their rat nests and left the brains behind it all to get on with it?"

"Maybe the video they took wasn't as damning as they hoped."

"Their plan probably didn't involve Patryk killing their guy."

"Or maybe they've already been in touch with Wilkanowicz, and he just hasn't told us. The meatheads could just be here in case he needs extra persuasion."

"After lunch, how about you see if you can find out what's going on in the police investigation, because there's something not right about what we've learnt so far."

"What do you mean?"

"Well let's assume, for the sake of argument that Patryk's account to me is truthful and accurate. How does that compare with the model that the cops are working on? For instance, who are they assuming actually fired the shot that killed Morales? Do they think Ruiz was the killer?"

"They won't think that; Morales' gun hadn't been fired. From what my contacts have said so far, they haven't got a clue, but because the two victims are what they regard as unimportant, they're not giving it top priority. There's been a double murder in Falls Church, and they'll be throwing everything they've got at that for the moment."

"What's all that about?"

"I don't know any more at the moment. I'll ask around, but I doubt it's connected to what we're working on. What are you going to do this afternoon?"

"I'm going back to Patryk's and I'm going to put the screws on him. In deference to his injury, I've been gentle with him up till now, but the time for that is over."

Chapter Six
Friday 2.30pm - Waverly Way, Mclean

"Ms. Price. How nice to see you. I didn't know you were expected today."

"I wasn't. This is what you might call a casual visit. Is he in the lounge?"

"No, he's in the study. I should warn you though he's not in a good mood."

"That makes two of us," she told him, heading off to find him.

"What the fuck!!!!" Patryk was shouting at his computer.

"Having trouble?"

He turned, obviously surprised to see her. "Saffie, you didn't say you were coming."

"No, I didn't, did I? We need to talk."

"Is there a problem?" he asked. "Other than the ones I know about, that is?"

She looked at him dubiously, "There's more to this than you know, or more than you're telling us."

"I've told you all I know, but I agree there's more than we know so far. I've spent the morning trying to recover some records, and it looks like some are missing. I've got all sorts of safeguards to stop that happening but with my arm the way it is, I'm really struggling."

"You need help?"

"Yes I do, but who do I get with the right level of clearance to be looking at this stuff."

"Outside my skill-set I expect."

"You're too busy anyway. I don't want to pull you away from what you're doing."

"How about Linda Baker? She's the best qualified person I can think of. Her clearance is more out of date than mine, but she's a safe pair of hands."

"I doubt she'd want to help; I don't think she thought I'd treated her very well over that business that caused her to walk out."

"It wasn't you that she blamed. It was the assholes at Professional Standards. I've already used her on this, although she doesn't know it's connected to you."

"I'll call her. Tell me what's worrying you in particular, and we'll see if we're on the same page."

"Leave that for the moment, come and sit somewhere comfortable."

Patryk conceded and when he led her through to the lounge, she could see how debilitated his movements were.

Saffie explained her theory about the fourth car.

"Fourth car?"

"There was yours, the Mazda that Morales was driving, the Ford owned by Ruiz' mother, and a Chevy that we're pretty certain is involved one way or another and whose details are restricted," she told him. "The cops aren't aware of that one yet." She went on to explain what they'd learnt about the Russian connections; and her theory about the attempt to blackmail or discredit him by filming him killing the Morales guy. "There must be something from back in your past, that if exposed now would have a huge international impact, or perhaps bring down an operation that's still ongoing."

"My thoughts have been much along the same lines."

"What I don't understand is, if it's the Ruskies, why they're using so much amateur muscle."

"That's not such a strange thing, when you think about it," he told her. "It's so they can step away and disown it, if it all goes toes up. Unless they're running an operation that hasn't been sanctioned by the Kremlin."

"So, are there any of our operations, such as the ones I described?" she asked, knowing that the only correct answer could be yes."

"I can think of at least four."

"Are any of them mentioned in that missing data you referred to earlier?"

"Yes, two."

Saffie's phone buzzed in her pocket. "It's Wolski, do you mind if I get this?"

"Go ahead."

"Wolski, something happen? ... Remember him, of course I do, hardly likely to forget, am I? Why do you ask? ... Oh Jesus. Who was the other one? ... Dear God, how old? ... We need to keep across this. ... Yes of course it's connected. ... Are you staying for dinner tonight? ... Okay, I'll see you in the morning."

Patryk had been about to call Linda, but held off, when he heard the start of Saffie's call. "What's that all about? Did you mean that what he was telling you about is connected to me?"

"Somebody murdered Felix Carter and his thirteen-year-old daughter."

"For fucks sake. Felix was an asshole, but he didn't deserve that, and his daughter for God's sake. I thought she lived with his ex."

"She did, but she was staying with her dad for a couple of days while her mom's in hospital."

Felix Carter had been family liaison officer when Brett had been on his final mission in Ukraine. Except for Saffie's personal intervention, the mission would almost certainly have ended in her husband's death. In the subsequent investigation it was found that Carter and Brett's controller, Karl Radwell had missed several opportunities to prevent things going wrong, and both lost their jobs.

"So, are you going to tell me, or am I going to have to actually ask you the question?"

"What do you mean?"

"Don't fuck me around Patryk. You know what I mean."

His shoulders slumped. "Two of them."

"So, records of two operations go missing from your archives, and both involve Carter, and then he gets murdered. When did you last access those files?"

"Last week."

"Why?"

"I had a call from one of our former colleagues that PS have been looking into a few ops from when I headed up Russian section."

"And it didn't occur to you to mention it until now?"

"I'm sorry, I wanted to see what, if anything they could find to use against me."

"Who was it that called?"

"Rupert Golightly."

"Jesus Patrick, he's been out of the service since before I joined."

"Yes, I know, but he'd been visited and asked about them."

"And are you sure that it was him that called? I mean unless you've been in touch regularly…"

"We went through the usual ID protocols."

"You need to get Linda or someone like her in here as soon as possible. It looks like your archives have been hacked. In the meantime, where can I find Rupert Golightly?"

"I don't know his address. He moved to Connecticut shortly after he retired."

"Give me his number; I'll find him."

Patryk dictated the number from his phone and watched Saffie type it into a number validator on her own.

"He called you from a landline - that's unusual, but an indicator it could be valid. Let's find out where that is. Area Code 203 - that's Greenwich. Give me a minute and I'll get an address."

She selected a number she'd called earlier.

"Dexter. … No, still on for later. I was wondering if there's something you can do for me very quickly now. … I need a precise address for a landline number. It's kinda urgent. … Fantastic, I'll text it to you now. I haven't had time to check my emails yet, but thanks. I'll see you later."

After a few more taps at her phone, she looked up at Patryk.

"Dexter? Is there a new man in your life?" he said.

"I don't have time for a relationship even if I were looking. Dexter's a new contact, and I'm still checking him out. Have you contacted Linda yet?"

"I sent her a text, but she hasn't replied yet."

A few seconds later her phone buzzed with an incoming text.

"453 Stanwick Road, Greenwich, CT. Let's have a look at that." Tapping at her phone again for a few seconds she was soon looking at the street view. "Jesus Patryk, either your pal Rupert won the state lottery, or they're paying senior execs in the CIA a lot more than I thought. This place is like a frigging palace. Is he married?"

"He was. I don't know if he still is."

"I think I need to pay him a visit."

"Do you want me to tell him you're coming?"

"No thanks. But let me give Linda a call, if she can't help we need to find someone else PFQ."

Saffie picked Linda's number from her contacts, "Linda. … Yes, hi. Did you get a text from Patryk Wilkanowicz a few minutes ago? … I'm working for him at the moment, and he's got a real big problem and needs help quickly. Trouble is that it's related to his old job, and there aren't many people who are qualified to help out. … That's great. Thanks

Linda." Turning back to Patryk she said, "She's in the middle of something at the moment. She'll call you back in the next hour."

"Thanks, Saffie. I should be doing all this stuff myself, but what with the gunshot wound and the cancer, I'm completely off my game at the moment. I can't seem to think straight."

"That's not all that surprising, I guess. I'm going to leave you now."

In the car she instructed her Bluetooth connection to call her long-standing friend, Mary Riley. Then just as she thought it would go to voicemail, she got an answer.

"Saffie, it's been too long. How are you?"

"I'm good, how are things with you?"

"Real good thanks. When are we going to see you?"

"It depends. How do you fancy having a couple of real enthusiastic young ranch hands coming to help for a few days?"

"You want to have the boys come stay again? I'd love that. When are we talking about?"

"I was hoping that tonight wouldn't be too soon."

"Sure, will you want dinner?"

"No thanks, we'll have eaten, so we'll be late. Is that okay?"

"No problem. How long for?"

"At least until Monday, but it may be longer. I've just taken on a really big case, and I need to be sure they're safe."

"I've got some news."

"Sorry Mary, I've got a bit to do. Tell me when I get there."

Leaving her car out of the garage, she went inside to find the boys using the big screen on the living room TV to play Rainbow Six Siege on the PS 4. "Okay boys. Sorry to interrupt, but how do you fancy a few days with Aunt Mary?"

"Oh yeah!" they shouted in unison.

They were keen to know when, and she told them the plan was to leave straight after dinner.

Josh, always the most down-to-earth one, reminded her, "But, Mom, we've got prep to do and school on Monday."

"Your tutor never tires of telling me how well you're both doing and how you're ahead of schedule on almost everything, so if you miss a day or two I doubt it will matter too much. As for prep, you can take that with you."

"Wow, this will be like an extra mid-term break," Ben enthusiastically observed.

"Well then, you better go pack some things then hadn't you?" They rushed off, "And don't forget all your ATV gear this time," she called after them.

Brett had bought them each a small quad bike to use while they were staying at the farm, and Mary had made space to store them in one of her outbuildings. Saffie worried that at the rate they were growing, they'd soon be too big for the junior-sized vehicles.

Dexter McDowell arrived in plenty of time for dinner. Saffie remembered his face, but not much else about him. He was about twenty-five years old, personable, good-looking in a clean-cut sort of way, but not athletic. His cheerful disposition made her take to him straightaway. They spent forty minutes talking through the services that he provided, and the sort of services that she required from time to time. By the time dinner was ready, they both agreed that there was plenty of scope for their business relationship to blossom. Over dinner she asked, "So Dexter, is there a future Mrs. McDowell waiting in the wings?"

"Not at the moment Saffie, but if you ever want to revisit that relationship thing, I'm open to offers."

Cindy giggled.

"I'm not in the market at the moment, and I've probably gotten a few years on you. You'd be better looking for a newer model."

"Are you asking our Mom for a date?" Ben asked.

"No, he isn't," Saffie quickly answered, "He's just letting me know that my question was a bit too personal, and he's right. How is business though Dexter? It must be tough starting out on your own."

"It's sporadic at the moment. I haven't got the cash to spread it around on fancy advertising, and there's a lot of competition. I'm relying mostly on word of mouth. Linda has been great putting things my way."

"But you're not competing with her?"

"Not really. There's very little crossover between what she does and what I do. Linda's mostly into hardware and large-scale security systems, whereas I'm more into data recovery, security and protection, that sort of thing. I won't work for anybody that wants to use my services for criminal purposes, so I vet all my clients before I take them on."

"You're the second person I've come across like that recently. Very refreshing."

"I expect you're talking about Patsy."

Saffie was taken aback. "What? How did you guess that?"

"Audrey is my little sister. Well half-sister to be accurate. Unlike her, I actually want to make a living out of what I do. This isn't something I do just for a few extra bucks."

"I'd be interested to learn what you discovered when you vetted me."

"Probably a lot more than you'd have wanted, but a lot less than I'd have liked to," he replied with a cheeky grin.

Cindy giggled again while Saffie blushed; she didn't remember doing that since high school.

"Okay boys, make sure you've got everything ready. We need to be on the road in half an hour. Dexter I'm sorry to be rude, but I need to chase you away."

"No problem, thank you for the meal. It was very nice, Cindy. Are you going on holiday?"

"I wish. No, the boys are going to stay with their Aunt while I'm away working for a few days."

It was a two-hour journey to the farm outside Harrisonburg, and the boys didn't stop talking almost the whole way, but then a few miles from their destination, when Ben was finally asleep, Josh spoke to Saffie. "Are you going to be doing dangerous things again, Mom? Is that why we're going to stay with Aunt Mary?"

"The main reason is because I'm going to be away myself. It's true that I want you to be somewhere safe, but Cindy's job is not to be a full-time childminder. I already feel guilty that I don't get to spend enough time with you both because of my work, but most of the time it's unavoidable. There's always been a degree of danger in the work I do, but no more so than a cop or firefighter. Would you want me to give up the only thing I'm any good at to be a full-time mom, because I don't think I'd be very good at that."

"You're the best Mom in the world."

She choked as she replied. "It's lovely to hear you say that sweetheart, but you and Ben make it easier than most kids do."

They didn't speak again until she turned into the drive of the farm. It was ten thirty, she and Mary hurried the kids inside and into the rooms that they'd now adopted as their own each time they came to stay.

Saffie was still carrying the boys' bags upstairs when Rusty, the ranch foreman appeared at Mary's bedroom door, obviously fresh out of the shower.

"Here Saffie let me give you a hand with that."

"Oh Rusty. I didn't realize you were… I mean, I thought you…" She awkwardly started to say when Mary appeared out of one of the boys' rooms.

"That was the news I was about to give you when you cut me off this afternoon."

"You and Rusty together? That's fantastic news."

"You approve then."

"Are you kidding? Of course I approve. I've watched you two skating around each other pretending there's nothing going on, every time I've been here for the last three years."

After they'd spent half an hour catching up on Mary's news and life on the farm, Rusty interrupted. "So where are you off to then Saffie?"

"Connecticut - I need to interview somebody who might not want to be interviewed."

"Sounds interesting. Will you be gone long?"

"I hope to be back home by Sunday, but depending on what happens up there I may ask you to keep the boys a bit longer. Will that be okay?"

"If I thought you'd let me, I'd have them here all summer."

Chapter Seven
Saturday 7.30am - Mary's Farm outside Harrisonburg, VA

The boys hugged their mother and watched her climb in her car. They waved as she drove away.

As always when she left the boys with Mary she felt a strong sense of guilt, and her eyes stung as she returned their waves. No matter how hard she tried to concentrate on what lay ahead in her investigation, the vision of the two boys in her rearview would penetrate her thoughts throughout the six-hour drive to Connecticut."

She'd booked a room at the Hyatt Regency Hotel about six miles from Golightly's home and checked in. There had been cheaper and closer options for places to stay, like guest houses and B&Bs, but she didn't want to be questioned about any comings and goings in the early hours should they prove necessary.

In an ideal world, she'd knock on his door, he'd invite her in, answer her questions with truthful and logical explanations, and she could go get a good night's sleep. Unfortunately, she doubted very much if that's what would happen. In the counter-espionage world, life was rarely that simple.

After lunch at an Italian restaurant in Greenwich, she drove to the property that Dexter had identified as the source of Golightly's call. The road was lined with tall trees and hedges along almost its entire length, so Google Streetview had given few clues what the approach to the house would be like. Nevertheless, she'd seen photos online from when the property had been marketed ten years earlier.

Saffie had been expecting something impressive, but when she turned into the driveway she was still shocked. The online photos hadn't done it justice. The paved driveway swept in delicate bends through immaculate grounds up to the huge, almost palatial, house. The building itself was reminiscent of a residence for a Far East colonial governor from the days of the British Empire.

A face appeared at one of the windows and watched her climb out of the car. Surprised that she hadn't already been challenged by some sort of security, she mounted the wide imposing steps that led to the tall double entry doors. There was no doorbell button, so she pulled the handle that presumably alerted people that there was a visitor.

After a long pause, a man's voice from a hidden speaker said, "Look up to the camera above the door and state your business."

Set into the doorframe was a tiny round semi-spherical object which she assumed was the camera. "My name is Saffron Price, I'm a private investigator working for Patryk Wilkanowicz. He's asked me to speak to Rupert Golightly with regard to their recent telephone conversation."

"Mr. Golightly is away from home at the moment. Leave your card by the door, and someone will call you to discuss whatever you need to talk about." The voice had an accent, that could quite easily have been Russian.

"I'm afraid the nature of the business is extremely confidential and can only be discussed face to face."

"You've had your answer. Leave your card and go away, or I'll call the police."

Instead of doing what the voice had said, she took out her phone and called the number that Golightly had used to call Patryk. She heard the faint sound of a phone ringing somewhere inside and waited until it went to voicemail.

"Mr. Golightly, this is Saffron Price, I'm outside your door. You know as well as anybody that the matters I wish to discuss could well impact on national security. If you don't speak to me I'll have to assume that you're either being deliberately obstructive or prevented from doing so. Either way it would necessitate the involvement of the FBI. That's something that I'm sure neither of us want. I'll wait in my car."

Half an hour later a police cruiser pulled into the driveway and stopped alongside her. She lowered her window and waited.

"Can you get out of the car Ma'am?" the cop asked.

"Sure." She climbed out and waited for the next question.

"ID." He demanded.

She produced her wallet showing her Virginia Private Detective and Investigator badge, her driving license, and offered him her business card. "What's your business here Ma'am?"

"I'm a retired agent of the CIA, as are both my client and Mr. Golightly. I'm not at liberty to reveal my business here as it concerns matters of national security."

"Are you armed?"

"I have a registered HK45, secured in the gun locker in the trunk. My concealed carry permit is in the wallet you're holding."

"I believe you've been informed that Mr. Golightly is not on the premises at the moment."

"That would be fine, except I saw him at the window when I first arrived."

"Even if that were true, he's not obliged to speak to you. So, if you don't leave peacefully right now, I'll have to arrest you."

"No problem officer, sorry to waste your time." Taking back the wallet, she climbed back in the driving seat, and smiled at him as she turned her car around. A quick glance in her rearview, revealed a man talking to the cop on the doorstep. It was the man she'd seen at the window earlier. Of course, she had no way of knowing whether or not the man in the house was Golightly, she'd only ever seen a photo, and that was probably taken twenty years earlier.

Unsurprised at Golightly's reluctance to talk to her, she began to make plans to revisit him later, plans which didn't include an invitation. Her preparations included making a couple of purchases that few would think of before making a covert entry into a residential building. They weren't something she'd used before, but the fruits of an idea she'd developed as a distraction when she was forced to work alone.

It was six pm by this time, so she returned to the hotel and made herself a cup of coffee in the room before making a series of phone calls.

Her first call was to Patryk. He had no news other than that Linda was in his study rebuilding the data he'd lost from backup. He expressed his lack of amazement at Golightly's reluctance to speak and offered to call and attempt to persuade him to cooperate, but Saffie asked him not to.

Her next call was to Wolski. "What's happening?"

"I spoke to your little lady with the toddler in Kincaid Avenue and convinced her that I was still on the job, and that our friends at 7811 were suspected of planning a bank heist. I told her that you were an undercover cop, and your visit had actually been part of the same operation. She's allowed me to put one of your surveillance cameras in her front bedroom, and to use it as a base when I make an entry later to plant a couple of bugs."

"I didn't expect you to do that. I was going to do it when I got back."

"I know that, but that would have been several days wasted, and I didn't have anything else on my to do list."

"Just take care, covert entry isn't something they teach at cop school, as far as I know."

"I know, but I didn't spend nearly fifteen years in the department without learning a trick or two."

"Where did you get the hardware? Cameras and bugs etcetera."

"The same place that you usually use. I told them to bill you for it. Is that okay?"

"Sure. I need to top up that ten grand I gave you, what with all the extra hours you're putting in and expenses you've incurred."

"I ain't gonna fight you for it. Thanks."

Her final call was to Mary and the kids. "How are they?" she asked her friend.

"Okay most of the time. Rusty's been keeping them occupied helping him. But Josh got a bit tearful at one point."

"What was that about?"

"He's terrified that something's going to happen to you."

"I'd better speak to him, is he there?"

"Just a minute, I'll fetch him."

There was a pause before he came on, "Hi, Mom."

"Hi sweetheart. How are you doing?"

"I'm okay, Mom. What about you. What have you been doing?"

"Not very much so far. I went to see a guy a couple of hours ago, but he didn't want to speak to me. I'll try again later. If it goes well I'll be on the way back to Dunn Loring tomorrow. What have you been up to?"

"Rusty's been teaching us how to round up cattle on our ATVs. Ben's really good at it, but I don't like to go too fast, and I sometimes let one get past me."

"It's only a bit of fun sweetheart. You're good at lots of other things."

"What do you mean?"

"You're good at math, art, and writing stories; but most of all you're really good at being the sweetest kid I know and making me feel good when I don't feel so hot. But don't tell Ben I told you that, he's good too, but in different ways, he just doesn't have that little extra something special."

"I love you, Mom."

"And I love you too. Go and get that brother of yours."

There was another pause while she heard Josh calling Ben to the phone. "Hi, Mom."

"Hi sweetheart. I hear you're learning how to be a cowhand."

"It's really good fun, Mom. I wish I could have learnt to do it on horseback, like back in the day."

"I bet you'd have been real good at it too. Have you been having a good time?"

"It's the best, Mom. Rusty's doing a cookout tonight, with steak from one of Mary's own cows, and Aunt Mary says some of her herd are nearly ready to give birth so we're hoping it happens while we're here."

"How's Josh making out?"

"He's okay, but he doesn't get as excited as me about things, does he? He's missing you a lot, but he's started a really good pencil-drawing of the old farmhouse. I'm missing you too though. I love you, Mom."

"Me too sweetheart. I'll let you go get yourself outside that steak. Speak tomorrow, I don't know what time."

She ended the call with a worse than usual bout of wet eye syndrome.

*****

At 11.30 pm, Saffie parked her car in a large construction site about half a mile from Golightly's house. She'd changed from the denim pants and sweatshirt she'd been wearing all day into an all-black outfit of combat pants and jacket, steel-toed sneakers, neoprene shooting gloves and ski-mask. Strapped to her right calf was a USMC combat knife. In her pockets she had her lock picking kit, zip ties, a small reel of duct tape, a fully charged high-output taser, as well as two spare magazines for the suppressed Heckler and Koch 45 she had tucked into her belt.

Apart from the absence of an automatic rifle and an assault helmet, to anybody observing she would have appeared to be a member of a SWAT or assault team. Definitely not just a caller who only wished to ask someone a few innocuous questions. However, that was the point. She wanted to intimidate, not only the subject of her interrogation, but anybody else she encountered whilst she was in the house.

Once out of the vehicle she went to the trunk and lifted out a plastic crate by its handle, ignoring the noises coming from inside as she carried it with her. Leaving the car unlocked to help with a quick getaway should the need arise, she made her way toward Golightly's home.

Stanwick Road was long and winding, but fortunately had very little traffic. Nevertheless in the short distance from where she'd left the car, to the decorative gateway of number 453, she was passed by two cars.

Each time she pressed herself into a hedge at the roadside until the vehicles were out of sight.

The huge beautifully kept grounds were enclosed in tall trees and thick shrubbery, allowing her to get close to the house without being observed and hopefully before any of the inevitable motion sensors detected her presence.

She was behind the garage, and only forty feet from the house, before the LED floodlighting blindingly lit the area surrounding the building as if it were noon on a summer day. Freezing behind a row of small decorative conifers, she waited until two men, armed with M5 suppressed assault rifles, cautiously stepped out of a side door and began a visual sweep of the area.

After a few words in what she recognized was Russian, one moved toward the rear of the building, leaving the second to search the area where she was concealed. The men appeared comfortable with their weapons, but their tactics were less professional.

Once the first man was out of sight, Saffie opened the crate, put her hand inside and pulled out a fully grown black cat, holding it by the scruff of its neck. The cat protested and attempted to claw it's captor. It was still screeching when she whipped the bag off its head and released it.

The cat hurtled away, crossing directly in front of the nearest man. Saffie watched him visibly relax and turn back toward the building enabling her to step silently up behind him and hold her hand over his mouth as she pressed the taser against the side of his neck. He made a brief noise and fell to the ground. She caught the rifle to prevent it clattering on the tarmac when it fell. It took only moments to truss him with ready-prepared zip ties and gag him with the tape. Then laying the rifle on top of him she dragged him behind the conifers where she'd hidden less than a minute before. It was more than another minute before her victim had recovered enough to understand what was happening. His wrists were secured behind him, his ankles together, and then his wrists and ankles to each other.

Speaking quietly in Russian she told him, "In a moment I'm going to remove the tape from your mouth, and I want you to call your friend and tell him that it was a cat. If you say anything else, I'll cut your balls off with this." She told him, brandishing the knife in front of his eyes. "Do you understand?" He nodded. "Do you believe me?" He nodded again. She pressed the knife into his crotch with one hand and pulled the tape away from his mouth with the other.

The man started to say something. Saffie didn't catch what it was, but it had nothing to do with cats. She slapped the tape back into position and pressed the knife further into his crotch, not enough to castrate him, but enough to penetrate the skin and make him reconsider his future masculinity. His protest from behind the tape led her to believe he was prepared to cooperate.

"Ready to try again?"

He nodded.

She pulled the tape away again and he called something that roughly translated as, *'It's ok, Gradsky, it was only a cat.'* She put the tape back across his mouth and more across his eyes. Then she waited for Gradsky to return.

When he did, Saffie attempted the same trick again using the second cat. but this time, the cat scooted away behind her, with an equally angry protest.

Unintentionally and without realizing it, she'd left the first guy's knees in sight. The cat's shriek drew Gradsky's attention towards her and he spotted his bound partner. "Volkov, are you okay?" he asked in Russian, and his approach towards his fallen comrade was slow and cautious.

In a perilous re-creation of a scene from a Charlie Chaplin movie, Saffie crept around the other side of the conifers, coming up behind him just as he realized what had happened to his friend. It proved the work of a moment to repeat the treatment she'd given Volkov, and she had him trussed like a second Thanksgiving turkey. Tying the two of them together face to face, she took the two rifles and their handguns before leaving her victims where they were.

In yet another sign that she was dealing with amateurs, she found the door they'd used to leave the building, had been left unlocked. Except for one of the M5s which she slung from her shoulder, she left the confiscated weapons on the ground outside the door. It led into a mudroom and utility area and through into the kitchen. Almost every surface was strewn with dirty plates, pizza boxes, half-empty fast-food containers, beer cans, bottles and used cooking pans. This wasn't a house where this would be normal. In one corner was a small puddle of what looked like dried blood.

Creeping through the first floor of the enormous house toward the vast two-story-high entrance foyer, she heard the sounds of a TV playing some kind of sporting event. Two voices speaking Russian were finding something very amusing.

Saffie waited and listened, not only to hear what they were saying, but for any sounds that indicated there were others in the house. She could see through a window that the movement sensors had stopped registering activity and the floodlights had gone out. When the two men realized that the lights outside were no longer alight it was likely, they'd expect their pals to return. She couldn't afford to delay any longer.

As she was about to burst into the room, she heard a young female voice from upstairs cry out in pain. Her scream was followed by loud instructions from a man and laughter from the two men in the room. Waiting was no longer an option. She exploded into the room, demanding in Russian, "Get on the floor with your hands behind your back."

The younger of the two dived for a gun on the amongst bottles and glasses on the coffee table. Saffie's lightning response was to put a bullet through his hand with her own suppressed handgun. The older one turned as if to run toward a door that led to the outside terrace.

"The next person that makes a move that isn't toward the floor gets a bullet in the head. What's it to be?" She knew that her Russian accent was a long way from flawless - she hadn't used the language at all since her trip to Ukraine three years earlier - but it was clear that the men had any trouble understanding her, or her intent and both dropped to the floor. She secured them in much the same way as the two outside, taping their mouths and eyes. Leaving them squirming on the floor like a pair of aborted lambs, she hurried to the staircase listening for clues to where the cry of pain might have come from.

At the top of the stairs, she heard whimpering, then a man's voice, in heavily accented English. "Now you get idea, bitch. Show me titties. That good. What you think Uncle Rupert? You think Alice have nice titties, yes? So, you going to tell me what I want to know, or shall we have a little look at Alice pussy? What you think?"

Saffie wasn't about to wait to learn what Rupert thought, she stepped into the room where a huge man was gripping a young girl by the upper arm, the girl naked except for a tiny pair of panties. So enraged by the sight, it never crossed her mind to issue any kind of threat or warning, she simply shot the man through the head and as his lifeless body fell to the floor, a second man grabbed her around the throat, taking her by surprise.

At any other time, in any other place, with any other adversary, the man would have had the upper hand, but with the adrenalin still pumping through her veins, and the blood lust of battle still ruling her responses, Saffie's cat-like instinct for survival took over. The steel-lined heel of one of her combat sneakers scraped down his shin, an elbow smashed back into his midriff, and her head did likewise onto his nose. Her attacker weakened his grip, allowing her to break free, spin and knuckle-punch him in the throat. Barely stopping to catch breath she restrained him as he fought for breath on the floor.

Rupert Golightly was naked, bound to a chair with a gag around his mouth. Ripping the gag from his head she said, "Are there any more of them?"

"There are four others, six altogether."

"I've dealt with them," she told him as she cut him free.

"My mother and sister are locked in the basement."

"Okay, I'll go and free them, meanwhile can you take Alice and find yourselves some clothes."

"Who are you?"

"We can talk about that in a minute, you just need to do as I ask, and try to find a room on the first floor that hasn't been too messed up by your guests. Wait there for me to bring your family to you and hold off calling the cops for just a few minutes if you can."

It took several minutes to locate the door to the basement, but when she eventually found it, she discovered the two distressed women locked in a small storage room with a lot of games equipment. They were tied, blindfolded and gagged, at least one had soiled herself and the room stank of urine and feces. Hurriedly she cut them free, belatedly realizing that the sight of her still wearing the balaclava must have been nearly as frightening as what had gone before. She rolled the mask up and apologized. "Come with me to join Alice and Rupert while we wait for the police."

"Are they alright?" the elderly lady asked."

"I'll leave it to them to tell you that."

"I can't see them while I'm like this. I've disgraced myself," she pleaded.

"Ma'am, the only people in this house who need to be ashamed are either dead or tied up like rotisserie chickens."

She was clearly stiff and struggling to move after being tied up for so long, but the other woman was nearly as bad, and hadn't spoken.

"I'm sorry, are you Rupert's sister?"

She nodded, clearly unable to speak. 'God knows what unspeakable torture these poor women have had to suffer,' Saffie thought.

Leading them up the stairs to the first floor, she reunited the women with Rupert and Alice in some kind of living room. "Just give me two minutes to check one thing before we call the cops. Is that okay."

She didn't give them an opportunity to reply but dashed to the back door and recovered a Glock that had belonged to one of the first two guys. Then rushing headlong upstairs to the room where she'd found Rupert and Alice, she checked to see if there were any obvious firearms. Finding a Remington in the dead guy's pocket, she put it in his hand, and went back downstairs. After replacing the Glock and M5 outside the side door, she stopped to gather her thoughts. She hadn't wanted to be accused of shooting an unarmed man, no matter how justified it was, and she needed to think of any other implications.

As she walked back to the living room she called 911, "My name is Saffron Price. I need to report a house invasion. 435 Stanwick Road, Greenwich. There are three occupiers requiring medical assistance, one dead intruder, another two also requiring medical assistance, and three further restrained intruders. … Yes Ma'am."

"The cops and paramedics are on their way," she told the others. "I'm going to wait outside for them to arrive. When they get here tell them everything you can remember. Rupert, when you feel up to it, I'll come back to ask the questions I came here to ask in the first place.

None of them spoke.

When she opened the front door and stepped outside, the movement sensors detected her presence and the grounds lit up again.

She laid her weapons on the ground beside her, and when the first police cruiser came through the gate she took one long step to the left and held her arms out to the side.

Chapter Eight
Sunday 8.05am - Greenwich Police Station, Greenwich, CT

Having failed to find any holes in her evidence, or anything that conflicted with what they'd been told by the survivors and the physical evidence, the cops handed her over to the FBI.

The Feds had been equally robust with their own interrogation. Saffie hadn't asked for a lawyer, nor requested a break. Other than claiming that the man that had been molesting Alice had been holding a gun, she was completely candid about everything. She explained her reasons for being there, for suspecting that Rupert had not been free to speak for himself, and for not calling the police earlier. The only thing she refused to reveal was why she needed to question Rupert, telling them it was a matter of national security.

The federal questioners had been reluctant to accept her reasons for secrecy but she guessed that someone from Langley must have eventually intervened to validate her credentials, and with all the bad grace they'd demonstrated over the previous hours, they released her without explanation, apology, or an offer of a ride to collect her car.

Free to go about her business, but without her weaponry, Saffie stepped into the waiting Uber that she'd ordered twenty minutes earlier. The cab dropped her at the construction site where she was grateful to find her unlocked car untouched.

The short drive to the hotel thankfully got her there in time for two helpings of what the establishment optimistically called *the full breakfast*. In her room she hung the *Do Not Disturb* sign on the outer door handle, and phoned the same three people she had the evening before, giving them only scant details of the previous night's events.

After a shower she collapsed on the bed and pondered her seven hours of interrogation by the feds and detectives of the Greenwich PD. They hadn't been gentle. Cops were notoriously hostile to private investigators, particularly if they perceived them to be muscling in on police work, and they were similarly antagonistic to federal agents for much the same reasons. As a former CIA agent turned PI, Saffie was particularly disliked. So, armed and dressed like a special forces operator, having confessed to killing two intruders (the guy with the throat injury had died), and wounding a third, she wasn't surprised they hadn't just let her walk away.

Near naked except she fell asleep on top of the bedclothes and didn't wake until 5 pm when her cell phone vibrated for the fifth time in just as many minutes.

"Hello."

"Ms. Price, it's Rupert Golightly. Can we meet?"

"Sure, where are you?"

"At home."

"Really? They let you back in already?"

"That's not my home, it's my mother's. I live in Branford, a slightly more modest place."

"How are your mother, sister, and niece?"

"Mom will be okay I think, but Judith and Alice are seriously fucked up."

"When do you want to meet?"

"Would tomorrow morning be okay?" he asked.

"Sure. Can we say nine-thirty? Text me your address."

After ending the call, she picked Patryk's number from her contacts list.

"All hail the conquering hero. Fucking Hell Saffie, how the fuck did you achieve that?"

"It was a combination of luck, and the fact that most of the opposition were just untrained gangsters believing they were invincible."

"I can't wait to hear the detail."

"We've got more important things to do than swap war stories. I don't think this is over, not by a long way."

"Why do you say that?"

"Instinct I guess, but I'll be able to tell you more after I've spoken to Rupert properly. I'm seeing him in the morning."

"He called me earlier to get your number. He was angry when I told him that you hadn't been released until eight o'clock."

"I'm guessing you played a hand in that."

"Greenwich PD called me to verify some of what you said. Later the FBI called me and began talking like assholes, so I called someone at the George Bush Center. They want to talk to me; I told them it would make more sense if they talked to us together."

"I intend to drive straight home after seeing Rupert tomorrow. Maybe Tuesday morning. How are you going to explain away your arm?"

"I'll think of something."

"How is it by the way?"

"When it's completely immobilized, the pain is just about bearable, but when I try to use it, it's indescribable. I doubt it will be much use for anything again, but as my life expectancy is somewhat limited, it's probably not that important."

Wolski reported that his camera footage and bug recordings were bearing a lot of fruit. He added that he'd overheard them talking about Gradsky being arrested by the feds after some sort of raid. But they were going crazy about someone called Baranov having been killed and weren't sure what to do next.

She tried to call Mary, but she couldn't understand anything she said because of all the background noise. Mary responded with a text message

Kinda tied up right now. We'll call you later.'

That was the cue for Saffie to go and try to find somewhere to eat. After a Google search she settled for another Italian restaurant, but slightly more upmarket this time.

It was ten pm when she returned to her room, and she still hadn't heard from Mary and the boys. She was about to call again when her phone rang.

It was Ben. "Hi, Mom."

She could hear they were in a car. "Hi sweetheart. You're up late. How's it going?"

"We've been having the best time ever. First Mary and Rusty took us to a fairground and then to a rodeo. There were pro bull and bronco riders, girls doing barrel racing, and a whole team of trick horse riders. It was amazing!"

"Wow!" What did you do at the fairground?"

"We went on a few rides and did some shooting and throwing games. Josh won a goldfish throwing softballs at a target that tipped a guy dressed as a woman into a big water tank. Rusty won a jar of candy at the horseshoe throwing."

"Sounds fantastic. Let me speak to Josh."

"Hi, Mom."

"Hiya darling. Have you been having fun?"

"It's been really great, Mom. Mary and Rusty are the best aunt and uncle in the world. We had hotdogs and cotton candy."

"Did you enjoy the rides?"

"I didn't mind the big wheel, but I didn't go on the fast rides; they make me feel sick."

"What are you going to do with your goldfish?"

"I didn't want it, so I gave it to a little girl who was clapping after I won. She gave me a kiss. It was embarrassing."

"Eleven years old and stealing the ladies hearts already."

"When are you coming home?"

"Hopefully driving home tomorrow, and maybe collect you Tuesday or Wednesday. Is that okay?"

"I miss you and I've done a couple of drawings that I want to show you."

"I miss you too, both of you. Let me speak to Mary."

"Hi Saffie."

"Have you been spoiling my boys?"

"I haven't had this much fun since we were that age."

"As long as they appreciate it."

"Nobody has said thank you to me this much since I took Troy Simmonds into the barn when we were sixteen."

Saffie smiled, "Thank you though, both of you. I really appreciate you looking after them like this."

"It's not a chore Saffie. Did I overhear you're coming to collect them Tuesday or Wednesday?"

"I hope so Mary, I miss them and feel so guilty for farming them out."

"They understand, they really do, and they're not a chore for us."

As she lay in her bed, Saffie had to admit to herself that she was a little jealous that she hadn't been there for their first rodeo.

Chapter Nine
Monday 9.30 am - Branford CT

Rupert Golightly was right; his home was a great deal more modest than his mother's. It was about the same size as her own but built in a far more traditional style. He must have been watching out for her, because as she pulled on to his drive, the front door opened, and he stood waiting for her to climb the steep stairs to his porch.

"Hi," she said, noticing his arm in a sling and severely bruised face.

"I thought we could chat in the garden if that's okay. I'd rather the ladies didn't have to hear us going over what happened.

"Are they staying with you now?"

"For the time being, anyway. I doubt any of them will want to move back there after what happened."

"Shame, such a lovely house."

"It's a fucking mausoleum. It belonged to my grandparents. I hate it."

"I thought you'd bought it ten years ago."

"What gave you that idea?"

"When I looked on the Internet, it looked like that was when it last changed hands."

"No that's when my grandmother died. They had to advertise it to value the estate. It's part of a family trust. When she passed my mother became the main beneficiary. In theory we're not allowed to sell it, but I expect we'll challenge that in the courts after what's happened."

Saffie nodded at his sling, "Is that from those bastards?"

"Yes and a great deal worse, but I don't want to go into all that. What they did to Judith and Alice was crueler than you can imagine, and worse still I doubt that either will ever want to speak to me again."

"Because you wouldn't tell them what they wanted to know, you mean?"

111

"Yes, but don't get me wrong, I'm not that much of a hero. If I'd have thought it would have stopped them hurting the women, I'd have told them every single thing they wanted to know. But we both know that as soon as they were certain they'd got what they wanted, they'd have killed us all anyway."

"I don't need to know the detail of what went on in that house. I just want to know what they were after and why, if you can tell me."

"It started about ten or twelve days ago; I can't be sure. I lost track of time. I'd been out fishing on my boat; I'd moored up and two guys met me at the end of the pontoon. They showed me a video of another guy mauling Alice about and told me if I didn't go with them quietly they'd rape her and slash her face.

"They drove me to Stanwick Road, took me to the basement, and tied me to a chair. Mom, Judith and Alice were locked in the little storeroom, I could hear them calling for help. Then, threatening to kill my mother, they forced me to call Patryk and warn him that there were four files that someone was trying to get access to.

"Did they name the files?"

"They gave me a list. I did what they told me of course, but the weird thing was, that they must have already had access to Patryk's archives to know which files to ask for. They just didn't know how to get into them. The weirdest thing was that it wasn't any of those four that they really wanted to know about."

"I don't understand."

"Four days ago, they started on me again. They sat me in front of a laptop with Patryk's archives open. They'd already deleted two of the four files. What they wanted was for me to tell them how to find a fifth file, code named *Improbable*. The thing is I'd never heard of an operation with that name, and there wasn't one with that name and I didn't know how to find the one they were looking for. They told me to show them how to get into some of the other files. I tried to tell them that I had no idea how to get into any of Patryk's files. We all have our own unique system of protecting them. At first they didn't believe that, so they decided to start trying to beat details of the *Improbable* operation out of me.

"After giving up trying to get me to tell them what they wanted to know, they locked me in a closet for a day or two with the women, only allowing us out to use the toilet. They fed us with bottled water and potato chips and other shit at first. Then they stopped doing even that.

"That's when Baranov and Gradsky arrived - a pair of perverted evil sub-humans they were. Between them and the others they subjected Judith to hour after hour of rape and degradations, so awful I can't describe. Much of it Alice and I were forced to watch. There was nothing I could do to stop them.

"Then Baranov and Gradsky went away for a day, and I began to think that the ordeal was over, and they'd just kill us. That was when you came to the door. They wanted to know who you were, and of course I didn't know that either. They broke my arm while they were beating me up after you left.

"Later, Baranov and Gradsky returned, and they dragged me up to the bedroom and told me I was going to watch while they did to Alice what they'd done to her mother, unless I told them what you were doing there. I've still no idea how you did what you did on your own."

"It's not important, what matters now is we stop these bastards before they do any more damage."

"But you have stopped them, haven't you?"

"I doubt I've come close. I don't know who Baranov was, although I've a pretty good idea who his immediate boss is. The others are just low-level gangsters. We can be confident that someone in Moscow is pulling the strings, or someone acting under their direct orders. I'm also pretty sure that there's someone inside Langley helping them out."

"At the moment I don't care who was pulling the strings, I only know that my life's mission has now shifted to ensuring that each of the four survivors of that gang, dies a painful death," he said.

"I don't know how you're going to achieve that; they're all going away for a very long time."

"That house in Stanwick should be an indicator, but my family are very, very wealthy, and whatever it costs to ensure they die is what I'm prepared to spend."

"One good way to make certain that that happens is for me to let it be known that they've talked. They'll be dead before they ever get to trial, that would save you the trouble."

"How can you do that without flagging yourself up?"

"What is it they say? 'This isn't my first rodeo'. Keep watching the story in the media. You've got my number now, if you think of anything I should know then give me a call."

She got up to leave and as they reached the front door, Alice appeared from somewhere in the house, put her arms around Saffie and whispered in her ear, "Thank you."

As the teenager turned away, Saffie said, "You're a beautiful young woman, Alice. The people that did this to you and your family, aren't fit to breathe the same air as any of you. If I have anything to do with it, they won't for very much longer."

Alice briefly turned back and gave a weak smile before returning to wherever she'd come from.

The drive home was almost as long as it had been from Harrisonburg, and it was nearly five when she pulled through the gates of her home.

When she threw herself on the bed, her thoughts went to the promise she'd made to Rupert. There was no question that she'd do what she'd said, but she knew it wasn't a foolproof way of ensuring all of the bastards would get the punishments they deserved. Ultimately, they were acting under orders, and those people were just as responsible as those who had been in the room.

Chapter Ten
Tuesday 7.30 am - Dunn Loring

Saffie collected the mail from the box in her front wall and along with it a copy of the free regional newspaper. On the front page, was an article that caught her attention right away.

VIRGINIAN P.I. MAKES DRAMATIC RESCUE OF FAMILY OF FOUR

Two home invaders have died in an extraordinary single-handed rescue when a female P.I. and former special forces operator intervened to end a two-week long hostage ordeal.

In the early hours of Sunday morning, an unnamed female former special forces operator, acting on her own initiative, effected the rescue of a 78-year-old woman, her son 58, daughter 43, and granddaughter 18. The four had been held captive in their home for more than a week by a gang of six home invaders. When the operator, now a Virginian private investigator, called at the home to make enquiries, one of the intruders, posing as the occupier, called the police who asked her to leave. According to the PI's information, the person who came to the door was not the legitimate occupier, but she had no evidence to support that at the time.

Later, she returned to the property, and after making a covert entry, she discovered that the family were being subjected to torture, painful inhumane treatment and sexual abuse. In the operator's ensuing efforts to rescue the family, two of the offenders died, one suffered a non-life-threatening gunshot wound, and the others were restrained.

Investigators have asked that the family and private investigator not be named at present, because it is possible that the incident may have national security implications.

The FBI, who are now leading the investigation, are giving little detail but have asked that anybody with information about this incident should contact them on the following number. 203-777-6311

As far as she was aware, there were only seven other female PIs in Virginia, five of whom only did divorce work, so she knew it wouldn't be long before somebody turned up asking for a comment. She doubted Rupert or the others would be any more cooperative than she would be.

Her phone rang, it was Wolski, "Hi, I was about to call you."

"Most people have to pay for the sort of publicity that you somehow always manage to get for free. Your phone must be ringing off the hook."

"I use an answering service to filter my calls. A bit old school perhaps, but it works for me."

"My calls always go straight through okay."

"That's because yours is one of a growing list of numbers that don't get diverted."

"I don't know how you manage to do all you do by yourself."

"With increasing difficulty. I've been meaning to speak to you about that. What would you say to coming on board full-time?"

"Partner you mean?"

"A bit too soon to be thinking about that,. I was thinking more like permanent employee."

"Doing what?"

"Washing dishes, what do you think? PI work of course, we'd have to talk through the detail, but there'd be none of that divorce crap you get mixed up in."

"How much would it pay?"

"We could talk about that, but how about what you were getting in the department plus 25%."

"Do I have to start now, or can you wait until I've got my pants on?"

"Wolski, I've just eaten my breakfast, what I don't need in my head right now is an image of you in your underwear."

"Who said I was in my underwear."

"Enough. Tell me what you've been learning with your little spy mission."

"I can't understand lot of it because most of the time they're speaking in Russian, or at least I think that's what they're speaking. They do resort to English from time to time. Apparently they're really crapping themselves about what happened in Greenwich. This Lipov character has got them running around like headless chickens."

"Have you heard them mention either of us yet?"

"Not yet, but I may have missed something. They've mentioned Wilkanowicz a few times though."

"I'll need to listen to those recordings when I have time. Maybe we should start thinking about going proactive."

"What does that mean?"

"Up to now we've been trying to find out about things after they've happened, we've done quite well, but we haven't found out what or who's behind it or why. Maybe we should make them reveal themselves."

"Listen lady you might be Jack Ryan in drag, but I'm not built for that."

"You're not Jessica Fletcher either, I was thinking more Andy Sipowicz. Wolski, I wasn't thinking of hiring you for your fighting skills; you're a detective, a good one. What I'm talking about is stirring the pot a bit so that it's not just us having to react to things."

"I thought you already did that in Greenwich."

"Can we talk more tomorrow, I'm seeing Patryk this morning, and collecting the boys this afternoon."

"Would it help if I was with you at Wilkanowicz's?"

"We're going to be talking agency stuff that you're not cleared for, but otherwise it would have been great. Think about that offer though, I don't want a spur-of-the-moment decision. We'll need to know what to expect from each other."

Patryk's front door opened before her foot had touched the ground as she got out of her car in his drive.

"Where have you been? The Langley guy will be here soon, and we need to get our ducks in a row."

"I didn't agree a time Patryk, and in case you'd forgotten you're no longer my boss and I work to my own timetable these days."

"I know, I'm sorry. I'm so anxious to get this thing done. Come in."

"If we're not ready when they get here they'll have to wait until we are. But first tell me how you are, then how successful Linda was in recovering your data."

"My arm still hurts like a bastard, and I can't increase my dose of painkillers too much because I'm already using Oramorph for the cancer. It does feel slightly better today because I haven't been trying to use the keyboard since Linda came and sorted things out."

"Okay, before we go any further…"

She led him back inside the house, took her bug detector from her bag and did a sweep of the study. Almost immediately it began to beep, and the closer she got to the bookshelf the faster the beeps went. Scanning each book individually, she found the culprit. It was 'The CIA World Factbook 2020-2021'. It was sitting adjacent to the 2019-2020 edition of the same book. When she opened the offending volume she revealed a black disk resting inside a circular hole that had been cut into the pages, it was slightly larger and thicker than a dollar coin. She levered it out with her thumbnail, turned it over and slid the switch to off.

Patryk looked aghast and was about to say something when Saffie held up a finger and began another sweep. As she got closer to his desk, the detector began to beep madly, and when she held it against a USB hub next to his laptop the noise became almost continuous. After unplugging all the cables, she opened a drawer and put it inside. Then when she started another sweep, the detector continued its regular beep until she held it toward the ceiling, when the pace of the sounds accelerated.

"The smoke detector," she quietly told him.

He nodded.

"Leave it for the time being, let's go somewhere else to talk."

Patryk led her to the lounge, where she did a quick sweep and found nothing.

"For fuck's sake Saffie."

"How did that happen?"

"I'm going to assume that you trust Hugo."

"With my life, quite literally."

"Okay then the logical conclusion is that it was the Data-Fort guy. When did he last come?"

"About three weeks ago."

"And before that?"

"Four weeks. They come every four weeks."

"Always the same guy?"

"Until four months ago, yes. They've changed a couple of times since."

"Now tell me what Linda found?"

"The two files she recovered hadn't been opened nor tampered with in any way, just deleted. There was mention of Felix Carter in both of them, but the contents are now redundant. I couldn't see how either could have prompted his murder."

"What about the rest of them?"

"As far as I can tell, they're untouched."

"That's consistent."

"What do you mean? Consistent with what?"

"Those files were never what they were after, although I suspect they would have quite liked to have seen what was in them if it became an option."

"So, what the Hell is it all about?"

"The deleted files were just a stalking horse to get you to reveal how you get into your files in general. The one they really want to get into is a file called *Improbable*, is that familiar?"

Patryk's already pale complexion turned ashen. He staggered and sat down. "Th-they know about *Improbable*? how the fuck did that happen?"

"I don't have a clue. They took Golightly and his family hostage, to get him to flag up the files in your archive, any files just to persuade you to check to see if all was okay. In doing so they must have thought they could track your actions, and you'd reveal a methodology that would be common to all your files. Then, using that, it would help them get into the *Improbable* file without you realizing it had been accessed. Somehow they had managed to penetrate the archive, but there was no file called *Improbable*."

"There's no way that Rupert would have any idea how to get into any part of my archive."

"Whoever they are obviously didn't know that, but you're missing the point here."

"Tell me then."

"First of all, they've got someone inside Data-Fort who either can or thinks he can, track your keystrokes.

"Second, they must have someone inside Langley, someone high enough to be able to give them some idea how to get into the archive. Also highly placed enough to know about the existence of the *Improbable* operation, whatever it is. I don't expect you to confirm it, but I'm guessing it must be about some high-level asset somewhere in the Kremlin, someone who's been in place for some time."

"Even if they get into my archive once, it would be no guarantee that they could do it again without me. But what the fuck…?"

"You need to dump Data-Fort immediately and get someone like Linda to go through every aspect of your security from the ground up. I doubt she had time to do that when she was here before. Don't tell Data-Fort they've been rumbled just yet, although I suspect the guy that planted those bugs, might already know."

"If they didn't want to get inside those files, why kill Felix?"

"Possibly there was something in them that showed how Felix could identify one of them. It's a brutal act, and of itself not something I'd put past the FSB. However, I don't think so. It was probably to lay a false trail to lead your suspicions away from the *Improbable* operation. On the other hand, whoever they are, they seem to be killing anybody with evidence that could lead back to one of them. They're completely ruthless.

They heard the electronic sound that indicated someone had arrived.

"I'll have to get that; Hugo is at the store."

"I'll go, stay there; you look bushed before we even start out. Take my lead, but while they're here, don't mention the names of any specific files, okay?"

He nodded, and she thought he looked broken, a man who'd always been an oasis of calm no matter how bad the storm, and to her who'd always epitomized strength.

When she opened the door there were two agents whom she'd never met before. Both held their badges ready for inspection.

"Agent April Daniels from Langley; this is Special Agent Francis K. Sinclair of the FBI. We're here to see Patryk Wilkanowicz."

"My name is Saffron Price. I believe you're here to see me as well, but we weren't expecting the FBI."

"This will be a joint investigation Ms. Price," Daniels said.

"That's as maybe, but it's likely that some things will be discussed that Agent Sinclair isn't cleared for access."

"I can assure you Ms. Price that I have clearance from the very highest level for access to anything we may need to discuss today."

"Unless that clearance comes from the Deputy Director of Operations at the George Bush Center or from the President then I won't be discussing anything with you at all. If you have a problem with that, then

I suggest you take it up with my lawyer Franklyn Cohen of Chesham, Chesham and Adelstein.

Daniels pursed her lips and turned to the federal agent. "It's okay, Frank. I got this. Go wait in the car."

If Sinclair had been the Medusa, Saffie would have turned to stone at that very moment, but he turned and walked back to the Jet Black Chevvy Suburban they'd arrived in and climbed into the driving seat."

"Come in, Agent Daniels."

"There was no need for that Ms. Price."

"I don't know how much you know about me, Agent Daniels, but if you've learnt anything, you'd know that the only reason I'm not carrying a badge just like yours is because my husband and I were victims of serious deliberate attempts to falsely incriminate us. Some of those involved in that, worked in the same building as you. I'm an old-fashioned girl, and I only like to get screwed by one person at a time. So, if Agent Sinclair needs to know anything from what you learn here today, then I'll allow you to take the chance of charges under the Espionage Act rather than me."

"Very well."

"Mr. Wilkanowicz is extremely unwell at the moment, and I'll ask you to bear that in mind."

The agent looked at Patryk, "I'm sorry to hear that, Mr. Wilkanowicz. What's wrong?"

He opened his mouth to speak but before he uttered a word Saffie offered an explanation. "Mr. Wilkanowicz has pancreatic cancer. It's spread to his bones and only last week they took a biopsy from his arm which is refusing to heal. He's been given only months to live."

"That's dreadful news. I'll be recording this conversation if that's okay."

"No, it isn't okay," Saffie told her. "By all means take notes, but I'd like you to turn your phone off and lay it on the table."

"But…"

"Do you want this interview or not?"

"Very well." She powered down the device and laid it where Saffie had said.

"Mr. Wilkanowicz…"

"Just call me Patryk. Much less of a mouthful, don't you think?" he weakly replied.

"Patryk, can you explain how you first became aware that something was happening?"

He described receiving the phone in the mailbox and the note referring to an email.

"What did the email say?"

"There was no email. That's why I called Saffron in."

"And what did you manage to find out Ms. Price?"

"It started to get weird from the word go, because while I was here, a police officer arrived to give Patryk's personal companion a speeding ticket he'd picked up the night before."

"They called here to do that? Isn't that unusual?"

"I thought nothing of it at the time but, later I realized there was more to it than met the eye. While they were here, somebody used it as a distraction to put a tracker on my car."

"Are you suggesting that person may have colluded with the cop?"

"Yes, or rather acted under his or his partner's direction."

"That's a serious accusation Ms. Price. What evidence do you have of that?"

"Only the video of it happening. Later when I tracked the crook that planted it down, he told me that's what happened."

"We'll need to follow that up."

Saffie told her how the father and son team had followed her, how she'd discovered who they were, and how they'd come to her home under orders to beat her up. She went on to explain how she'd restrained and questioned them, then driven them to Vienna, omitting mention of sugar in the fuel tank.

"That's a bit severe, and I'm pretty sure it's illegal."

"Call it humane pest control, like putting a rat in your neighbor's yard and hoping it'll stay there. Anyway, as for following it up, good luck with that, I read in today's paper that the two Scotts were found shot dead in Clay the elder's home yesterday afternoon."

"Are you able to account for your whereabouts for that?"

"Seriously?" Saffie asked. "You'll recall that the reason you're here is because of the rather conspicuous incident in which I was involved in Connecticut. I'm using Scott's gun at the moment, because the Greenwich PD have held on to mine. You're welcome to have the gun tested against the rounds found in the Scotts if that helps."

Daniels ignored the jibe. "What happened next, Patryk?"

"I had a phone call from Rupert Golightly who told me that Professional Standards had been looking into a few ops from when I headed up Russian section."

"I'm quite certain that wasn't true."

"I didn't know that at the time, but when I checked I found some files had been deleted, two of them had mentioning Felix Carter, and it was the day after his death."

"Why didn't you report it?"

"I discussed it with Saffie, and between us we thought there could be some ongoing conspiracy to discredit me, and I decided to ask her to investigate further before I made a decision."

"Conspiracy, between whom?"

"How would I know. Let's be honest, I'm not exactly mister popular over there am I?"

"So, are you saying you don't trust Professional Standards to conduct a full and fair investigation?"

"Let's say I trust Saffron a whole lot more."

"What did you do Ms. Price?"

"I recommended that Patryk call-in expert IT advice, which I believe he did. In the meantime I undertook to speak to Rupert Golightly."

"Who did you call in, Patryk, given that your files are almost certainly about as confidential as any are likely to be?"

"I asked Linda Baker. Her clearance isn't up to date, but I regard her as at least as reliable as Saffron."

"More reliable than PS?"

"At that point I wasn't sure whether Langley was involved or if this was motivated by other people."

"What about you Ms. Price?"

"I think you're aware of what happened when I went to visit Golightly."

"Is that it? Is that all that either of you have to say?" the agent said looking from one to the other.

"Feel free to ask any questions," Saffie offered.

"Does this mean you've completed your investigations then?"

"I've barely started, but if there's nothing more I have a busy day ahead of me. Thank you for your time."

After Daniels had left Patryk pointed out that there was more than one error in the timeline they'd given her.

"That's why I didn't want her to record it, and why I didn't want the Feds sitting in. It's so much easier to make a mistake in written notes."

"You're running rings around them at the moment, but I hope you're not putting yourself in more jeopardy by doing so."

"My head is well and truly above the parapet now, so I have little choice but to continue what I started."

"You're an extraordinary woman, Saffie. I should have appreciated you more when you were an agent."

Hugo had returned while Daniels had been there, and when Saffie was ready to leave, he showed her out. "Ms. Price, I'm really worried about Patryk; he's not himself."

"Hugo, I think we know each other well enough now for you to call me Saffie. But yes, I agree, he's not as sharp as he once was. In the past he'd have been way ahead of me with some of this. You can always call me if there's anything you need help or advice with."

"Thank you, Saffie. You're very kind.

As she went to get into her car, something occurred to her. Taking out the scanner she ran it over the car, quickly locating a tracker under her nearside rear wheel arch. She pulled the magnetic device off and put it on the passenger seat.

When Saffie stopped at the lights to turn left from Chain Bridge Road into International Drive, a truck loaded with the shells of cars looking as if they were headed for a scrap yard pulled up beside her. Smiling, she lowered her window and tossed the tracker through the window of one of the car shells.

As she approached her home she spotted a man sitting in a car near the gates. She recognized him from three years earlier. She pressed the remote control, the gates opened, and she drove through. Watching in her rearview, she was astonished when the guy followed her through, just as Clay Scott had a few days earlier.

After driving her car into the garage, the door closed behind her, and she went inside and waited. It wasn't long before the doorbell rang.

"Hello," she answered, through the entry phone.

"Hello, my name's Brian Newgate. I'm a reporter with…"

"I know who you are Mr. Newgate."

"I was wondering if you'd like to comment on the speculation about you being the Virginian P.I. involved in the hostage rescues in Connecticut."

"I'm fascinated to hear that."

"What?"

"What you were wondering about."

"Do you have any comment to make?"

"Why would I?"

"Maybe you would want to clear up any confusion."

"I'm not sure which newspaper you read Mr. Newgate, but it's clearly not your own, which said, and I quote, 'Investigators have asked that the family and private investigator not be named at present, because it is possible that the incident may have national security implications.'

"I wasn't proposing to name you Ms. Price."

"If I were to comment with anything relevant what do you think the effect would be? It would reduce the list of possible contenders to two, increasing the possibility of a threat to their lives by 33%."

"How?"

"Because by commenting either way I would be either ruling myself in or out; and given that we appear to be talking about matters of national security, we'd leave ourselves open to charges under the Espionage Act. So, my advice to you is to fuck off and go take some lessons about how to do your job."

"Can you open the gate then?"

"I'll open it when I'm good and ready."

She left him to sweat and went upstairs to change and pack a bag. Newgate periodically rang the doorbell, but she continued to ignore it while she composed a press release in Newgate's name. It said that there were reports that the suspects arrested in the hostage case all had connections to Baltimore nightclub owner Sergei Lipov. Those in custody were cooperating with the FBI, and indications of a connection to the FSB, the Russian Secret Service, were being investigated. There were hopes of an early breakthrough in the investigation.

Using a spoof email account, she posted it to all the country's leading press agencies. It was doubtful that anyone would directly name Lipov without evidence, but it would flag him up to the Feds, and the gangster's name would inevitably leak out.

Grabbing her bag and a couple of energy bars she got into her car and opened the garage door. As she reversed out of the garage, Newgate came to her window, so she stopped and waited to hear what he had to say. "I've called the police Ms. Price. You've kept me unlawfully detained for over an hour."

As she opened her door she watched him shrink backwards. He was holding his phone, obviously wanting to record what she was about to say. Without speaking a word, she snatched it out of his hand, dropped it on the floor and stamped on it several times.

"Whoops, your phone got broken again, didn't it? You really should take more care."

"I'll sue you for criminal damage and false imprisonment."

"Would you like to add assault to those charges? This is the second time you've attempted to put my life at risk. Last time, if I recall, I saved you from getting shot; next time I won't bother. You are not being falsely detained. There's a sign on my gate that reads 'No Entry Unless Authorized, therefore you entered my property against my expressed wishes. Then you attempted to record my words without my permission after I'd told you that I did not wish to comment. So let me tell you this now; if your actions have put mine or my children's life in danger in any way, I'll hunt you down like a rabid dog and kill you in the most painful way I can think of. If you've learnt anything about me you will know that I am quite capable of carrying out that threat. Are we on the same page now?"

The man was visibly shaking now, "Yes."

"Good, because I'm going out now, and if you're not off my property before the gates close behind me, you'll be here until I get back in three days' time."

Newgate was practically running to the gate and got there just before she did herself. The garage door had closed behind her, as would the gates.

It was 12.15 pm, and she called Mary on hands-free. "Hi, sis. I'm on my way. If you can save me a sandwich, I'll be with you in two hours."

Chapter Eleven

Tuesday 2.30 pm - Mary's Farm

Saffie's arrival at the farm coincided with Rusty, Mary, and Ben getting ready to go out on their ATVs and round up some cows to go for market. She waved them off then turned to her other son.

"Didn't you want to go too, Josh?"

"No, I've finished my drawing, and I wanted to show you."

"Ben told me that you were doing a drawing of the old house, I'm looking forward to seeing it."

"Not that one. Another one. I've been working on it for over a week, it's for your office. I haven't shown it to Ben in case he got upset."

"Why would he be upset?"

"It's of his dad."

"You made a drawing of Brett? That's wonderful. I can't wait to see it. Help me bring my bags inside and you can show me." They took her bags up to her room. "Come on then sweetheart, show me your drawing. You've got me excited."

He led her to the room he'd been using, lifted the mattress and pulled out a tabloid-sized pad of heavyweight drawing paper that he only used for his best work. The expensive professional quality materials he used were his only real indulgence, unlike Ben whose preferences were video games and sportswear.

Saffie tried as hard as she could, not to compensate for the loss of their father and her own frequent absences by giving them expensive material substitutes. She was fortunate that the boys were mutually supportive, and neither were particularly demanding, but there was no question that Josh was far more insecure than his brother. Holding the pad out, he nervously awaited her reaction.

When she peeled back the cover, she caught her breath. It was a head and shoulders drawing of her husband in landscape orientation. Nobody who'd ever met Brett could mistake it for anybody else. She recognized the picture; it was from a photograph Josh had taken when they were at a football game. Chase Soper had just scored a touchdown to put their team in the lead, and they'd been on their feet cheering. In the original photo, she'd been seated on the other side and Ben had been in the foreground. Her eyes were full, and she choked up, failing to say anything. Instead, she laid the pad on the bed and pulled her son into a tight hug. Eventually, she managed to speak. "That is the most beautiful thing I've ever seen darling. Thank you so much."

"I had to do it three times, but it's still not very good."

"Josh Price that is the dumbest thing you've ever said. Either that or you're the only blind artist in Virginia."

"It's only a copy."

"What, you think that landscape and portrait artists think up their subjects in their heads?"

"But I had to try three times."

"Even the very greatest artists are never satisfied with their first efforts. Stop putting yourself down for goodness sake. Have you shown it to anybody else?"

"Cindy saw the first one when I started. She said it was good, but then I went and messed it up."

"I bet your idea of messed up is different to mine. Why do you think Ben would be upset?"

"Brett was his real dad, but he wasn't mine."

"You listen to me. If Brett could have gone to a store and bought two sons designed just the way he wanted them, then he would have come away with a couple of kids who were just like you and Ben. When I first suggested that we adopt you permanently, it was like he won the lottery. Don't ever suggest he wasn't your real dad again. When you came along you made our family complete."

131

"I'm sorry, Mom."

"Don't be sorry, just try to remember that I'm not, and never was, a girly girl, whose life plan was a home, husband, a house full of kids, and flowers in the yard, and I never will be. That's why I still do the job that I do. But now you're part of me, like vital organs; if you or Ben weren't around I'd no longer be able to function."

"Thank you, Mom."

"There's a couple of things I want you to do for me though?"

"What's that?"

"First of all, sign it, and second, make it a gift to Ben as well, because when we get home I'm going to have it framed, I want to hang it in the family room. That way I can look at it when I get bored with watching *Olympus Has Fallen* with you two for the 119th time."

She ate the steak sandwich that Mary had made for her while he showed her the rest of his work. "Is this what you want to do when you leave school?" she asked him.

"I don't know what I want to do yet, but when I'm drawing, I don't think of anything else, and I don't worry."

"What do you worry about?"

"I worry that you'll get hurt when you get mixed up with dangerous people, and about Ben when he plays football or drives his ATV too fast. I worry that my real dad is going to get out of prison and come and get me."

"Oh sweetheart, you shouldn't have to worry about any of those things but let me put that last one to bed. Firstly let's stop referring to Bridger Davis as your real dad. No real father would attempt to fuck off to another country and abandon his only child without even saying goodbye. Same goes for your mother. How many times has he written to you since he left?"

"Never; nor has my mom."

"I rest my case. Furthermore, Bridger is a coward and a traitor, very lucky to have escaped the death sentence. By the time he gets out of Pennington Gap Federal Penitentiary you'll be in your forties, and he'll be over seventy. He was more interested in saving his own skin than he was in you, and the same could be said of Brooke."

"Why are they like that?"

"I'm sorry, I'm going to curse again, but the answer is, I have no fucking idea. Some people only ever consider the world from their own point of view. They're called narcissists. I guess your Brooke and Bridger are a bit like that."

"I once heard Mom, I mean Brooke tell Bridger that she never wanted kids and only had me in case they needed a reason to stay in the country."

"It's awful that they allowed you to overhear them talk like that."

"They didn't know I was there; I was supposed to be in bed."

"I'm sorry if my job distresses you, but when you think about it, it's no worse than if I were a cop or firefighter is it? Probably less so most of the time."

"I guess."

"And finally, if you haven't spotted it by now then you're walking around with your eyes shut. Ben is devoted to you; he would never ever resent you for loving me or Brett as much as he does." Even as she spoke, she knew that he'd still need reassurance from time to time.

"So how long have we got you for this time?" Rusty asked over dinner.

"I hope for a couple of nights at least, if it's okay with you two."

"Haven't you got to get back to your investigation?"

"I've thrown some chum in the water; I want to see who bites. But I might want to leave the boys with you for a bit longer if that's okay as well."

Ben had just started to ask something, when her phone rang.

"Mrs. Price?"

"Hello, who's speaking?"

"It's Brian Newgate. What the fuck have you done?"

"I'm not sure I know what you mean."

"You know exactly what I mean. You've sent out a press release in my name?"

"Slander can be a very expensive hobby Mr. Newgate so be very careful about what you say next. Perhaps if you tell me what happened, I might be able to advise."

"Two FBI agents came to my office this afternoon. They suggested that I've put out a press release accusing a gangster nightclub owner from Baltimore of being responsible for the hostage-taking in Greenwich."

"And did you?"

"No, of course not. I don't know anything about it."

"That's the problem when you write stories based on guesswork and pretend you know what you're writing about."

"I didn't write it."

"I suppose your biggest problem is whether or not the accusations are true. Did the agents say?"

"They said it's likely to be true. They wanted to know where I'm getting my information."

"Don't you normally refuse to reveal your sources?"

"I haven't got any sources. I told them that. Eventually they believed me."

"That must be a relief for you."

"No, it isn't a fucking relief. Now my name is out there attached to this false press release."

"I thought you said it was true."

"It is true."

"So, what's the problem?"

"If the gangster thinks that I put this information out there I'll be the next one he comes after, won't I?"

"So, you're saying that you're worried that you might be at risk because somebody has leaked your name implying that you might know more about something than you do. Yes, I can see your concerns. I could look into that for you if you like, but I have to tell you that I'm not cheap. My charges are…"

"I don't want to hire you."

"Then what do you want Mr. Newgate?"

"I… I just wanted you to know that I figured out that you're behind this, so if anybody else comes asking I won't hesitate to tell them."

"Mr. Newgate, I'm sure that when it comes to light that you had the world exclusive on this horrific story, you won't be wanting to give the credit to anybody else but thank you for the offer."

"What? Eh? No wait a minute…"

She ended the call.

"What was that all about?" Mary asked.

She gave them all a precis of her run-in with Newgate, and how she'd used his name to accomplish something she was intending to do anyway.

"Won't that put you in the frame though if he says that?"

"Sergei Lipov, the nightclub owner in question has been aware of my involvement in this for nearly a week now and I'm not the one that can give him the information he wants."

"Won't he see you as a threat to him?"

"I hope so, but I doubt he'll think I'm worth exposing his involvement in what I'm working on yet."

"Isn't he already exposed?"

"So far, all he's got is a couple of feds sniffing around him. He'll have had them and the cops after him dozens of times in the past. He'll wave them away like flies."

"So, what was the point?"

"By the time I'm finished with him, he'll wish he'd stayed in Russia."

"How the Hell do you think you can achieve that, if the cops and feds have been after him and they can't make anything stick?" Rusty wanted to know.

"Two reasons; first because unlike our friends in the law enforcement community, I don't play by the rules; and second because he hasn't committed the crime they'll get him for yet."

"This sounds real dangerous, Mom," Josh remarked with trepidation.

"Not as dangerous as you think, sweetheart."

"Does this mean we get to extend our mid-term break?" Ben asked wearing a big grin.

"Here's the bad news. I spoke to Emily, and she tells me that she's happy to work with you online for the time being. You've done it before during Covid, so it won't be a problem."

"Aw, Mom. I was hoping we would get to see some calves being born."

"I expect Emily won't mind if you interrupt your lessons for something as important as a birth. Why not film it on your phone, then if she wants to talk about it you can."

"We already did sex education."

"Not for cows you didn't."

Chapter Twelve
Wednesday 07.30am - Mary's Farm

Saffie chased the boys out of bed just as she usually did at home.

Emily, their tutor wouldn't want to alter her schedule just because she was working online rather than face to face. It had been the biggest stroke of luck when she and Brett chose her to be the boys' first tutor. She was a young widow, only two years out of grad school. But with a then six-month-old baby and no husband, she needed good money and flexible hours. She'd come with first-class references, the boys had taken to her straight away, and both were achieving despite the high expectations for their age.

Without bothering to shower, Saffie dressed in her training outfit and went out into the yard. After a few stretching exercises she began one of her regular workout sessions which consisted of three sets of five Squats, three sets of five Bench Presses, three sets of ten Pullups, and twenty-five Press-ups. They didn't have gym equipment at the farm, but over the last three years since she'd become a regular visitor, they'd adapted various equipment to substitute. As she took a breather after her final set of pullups, which she'd done using the tines of a backhoe loader she turned to see Rusty watching her.

"You must be some sort of masochist," he told her.

"Why, because I enjoy it?"

"Looks like unnecessary pain with very little to show for it if you ask me."

"I need the endorphins. They're a great stress reliever."

"If you say so. Mary said to ask if you want breakfast."

"Tell her I'll get my own when I get back from my run. Thank you."

Having completed her press-ups, she strapped on her running belt with water bottles and set off on her run. On previous stays she'd calculated that the perimeter of Mary's original farmland was about five miles which she aimed to do in less than forty-five minutes.

That day's workout had been her first tough one for a week, so by the end of the run she was breathing hard as she stopped behind the barn to catch her breath and check her time on her watch. Just as she congratulated herself for coming in at less than forty-four minutes, she heard a shot ring out from inside the house.

Hurrying to the yard she found a new GMC Sierra pickup parked next to her own car. Ignoring the other car, she opened the trunk of her own and punched a code into the gun safe allowing her to retrieve the gun she taken from Scott senior. She was thankful that she'd stripped and cleaned it, so she was confident it would work.

Approaching the open front door, she could see a masked man standing in the doorway to the family room, holding a small semi-automatic handgun with one hand. He had his other around Ben's mouth.

"Tell us where the bitch is right now, or we'll kill the kid," the man holding Ben said.

"Look Blink, there's no need to kill the kid yet, she's gonna tell us aren't you?" the voice inside the room said.

The man holding Ben, gripped him tighter than ever and angrily said, "I told you, no names. We started this, now we've gotta finish it. Well bitch, are you gonna tell us or what,

"I told you; she went out for a run over an hour ago," she heard Mary say. "She's late getting back; she might have fallen and be hurt."

"Do you think we're fucking stupid or some…"

"His speech was interrupted by the 9 mm projectile that passed through the masked man's head.

"Run, Ben!" Saffie yelled at her son.

Three long steps brought her to the door, but she tripped on the outstretched leg of the dead man. As she fell a bullet passed over her head and shattered the mirror on the wall behind her. In the split second that followed, Saffie brought her gun to bear and loosed three rapid shots into the second man.

"Are there any more of them?"

Mary shook her head, "No, I don't think so."

"Where's Josh?"

"In his bedroom I think."

Saffie turned, and scaling the stairs three at a time, she found Josh hiding behind the door holding her taser.

"It's okay sweetheart, you can come out now, it's all over," she said, taking the weapon from him and tucking it in her belt.

"Where's Ben, is he alright?"

"I sent him outside. He's okay. Let's go find him." As she spoke they heard the sound of approaching, sirens.

"I asked Emily to call the police, Mom. Is that okay?"

"That was absolutely the right thing to do. You're a brave and clever boy."

"I wasn't brave, Mom; I was really scared."

"Fear and cowardice aren't the same thing. I was terrified too. Do you remember the book I gave you for Christmas?"

"*To Kill a Mockingbird*? Yes."

"There's a line in there that has stuck with me my whole life since I first read it when I was your age, it's when Atticus tells Jem that real courage is seeing things through even if you're pretty sure you're going to lose. You were scared but you fetched my taser, and you thought to get Emily to call the police. That took real guts, and smart thinking too. I'm proud of you."

By the time they were downstairs, Mary had called the cops a second time, and Ben had located Rusty somewhere on the farm. They'd returned on a tractor after making yet another 911 call. Rusty told her they'd been just in time to see the GMC accelerating away down the drive.

Ben rushed into her arms, "Did you get them, Mom?"

"Yes sweetheart, I did."

"Are you okay Josh? I was real scared."

The two boys hugged and were still clutching each other when the first cop car swung into the drive.

"Who were they?" Rusty asked.

"I don't know, I haven't had time to check their IDs."

Over the next hour or two, the farmyard became packed with regular emergency vehicles plus Sinclair and his partner from the FBI, and April Daniels from the CIA. It was like the Tower of Babel, everybody shouting over each other claiming supremacy over the crime scene and/or the investigation, until Saffie finally lost her patience and shouted at the top of her voice, "WILL YOU ALL JUST SHUT THE FUCK UP!"

There was a momentary stunned silence, and before they could start up again she added, "You've got a woman and two traumatized children here. Why the fuck don't each of you agencies nominate an investigator and form a team to interview all the principal witnesses one at a time? It will save time and allow these innocent people to start recovering from their ordeal."

"You're not in charge here Ms. Price," Sinclair said.

"And neither are you at the moment Sinclair. You're all behaving like a bunch of drunks at a football match with your petty squabbles about jurisdiction. If you've all got all of the evidence, then you can fuck off somewhere else to argue amongst yourselves about who's got the shortest dick."

There was another ten minutes of wrangling until they agreed to do as Saffie had suggested, and the team became Agent April Daniels, Special Agent Frank Sinclair, and Detective Sergeant Hendryx from Harrisonburg PD. Saffie remembered Hendryx from three years earlier when he'd come across as an old-school cop out of the same mold as Wolski.

They used the dining room as an interview room.

Each of the interviews was going to produce a different perspective because when it started, the two boys had gone to separate rooms to do a test, Mary had been in the barn collecting eggs, and Rusty had been overseeing the birth of a calf in the cattle shed.

Ben had been the first of them to know that something was wrong when one of the intruders came into the room holding a gun. He had shouted to his brother to hide before his captor had put his hand over the boy's mouth. Ben bit his hand and almost escaped before the second man hit him around the head so hard it made him dizzy.

Josh heard Ben's shout and saw what was happening as the second man grabbed Ben. He went back to the video link and told Emily to call 911. Nobody knew if she'd already called.

Mary returned from the barn and the two men holding Ben ordered her into the family room and demanded to know where Saffie was. When that didn't work they resorted to threats and fired a shot over her head, and when she still wouldn't say they began to threaten Ben.

That was when Saffie intervened. None of them knew where the third man had been while this was going on.

As each of the interviews ended the interviewees gathered in the kitchen. To Saffie's surprise they'd allowed Rusty to be with the boys while they were questioned. As the shooter, it was inevitable that Saffie's interrogation was going to take longest. She'd been in handcuffs since the first cop car had arrived and refused to answer any questions until they were removed. Reluctantly, in Sinclair's case, the inquisitors agreed.

"Before you lot start. I need you to tell me who those two assholes were."

Sinclair huffed, "You shot two people without even knowing who they were?"

"A shot had already been fired, and one of them was threatening to kill my son. Do you think I should have asked them for ID first?"

"Just tell us what happened, and we'll tell you who they were when we're ready Ms. Price."

"Is it a secret?"

Hendryx was clearly pissed off with all the fucking about and announced, "They were cops from Fairfax PD."

"Cops? Jesus! What sort, detectives?"

"Not street cops."

"That makes no sense at all. I've never had anything more than slight disagreements with cops in the USA, and not even that recently. What were their names?"

"Patrol Officers Tobias Blenkhorn and Graeme Seymour."

"Ah that makes a bit more sense I suppose, but I still don't understand the motivation."

"Explain," Sinclair demanded.

"Blenkhorn's name came up in a case I'm working on. I've never met him face to face, and I've never heard of Seymour."

"What case?"

"I'm afraid I can't talk about the case, Agent Sinclair."

"Don't give me that bullshit. You're looking at double homicide charges here."

"Hey, hold on right there, Special Agent Sinclair," Hendryx interrupted. "Unless you've been seeing and hearing a different lot of evidence to me, all I can see are two justifiable shootings. What's more, I've seen no evidence of a Federal crime, so if anybody was charging anybody with anything it would be the Police Department."

Daniels interrupted, "I'm sorry Frank, but I tend to agree. Can we get on now, otherwise we'll be here till nightfall?"

"Just tell us about your case then," Sinclair said.

"You know what case I'm talking about agent, and you're still not cleared for me to discuss it with you. Neither is Sergeant Hendryx for that matter. However, in so much as Blenkhorn has no bearing on the case, I can explain how I came to be aware of him."

Hendryx explained, "Blenkhorn, Seymour, and a third Patrol Officer, Chester Boggs, were suspended two days ago. The first two were on final warnings and likely to lose their jobs.

Saffie explained how she'd captured the two Scotts and extracted their confession. She went on to explain how Blenkhorn and Boggs had been implicated.

"So, you're saying that you did have some sort of beef with Boggs then?"

"You really need to get that hearing problem sorted out, Agent Sinclair. Like I said I've never met any of them. I would never have heard of them either, were it not for the fact that they colluded to fit a tracker to my car. Blenkhorn and Boggs figured low on my to-do list, but I was given to understand that Boggs held some sort of grudge against my client Patryk Wilkanowicz. Patryk's assured me that, until he was mentioned last week, he'd never heard of him either. I have no reason to disbelieve him."

Saffie was an experienced agent; she gave a detailed firsthand account of precisely what happened at the farm, leaving nothing out and without offering any explanations or excuses for her actions, and like all of the interviews, it had been recorded.

"Have you any other questions? If not can you leave us alone to get on with our day. It's nearly two-thirty, I haven't eaten since last night, and I need to spend some time with my children."

"We'll need to hang on to your gun I'm afraid, Mrs. Price," Hendryx told her.

"Keep it. It wasn't mine anyway. I confiscated it from Clay Scott senior when he used it to hold me up."

"By the way, I just spoke to my Captain," Hendryx said. "He told me that the three suspensions last week were as a result of complaints made on your behalf by your Patryk Wilkanowicz."

"As far as I know only Blenkhorn and Boggs were involved in that. Where does Seymour come into it?"

"He tried to alibi the other two, but Wilkanowicz had provided video evidence, and there was no way they should have been hand-delivering a speeding ticket for such a trivial offence," Hendryx explained. "It was one of Seymour's tickets and he has a long history of using tickets for extortion of money and sex. It was a last straw for the Captain."

"How did they find me here though?"

"I don't know yet, but I intend to find out. I'll let you know as soon as I do."

"Thank you Sergeant.

By the time the interview had been concluded, the bodies had been removed, and the only strange cars left in the yard belonged to the three questioners. Mary, Rusty and the boys were in the kitchen eating sandwiches and drinking coffee or soda, along with Sinclair's partner, Agent Reynolds.

When the last of them had left, Saffie turned to her old friend, "I don't know what to say, Mary. I'm so sorry for bringing all this into your home again. Do you want me to stop coming?"

"Don't you dare deny me access to my godchildren now, not after I've finally got to know them so well. This wasn't your fault. Those assholes brought this upon themselves. If they'd had half a brain between them they'd have known not to tangle with you in the first place."

"How are you two boys?"

"We're okay, Mom," Ben said, "I've just been telling Josh how smart he was getting Emily to call 911."

They weren't to find out until later that Emily had spotted the gunman over Ben's shoulder but not in time to stop him being grabbed. She'd panicked and hadn't thought to call 911 until Josh asked her to and told her where Mary's farm was.

"He grabbed my taser from my bag too. That would have given them a surprise, if they'd found you Josh. Where were you going to use it on him darling?"

"I was going to shove it in his balls," Josh shyly replied.

There was a slight pause and then everyone burst out laughing.

"Come here young man and you, Ben. I love you both so much."

She hugged them tightly until Ben told her, "Your tummy's rumbling, Mom."

"You haven't eaten, have you?" Mary said. "Sit down, I'll make you some ham and eggs."

"That'd be great, but do you mind if I make a few calls first?"

"Go ahead. It'll be a few minutes."

Saffie smiled her gratitude. "Boys can you bring me your phones?"

They fetched the devices. She checked and found that both had their locations turned on. She cursed. She routinely checked to ensure her own were always turned off but realized that she hadn't been checking the boys. "It was my fault that those assholes were able to find us here, because I hadn't told you to switch your phone locations off. I'm real sorry."

"It was an easy mistake to make, Mom," Josh told her.

"All the more reason that someone with my training shouldn't have made it."

"We'll remember next time won't we Ben?"

"Don't keep them turned off all the time though, because I need to know where to find you if you're getting up to mischief."

"We don't get up to mischief, Mom."

"You're boys - it's in your DNA."

Next she called Wolski and brought him up to speed with events at the farm.

"It hasn't resolved anything though has it?"

"No, I don't think it has. All it's done is put Blenkhorn out of the way. It hasn't explained what Boggs's problem with Patryk is, and he's still out there."

"I've been doing as much as I can to find out more about him, but I've hit a brick wall."

"No offence, but I think we're going to need to use someone that has the resources to go a bit deeper. I'll have a word with my British contact."

"What can he do?"

"You have no idea, but let's just say, I wish I'd known about him when I was still with the agency. Just email me with everything you've got."

Patryk sounded dreadful when he picked up the phone.

"Are you alright?"

"Feel like shit."

"Okay, I won't bother you for long, I just wanted to chew you out for reporting the tracking attempt in my name. It didn't help."

"Okay sorry."

"You need to see a doctor."

"Yeah, maybe when Dr Oppenheimer is next in town."

"I'll let you go."

Frantically she looked for Sinclair's number in her phone, before remembering that she hadn't had any reason to record it. Rushing through to the kitchen she asked, "Did that asshole from the FBI leave his card?"

"It's on the side over there," Rusty told her.

Hurriedly she typed his number into the phone and called, "Sinclair you've got an emergency on your hands."

"That's Special Agent Sinclair to you Ms. Price."

"Just shut your self-important mouth and listen to what I have to say. I have reason to believe that Patryk Wilkanowicz is being held hostage in his own home."

"What makes you think that?"

"Because when I was an active field agent, he was my controller, and we had a codeword we'd use if we were compromised, and he just used it in a call we had a few minutes ago."

"How long since you last used this codeword?"

"About eleven or twelve years."

"How do you know it's still a valid codeword."

"Because it's a personal word, agreed between us and only changed if we both agree to change it, and we haven't. Are you going to do something or not."

"I'll run it up the line."

"Asshole," she told him.

She ended the call and then phoned Daniels to give her the same story and added the bit about Sinclair.

"I'll light a fire under his ass, don't worry. I'll let you know what we find out. Thank you."

Saffie was terrified about what might be happening to Patryk. Although relationships had been soured by what happened in Ukraine, she and her old controller had worked closely together for so long that he felt like a member of her own family, an older brother almost.

Starving hungry she could only nibble at the plate of food in front of her and in the end she pushed it away and sent a text to Digits.

Need help ASAP.

Four pm in Virginia, was midnight in London so she wasn't expecting a reply until the morning, therefore she was surprised when he texted straight back.

Call me back as soon as you're ready.

She called immediately.

"Good evening Mrs. Price, or good afternoon where you are. How can we help?"

Saffie was surprised to hear a young female voice, "Oh hi, I was expecting to speak to Michael, is he not around?"

"Digits is sitting here right next to me. I'm Minerva, until yesterday his apprentice, but as of today his full-time associate."

"Nice to speak to you Minerva, I'm sorry I didn't catch your second name."

"It's just Minerva. I'll hand you over to Digits, in a moment Mrs. Price, but it will probably be me who deals with your problem. We just thought I ought to introduce myself.

"And it's just Saffie for me."

Digits took over the call. "Hi Saffie. What can we do for you?"

"I'm working on something for a former principal officer in the agency. It's a difficult problem and it looks like it may involve some Northern European people, if not their headquarters. Now I'm private I don't have access to the sophisticated deep-search facilities I used to have. One seemingly unimportant actor in this business revealed a personal enmity toward my client that doesn't make sense, because we can't find any way they could have been connected in the past. We're also concerned that there may be one or more people in the local HQ not acting in our best interest, so we want to keep our curiosity under the radar for the moment. The actor is currently in the wind, making it difficult to pin him down."

"I get your drift. Send us what you know already, and Minerva will start work on it first thing tomorrow. In case you're concerned, she's turning out to be one of the best I've ever worked with. She's capable of doing almost everything that I do, and a lot more besides. She just graduated MA in Intelligence Analysis at King's College London, and her father is ex-Delta."

"There's one last thing I'd like you to do for me, but it may not be possible given who the target is."

"I'm always up for a challenge. Tell me what you want." After she'd explained her request, she could hear the relish in his voice when he replied, "Oh yes, I'm tempted to do that free of charge. I'll let you know how I get on."

Saffie typed a quick email and sent it off, curious about the new addition to Digits' team. She'd never worked with him personally, but he'd been very highly recommended by a number of others in the private intelligence world.

Since leaving the agency, all of Brett and Saffie's work had been domestic private investigation. Nothing small time, but missing persons, suspected child abuse, kidnappings, insurance fraud, high-price industrial espionage, and corporate extortion. She'd even done one or two brief spells as a CPO, but nothing that crossed the line into international intelligence, not that there hadn't been offers. She had extensive experience in intelligence to draw on, but Minerva didn't sound much more than a kid.

She put her curiosity to one side while she waited to hear what was happening with Patryk. Given the traumas of their own earlier in the day, she appreciated Mary, Rusty and the boys' efforts to distract her, but she still couldn't think of anything else.

At gone six pm, her phone finally rang. It was Daniels, "What's happening?" she demanded, taking the phone out of the room.

"By the time the Feds got there it was over. Wilkanowicz had been badly beaten, and he's in no condition to be interviewed. He's been taken to the Virginia Hospital Center in Arlington."

"What about his personal aide, Hugo?"

"He got a minor beating when they first forced their way in. Then they tied him up while they worked his boss over."

"Has anybody put a guard on Patryk?"

"The Feds are leaving two armed guards with him 24/7 until this is sorted out."

"How bad are Patryk's injuries?"

"Pretty bad, even for somebody without pancreatic cancer, I can't say what his prognosis is. What do you know about the bullet wound in his left arm?"

"You'll have to speak to Patryk about that. Can I visit him?"

"You'll need to ask the medics, and I'm not sure if the Feds would have a view. One more thing though. The cops are pretty certain that the third person present at the farm hostage situation was Chester Boggs. They identified his prints from the steering wheel of Blenkhorn's car after it was found abandoned near Springfield."

"Is that where he lives?"

"His home is in Woodbridge. He's not there at the moment, and there's a federal APB on him."

"Thank you, Agent Daniels."

She ended the call and went to rejoin the others.

Chapter Thirteen
Thursday 07:30am - Mary's Farm

Saffron started the day with yet another workout routine and a run before breakfast.

"You boys might need to retake those tests again today. Do you both feel well enough to do that?"

"Yes, Mom," they chorused with the weary sigh of tolerance that school kids the world over have perfected.

"I'm really trying to bring this whole thing to an end as soon as possible so we don't have to keep spending time apart. I'm sorry."

"We understand, Mom, and we love it here at the farm, so you shouldn't worry," Ben said.

"Try not to get into any more gunfights, Mom," Josh told her.

Mary was looking on, "You listen to that son of yours, missy. He knows what he's talking about."

"I'm sorry for using you as an unpaid child carer again, Mary," she said noticing the gun strapped to her friend's hip for the first time for years.

"This is in case we get any more rattlers. Can't be too careful in cattle country eh?" Mary winked. "As for the boys. If I'd known kids were this easy to look after, I might have had a couple of my own."

Saffie laughed. "It's not too late," she said nodding at Rusty. Still smiling she threw her bags in the trunk of her car. As she got in the driving seat, her phone rang, unknown number.

"Morning Saffie."

"Minerva?"

"For future reference, this is my direct line."

"Is everything okay?"

"I just called to give you my report. I've emailed it, but I thought it best to talk you through the summary because it's a bit long-winded. I'm going out tonight, so I thought I'd call in case you have questions."

"You've done it already?"

"Well, I've had all day. It's quite interesting."

"Wow, that's fantastic. Yes please go ahead."

"Okay, here goes. Chester Boggs, born Woodrow Wilson Perry 1989. Following his parents' divorce in 1990, his mother Ella-May remarried in 1992 and changed their surnames to Lee. She and her husband died in a home invasion in 1995 when Woodrow was six, The shooters were never caught, although the boy's father was questioned. The boy was placed for adoption with a Mormon family called Leavitt from Salt Lake City who renamed him Brigham. He became increasingly unruly and unmanageable, and when he was nine the adoption failed, and he was re-placed for adoption again, this time with a family from West Virginia called Harper and renamed Noah. That's where official records ran out.

"For the next bit I've had to speculate and join dots using newspaper reports, adult and juvenile court records. He was recorded as a runaway when he was ten years old, and for the next eight years, kids matching his description popped up in schools and courtrooms up and down the Blue Ridge Mountains with a variety of given names, usually Chester, Jed, Buck, or Wade; and surnames Cobb, Fisher or Boggs. His Juvenile records are sealed, although if you need me to, I can probably get somebody to take a look. He has no record of schooling beyond 7th grade until he was nineteen when he achieved 155 in a GED from Northern Virginia Community College.

"His employment is pretty checkered. Truck driver, bartender, warehouse worker, tire fitter etcetera. He joined Fairfax PD in 2021. He has no adult criminal record. Arrested once after a bar fight in Lexington in 2018, but no charges. I can't find any references to women in his life. He has a checking account with rarely more than five thousand or less than a thousand dollars; and a deposit account opened two months ago with a single ten-thousand-dollar cash deposit which hasn't been touched since.

"He rents a small one-story house in Kenwood Drive, Woodbridge, lives alone, and eats at Brittany's Restaurant & Sports Bar, once a week. All in all, a pretty boring character. The only anomaly is that ten-thousand-dollar cash deposit in March this year. I suppose it could have been winnings from a bet."

"I can't believe you found all that out in one day."

"Well, I had a lot of help using Digits' contacts. It would have taken a lot longer to do it on my own. He's doing fieldwork today, otherwise he'd probably have talked to you himself."

"Thank you Minerva, that's amazing, I can't thank you enough."

"I get paid well and I love my work, so you don't need to."

"Is there any more to find do you think?"

"There's always more to find. It's whether it's worth the trouble looking that's the question."

"I don't want to monopolize you, but can I ask you to keep digging."

"How about I do it as an ongoing project that I just pick up when there's nothing else going on? I'll only bill you for the time I spend on it."

"That would be fantastic. I don't know why yet, but I get the feeling that Boggs may be a key to open this whole thing up."

After ending the call, she started the engine just as her phone beeped with a notification from her bank. Someone had just deposited ten million dollars in her account.

'*Shit! What the fuck is that all about?*' A quick look at the account answered her question but angered her just the same.

Slamming the lever into drive she drove off in a temper, not needing the GPS to tell her how to get to the Virginia Hospital Center. She thanked God for automated parking payment after finding a spot in the garage, and knowing she could just drive out when it was time to leave.

Striding through the vast ultra-modern building of Zone A, which she knew to contain the Emergency Department, she located an Information Desk where she learnt that Patryk was on the fourth floor in Room 443.

When she stepped out of the elevator she was stopped by a man about twenty-four years old wearing a dark suit and reflective sunglasses. "Can I ask your business Ma'am?"

"You can ask; whether I tell you or not, is another thing. Tell me who you are."

"I'm with the FBI," he said, opening his jacket to reveal a badge on his belt and a gun in a shoulder holster.

"No kidding. I'm here to visit a patient."

"Which patient?"

"Dr. Patryk Wilkanowicz."

"Mr. Wilkanowicz isn't allowed visitors at present Ma'am."

"Is there a medical reason for that?"

"No, Ma'am, it's for his protection."

"He doesn't need protection from me. We're long-standing friends and colleagues. If Patryk's not suspected of a crime, he's not under arrest, and there isn't a medical reason to exclude me, I'm quite sure he'll want to see me, if you ask."

"Okay lady, what's your name?"

"Saffron Price," she showed her ID.

"Private dick eh?" he grinned at his own use of the outdated euphemism.

"As opposed to a state-employed one; yes?"

The man put a finger to his ear and spoke into the almost invisible mike by his cheek.

"Got a lady here called Sapphire Price or something, says the old guy will want to see her." There was a pause. "Okay lady, you can go in, Room 443."

"Thanks."

At the door to Patryk's room, she was stopped once again by a man who could have been the other one's twin who searched her bag.

"Is it just you and your pal outside here to look out for Dr Wilkanowicz?"

"Yes, Ma'am."

"How many entrances are there to this floor?"

"I don't know, Ma'am."

"Then I suggest you find out. I'd hazard a guess there's at least two. That being the case you need to have both of you on the door to the room, not one of you in the elevator lobby dressed like one of *The Blues Brothers* and behaving like a maître d.'"

"We're professionals, Ma'am. We know what we're doing. We don't need wannabe cops telling us how to do our jobs."

"Oh really? So, if two or more bad actors dressed in scrubs come into the floor using one of the other access points while you're stood here polishing your Aviators, you'll be okay on your own will you? The truth is you could easily be compromised or overpowered before your pal had the first idea what was happening. I was an agent before you finished fifth grade so don't patronize me. I'll be wanting the door closed while I'm with Dr Wilkanowicz, so we won't disturb you while you sort your security detail out. You'll need at least two more agents if it helps."

Patryk's bedhead had been raised and he was laying still. He didn't look up. It was difficult to see if he was awake or not. His blind eye was covered, and the other was extremely swollen. His left arm was in bandages, and he was attached to the numerous obligatory tubes and wires. A nurse was taking notes from the various pieces of beeping and flashing machinery.

She leaned over him and touched his right arm. "Patryk, it's Saffie."

"I know, I heard you ripping that kid a new one."

"How bad is it?" she asked, shocked by his appearance.

"It's pretty bad," he coughed.

"What have they told you?"

He coughed again.

The nurse interrupted, "Mr. Wilkanowicz is a very sick man, Ma'am. Please try not to tire him too much."

"Of course. Can I come and speak to you when I leave?"

"Sure, just ask for Nurse Richmond." She left them alone.

"Ten million bucks, Patryk. What the fuck?"

"Just shut up and let me speak while I still have energy will you?"

"But…"

"Quiet. First take my phone and work with me to change the biometrics to yours…"

"But Patryk…"

"Shut up. This is important."

Together they added her print, voice, and face profiles to the phone.

"Right, now put the phone in your purse and take it with you when you go. I won't be needing it again." He gasped. "The money is to pay you for the work you've done and the… " He paused to catch his breath. "… work I know you still have to do." Another pause. "This thing is a long way from over, and I may not be around to see it through."

"Don't talk shit, Patryk. You're a tough bastard…"

"Please don't interrupt. There are things you need to know." Pause. "I only realized their importance when they were beating me up." Pause.

"Ask Linda to get you into my archive; the key to it is in there. Just remember this. *'She had not known the weight until she felt the freedom.'* Got that?" Pause. "I don't know how it fits together, but the answer is in there.... There's a mole in Langley and another in the State Department... I don't know who they are, nor who to trust. [pause] I've sent Hugo away to stay with his brother. He'll call once he's settled.... Two of the bastards that beat me up were Yanks, I'm sure of it, bikers probably. One had a long beard and hair, lower left ear missing, and his pal was about six five and 240 pounds... and had the words *Full Throttle* tattooed on his right hand.....The third guy was Latino; he had a bandana and a covid mask." He coughed violently. "I thought his eyes...looked familiar..."

There was a shout from outside the room. "Excuse me, sir I need to see some ID before you go in there..."

Saffie heard the familiar phut of a silenced firearm, followed by a succession of screams. She instantly looked around for a weapon, but the only thing to hand was a spare drip pole, with a heavy five-wheeled base.

There were more cries interspersed with the sound of people or furniture being thrown about, before the door burst open, and a man in biker clothes stepped through to be met with the swinging base of the drip stand. Unfortunately, the improvised weapon was far too unwieldy to finish his involvement, although one of the legs caught him across the nose, sending him staggering to the floor but in swinging the stand in the way she had, it threw her off balance as well.

The door stayed partially open for only moments before it was thrown back on its hinges and an enormous man filled the doorway. His eyes settled on Saffie. When he came at her, all her training, moves of attack and defense seemed to have no effect, and his hands grasped her around her throat. Grinning wordlessly as he pressed her against a surgical instrument trolley at the side of the room, his giant hands tightened, and she knew she only had seconds to live unless she could do something.

With her left thumb, using all the strength she could muster, she hooked out his right eyeball. The outcome was bellows of pain and his grip weakened slightly but he didn't let go. Flailing around with her right hand, hoping to find something else to use as a weapon, her fingers closed on one of the surgical instruments that had been covered by a sterile cloth awaiting a procedure. She didn't know what it was but using every ounce of strength she had left, she hit him with it in the left temple. The effect was instant. His Titanic scream must have been heard right across the hospital campus. Releasing Saffie, he somehow remained upright clutching his head and staggered out of the room with a scalpel embedded three inches into his brain and one eye hanging down his cheek.

Saffie had no time to take in what had happened because the first man stumbling to his feet, had picked up his gun from where it had fallen and shot Patryk. He attempted to fire more rounds, but his gun jammed. Moving in to tackle the now unarmed man she tripped on the discarded I.V. stand and the man threw the gun at her and ran through the door, leaping across the huge body of his pal.

Pausing for a few seconds to take in what had happened she yelled, "We need medics in here right now; your patient's been shot." She leant over her friend. "Help's coming Patryk."

Wheezing like worn-out fireside bellows he managed to tell her, "It's too late you crazy woman. You need to ask Linda to find these two names, Perry and Esteban..." He attempted to say something else, but the rest was unintelligible as he slipped into unconsciousness,

Frantically she pressed the emergency call button and shouted, "Help, I need fucking help!" She had never felt so helpless. It seemed forever but was probably only moments before a team of health professionals had gathered. From the corner of the room, she watched them work on Patryk for more than twenty minutes without effect until the man who was clearly the most senior member of the team asked if they all agreed it was time to call it. Nobody objected.

Sliding down the wall onto her haunches, it felt like every muscle and sinew in her body gave way, and she wept.

Another five minutes passed before Sinclair said from the door, "This is a crime scene Price, and this time there's no argument about whose it is, except that it's certainly got nothing to do with you."

"If one more syllable comes out of your offensive mouth, Sinclair, I'll take that badge of yours and shove it up your ass. Your incompetence just cost the life of the most valuable witness you're ever likely to have."

"What the Hell are you talking about?" he demanded to know.

Saffie heard a voice from behind them. "Sinclair, she's probably talking about the two still wet-behind-the-ears agents you posted to guard the former head of the CIA, a vital witness in an attempt to interfere with the security of the nation."

"You're talking about two courageous agents who just heroically died in pursuance of their duties. Who are you Ma'am?"

"My name is Special Agent in Charge Sofia Ramirez, and I know exactly who I'm talking about. Two men who would probably be alive now were it not for your actions. You're suspended. Hand your gun and your badge to my assistant. You can answer for your actions at the congressional enquiry that will inevitably follow this shit-show. Your partner, Agent Reynolds, can stay for now and help us understand what the fuck went wrong here."

Left with no choice, Sinclair complied and slid out of the room.

"He's right though Ms. Price, this is a crime scene, and none of us should be in here right now. Come, let's find somewhere quiet and you can talk me through what happened."

They walked out of the door, and for the first time Saffie saw the carnage that the two thugs had caused. The huge gangster that Saffie had killed, lay sprawled across the body of a young FBI agent. Not far away was a male nurse with his head twisted at an unnatural angle. Beside him, lay Nurse Richmond with a neat bullet hole in the center of her forehead, and by the entrance to the ward the second FBI agent's body lay sprawled outside the door.

Somehow, the remaining staff of the Intensive Therapy Unit were trying to recommence their care of the seriously ill patients they hadn't yet been able to move to other parts of the hospital. Everywhere she looked there were agents in their distinctive FBI over-jackets, interviewing tearful staff members. CSI teams had begun to arrive and were already commandeering individual parts of the crime scene.

Ramirez didn't speak. She quietly led Saffie to the elevator that the bureau had appropriated for the exclusive use of law enforcement agencies and on the ground floor a cop directed the two of them to a small meeting room.

"Saffie, is it okay to call you that?"

"I think we know each other well enough to dispense with bullshit, so yes," was the steely response.

Ramirez had been the senior FBI agent involved in the investigation into the events surrounding the kidnappings of Brett and Ben, three years earlier. They'd developed a mutual trust and respect for each other that had played a big role in successfully bringing the investigation to a conclusion. "First of all, this is not on the record, so if there are any discrepancies, when the time comes to give your statement, then nobody will hear about them from me. You and I learned enough about each other over the Walt Bannerman affair to know that we can be trusted to operate in the nation's interest, with all due regard to natural justice."

Saffie looked her up and down, "First tell me what you know about what's been happening with Patryk, because something stinks."

"I agree. I only became aware that something with CIA implications was happening late yesterday, after news of his home invasion went down. I should tell you that after the Bannerman business, I was appointed to a new role. By new, I mean one that hadn't existed before. I oversee any and all investigations where there might be a conflict between the FBI and the Agency. Though I say it myself it's been going well until now. I don't know how that jerkoff Sinclair was given this investigation, but he's going to lose his job over this."

"I warned that agent on the door that they needed to do things differently, but he wouldn't listen."

"To be fair to him, I heard that he reported what you'd told him to Sinclair, but he was overruled."

"Is Sinclair crooked, or just dumb?"

"At the moment I don't know, but back to the business in hand, tell me about today."

Saffie started her tale with the events of the day before, because although she didn't believe they were directly connected, she knew that at some point they would form part of the whole portrait. After she'd finished giving her account, omitting only Patryk's description of the Latino guy, and his final dying words.

"You're racking up quite a body count again Saffie."

"I won't lose any sleep about the passing of any that died at my hand this week."

"April Daniels is champing at the bit to get you into an interview room, but I can assure you that if you tell her what you've told me there won't be any issues. The FBI are taking over every aspect of this investigation, including the events at the Harrisonburg farm. I know you well enough to be aware that you probably haven't told us absolutely everything, and I trust that you haven't done so for all the right reasons. My problem is that if something happens to you, then what you know will die with you."

"It won't," Saffie assured her. What she didn't say was that she maintained a journal of everything she did, that her lawyer would have access to in the event of her death.

"I've persuaded the directors of both the Bureau and the Agency that it will be okay to keep you appraised of any developments. Daniels won't have the same faith in you that I do, and she's not happy with the arrangement, but she'll have to live with it. We're not asking for you to commit to anything, but we're hoping you'll share your findings with us."

Saffie was not in a mood to communicate, and other than a perfunctory acknowledgement, she said nothing until she was sure that Ramirez had finished. "The first piece of information you can share is who were those two pieces of shit."

"The guy you killed was called Tyson Sturgis, AKA *Gulliver*. We believe the one that got away was called Damian Bramwell, AKA *Handlebar*. They were members of the Pagans biker gang, although we think it's unlikely that this was a Pagan sponsored operation. There's an APB on

Bramwell as well as one on Chester Boggs. In theory Boggs should be easy to find because he doesn't have backup support like the biker gang."

"Maybe, but cops can be just as protective of their own."

Daniels and Ramirez sat in and took notes while two agents took Saffie's statement. She told them what happened and answered their questions but volunteered no help. Foremost in her mind throughout was how to locate Bramwell.

It was three pm by the time she left the hospital, she was tired, hungry, and in need of a shower. Nonetheless, she stopped at a shop to replace the gun and silencer that were still with the cops in Greenwich. She was expecting to need it.

Cindy hadn't been expecting Saffie back, because she hadn't bothered to call ahead. "Haven't you brought the boys with you?" she asked.

"They're going to be staying up at the farm for a few more days. I'm sorry I haven't kept you up to date."

"You look awful, if you don't mind me saying so."

"I'm not surprised, I've just seen one of my oldest friends murdered in front of my eyes, and yesterday somebody threatened to kill Ben and my other oldest friend."

"Dear God! Tell me what happened."

"Do you mind if I take a shower first, but I'd be eternally grateful if you could rustle up some food. I haven't eaten since seven-thirty, and I sense it's going to be a long time before I get another chance."

On her way upstairs, her phone buzzed, "Minerva. What can I do for you?"

"Since we spoke I've been monitoring events over there. I'm guessing you were mixed up in that nasty business at the Virginia Hospital Center. Are you okay?"

"I'm fine, thanks for asking."

"I rang because one of my search queries about Chester Boggs threw up a surprise result that I thought you might find interesting."

"I'm interested in everything about him. What have you got?"

"Boggs is a survivalist, or what I believe you call a prepper. I probably should have mentioned that before. Anyway, I've been running property searches on him and some of the families he lived with growing up. The last family he's known to have lived with were the Sayres from a little place called Abbot in Upshur County, West Virginia. They died in a house fire in 2005. They also had a reputation as preppers, and were the registered owners of a small patch of land near a place called Wildcat. It's remote - appears to have little going for it. No regular roads, so it's doubtful if it has any amenities like power or telephone, but by the looks of it on Google Earth there's still a small cabin there."

"Minerva, I think I love you."

"I'm spoken for but thank you anyway. There's no address but I'll send you the coordinates."

"While you're on the line, I'm wondering if I can employ your services to look for another guy in a similar way."

"Why not? Tell me what you know."

"His name is Damian Bramwell and he's a member of the Pagans biker gang, known as *Handlebar*. He's about thirty-eight years old, 5 feet 9 tall and 150 pounds, with a long beard, brown hair and the words *Full Throttle* tattooed on his right hand. That's all I've got, I'm sorry. It's a long shot I know."

"I might be able to do something with that. I won't be able to get you an answer until tomorrow at the earliest though."

"I can't thank you enough."

After her shower and something to eat she began to feel almost human again. She was anxious to get after Boggs, but she knew that she needed to speak to Mary, the kids, Linda, and Wolski first.

Mary was horrified to learn about Patryk's murder, but between them they decided not to mention her involvement to the boys. Ben and Josh were excited to speak to her. They'd both scored really high in their SATs, but most of all, because twin calves had been born that morning and they'd been able to watch.

Her call to Linda revealed that she had already heard the news about Patryk and had guessed Saffie's involvement. Although she hadn't been named, the piece on the website of the regional newspaper left little room for doubt by anyone who knew her. This was national if not international news. She knew that soon it wouldn't only be the idiot reporter Newgate waiting at the gate for comments. They made a tentative appointment to try to make some sense of Patryk's archives in two days' time.

Lastly she called Wolski.

"I was beginning to think I'd been let go. Did you have a good couple of days off?"

"I take it you haven't heard what's been happening then?"

"What're you talking about?"

She explained the events of the last two days in chronological order. Almost every sentence elicited an expletive. By the time she got to Patryk's murder he was reduced to good old-fashioned blasphemy.

"Jesus, Mary and Joseph Saffie what the Hell are we dealing with here? Does this mean that the Patryk investigation is over?"

"I'm reading between the lines but I'm pretty sure there are two things going on. The Russians or an as yet unidentified Russian agent - we'll call him Vlad - is after information from Patryk's archive, and in terms of them thinking they're going to succeed, it's over. As far as I'm concerned though it won't be over until every one of them is either in prison or dead." Dead would be her first preference, but she didn't tell him that. "The other thing happening is that Vlad has been using local low-level criminals to provoke Patryk into revealing what or where some sort of information is. Logic would dictate that they would now fuck off and go away but I doubt that will happen."

"What do you mean?"

"None of the people that Vlad's been using have the brain power of lobotomized bonobos, with testosterone levels in inverse proportion to their intellectual abilities. So far they've all been spectacularly defeated mostly by me acting on my own. The likelihood that they'll just give up and go home now is pretty remote."

"So, what are you going to do?"

"I'm going to need your support to watch my ass. Metaphorically speaking of course and providing you're up for it."

"When do we start?"

"Tonight, if that's okay with you."

"You're on. What time, where."

"We're going on a little field trip. Wear black or very dark clothing, and pack enough to stay over for a few days. Make sure you're well-armed."

"Long gun?"

"With suppressor, if you've got one. If not I've got a spare."

"I'll be with you in about an hour."

Her next task was to locate the Wildcat cabin. Using Google Earth she found it okay, but it was a four-hour drive away.

When Wolski arrived and she'd explained her plan, he wasn't enthusiastic. "It's not that I don't think it's a good plan so much, but that I'm not sure that I'm the best guy to help out."

"You'll be fine. I'll be doing 90% of the spearhead stuff. I just need you nearby, in case I need an extra pair of hands."

With Saffie wearing her nighttime combat gear again, and Wolski similarly dressed in some of Brett's hunting clothes which fitted in places, they prepared to leave.

"Run it by me one more time. You're going to creep up on this guy's cabin like Lara Croft on steroids, lob a smoke grenade through the window. Then when he comes out, you're going to hogtie him and force him to tell you what you want to know. Is that about right?"

"That's about the size of it, yes."

"So, where do I come in?"

"You know what they say, 'No plan survives contact with the enemy.' You're there if something goes wrong."

"When I went private, I didn't envisage anything like this."

"Would you rather be alone, waiting outside someone's home hoping to catch a photo of an illicit liaison between a bored housewife and her married lover?"

"Fair point."

Chapter Fourteen
Friday 00:30am - Remote wooded area outside Wildcat, WV.

The GPS took them to the poorly maintained track that led to the cabin which Saffie had assumed was Chester Boggs hideout. A hundred yards along the track, she reversed among some trees near where the track met Bull Run. Leaving it where it wouldn't be spotted by anybody driving the main road, she killed the lights.

"If I'm right, the cabin is at the end of the track about one and a half miles from here. There's another cabin about halfway, so we can't drive any closer. These hillbillies use CB radios to talk to one another, and although they mostly hate the sight of each other, they hate outsiders even more. I'm hoping he's either asleep, stoned, or drunk on moonshine when I get there so this will all be over very quickly. You wait in the car, and keep listening to your headset, and keep your gun ready in case the Clampetts in the other cabin come home late."

"You're going to walk there? It's frigging pitch black."

"I'm going to use night vision glasses. This won't be my first time."

After donning her NVs and headset, they tested their mikes and earpieces, and she set off.

When she'd told Wolski that this wasn't her first time it was true, but the last time had been before Ben was born. It wasn't that she was unfit, in fact she was probably in better shape now than she'd ever been but opportunities for training when you were in the field were few and far between. Nighttime incursions were a special forces discipline, and on the few previous occasions she'd always been accompanied by at least one Ranger, Delta or SEAL operator and the AR15 hung from her shoulder was an encumbrance she was regretting even before she reached the house halfway to her destination.

She moved deep in amongst the trees so as to avoid disturbing any dogs inside the house, hoping there were none kenneled outdoors. The undergrowth was thick in places, and there was always the risk of snakes, so skirting the house had taken longer than she'd hoped. Rebuking herself for expecting things to be easy, she sent a progress report to Wolski, then told herself again that there wasn't a schedule.

When the app on her phone vibrated to let her know she was 500 yards from the cabin, she increased her caution. Making certain with every step that she didn't snap a twig, or trip a booby-trap to trigger an alarm, she made slow progress.

At 400 yards a huge green heat source began to emerge ahead of her. Too big to be a boar or human she was searching her mind for other options, but when the shape turned, she could see it was a huge elk, and from its antlers, obviously a bull. If she tried to pass and it spooked, its rapid movement might alert Boggs to her presence. Downwind, she sank to the floor and waited for the animal to move off. Then without warning a gunshot rang out and the creature stumbled and fell.

What happened next caused Saffie's heart to leap into her throat. Between herself and the fallen elk, a man-shaped heat source rose up from the floor and began to move towards his fallen prey.

Her pulse leapt, when a deafening roar came from behind her and off to her right. She turned to see another huge heat source charge past.

A bear!

The massive creature was upon Boggs in moments. Its human victim screamed. Probably too late to draw a handgun or knife, he was defenseless against the enormous creature's massive jaws and claws. Saffie pulled her handgun, rapidly unscrewed the silencer, and fired six shots into the air. With another roar, the bear momentarily reared up on its hind legs before charging away, abandoning Boggs' motionless body.

Her heart was still pounding when she spoke, "Wolski, call an ambulance and the cops, and get up here fast. Boggs just got attacked by a bear."

"Is he alive?

"I don't know. Just get everybody here before we're surrounded by pissed-off hillbillies."

"Copy that."

Her next call was to Ramirez.

"What the fuck Saffie, it's two o'clock in the morning."

"I've found Boggs, but he's been attacked by a bear."

"Is he alive?"

"I don't know yet; just send the cavalry, the natives probably won't be friendly. I'll text you the coordinates. I'm outside Wildcat in West Virginia."

Cautiously watching for signs that the bear was still around, although she didn't think it was likely, she made her way toward Boggs. When she reached him there were no initial signs of movement, but when she touched his body he groaned. Lifting the NV lenses, she turned on the LED torch she'd taped to the side strap. Immediately she could see that the man was seriously hurt. One arm lay at an impossible angle, there was a deep gash from his hairline to the side of his mouth, another through all his layers of clothing exposing his ribs, and what looked like teeth marks in his right leg.

There was only limited space for first aid equipment in her combat clothes, but she did have two field dressings and a tourniquet.

"Lay still, I'm going to try to help."

"Who are you?" he said, his words distorted by the torn muscles in the side of his face.

"Never mind for the minute, let me try to stop the bleeding first."

After cutting away the leg of his pants, she used the tourniquet to reduce the blood flow from the deep lacerations underneath. Then she pressed a large field dressing against his chest wound and taking his good hand she placed it on top. "Hold that."

Then using the second dressing she wrapped it around his head. She could hear a vehicle approaching, and she prayed it would be Wolski.

"What have you got against Patryk Wilkanowicz," she asked.

The wounded man groaned.

"Just tell me. I just saved your life - it's the least you can do."

"After what he did."

"What did he do?"

"Betrayed me…"

He was struggling for every word when a voice from the track about twenty yards away called, "What the Hell is going on there mister?"

'Shit!' she thought, and hurriedly replied, "A man's been attacked by a bear."

Obviously wary of coming closer he shouted back, "Who's been hurt?"

"I think his name's Chester Boggs."

"Who are you, bitch?"

"My name is Saffron Price, I'm a private investigator."

"You armed?"

"Yes."

"Drop your weapons and come on out, or we start shooting."

She turned off her torch. "What for? I'm not threatening anybody; and as things stand I can see you, but you can't see me."

"We stopped your partner down the hill, so you ain't getting any help. Get in there after her Thaddeus, and you Beau."

"First I should warn you that it won't be long before these woods will be swarming with cops and Feds. I called them straight after the first shot, and second I'm a pretty good shot with a rifle myself."

The man laughed, "Yeah, sure you are, bitch."

"Unless your boys are trained in advanced first aid, they won't be much help to Chester, so I'm advising them to stay away. If I'm approached by anyone armed, I might be obliged to defend myself. I've an automatic handgun with eleven rounds remaining, two spare clips, an AR15 with a full magazine, a twelve-inch combat knife, and night vision glasses. What's more I've been trained to use all of them."

"Like I'm going to believe that."

"That branch you're standing under, if you don't want it to fall on your head, stand back."

Hoping her shooting was as good as her boast, she took aim and fired. The branch of the red maple didn't fall, but the guy jumped back so it obviously shook enough to convince him, whoever he was.

"Fucking bitch…"

The man was interrupted by the arrival of another car; he was lit up by the headlamps and a gunshot rang out.

"Drop your guns on the floor and step away from them, now. That includes you asshole." It was Wolski.

"You two are in deep shit, when the cousins get here," the guy who'd been talking said.

"They better get here before the cops then, because if you pick that gun up again you're gonna get another hole in your body."

The sound of approaching, sirens negated the need for more threats.

"Can I concentrate on keeping your pal alive now?"

Turning her torch back on, she looked at the injured man, and immediately saw that he was unconscious. She'd learn nothing more from him.

"What have you done with Daisy Mae, asshole?"

"She's cuffed to a tree. Now shut the fuck up and wait for the cops," Wolski said. "Are you alright Saffie?"

"I'm fine but Boggs doesn't look well."

The first cop to arrive on the scene insisted that Wolski disarm himself but was otherwise surprisingly nonthreatening. Another two cars and an ambulance were next and paramedics took over from Saffie, stabilized Boggs and transferred him to their vehicle.

It was two more hours before a pair of agents from the FBI offices at Beckley arrived, by which time the family had been chased back to their house. They'd gone with few objections, having been granted permission to return later to butcher the out-of-season elk carcass. Having been banned from approaching the cabin, the agents and cops passed the time with Saffie and Wolski, until Ramirez and Daniels arrived at six-thirty although the agents from Beckley couldn't understand why two private detectives and a CIA operative were being allowed into a potential crime scene while they were being told to stay outside.

The four of them conducted a careful search of Boggs' cabin and the cunningly disguised underground hideaway below. It revealed how much of a committed prepper he was. There were enough boxes of energy bars, canned goods, and dried food, to feed a person for more than three months. He'd also accumulated enough guns and ammo to start a small war, with automatic handguns and rifles, pump action shotguns, sniper and hunting rifles, and even stun grenades, smoke bombs, and gas masks.

Boggs had thought of everything. There was a 4-kilowatt petrol generator with a piped exhaust, a 12-volt battery bank, and a 40-gallon petrol tank with a facility to refill from above ground. Water was provided by a rainwater collection arrangement, and the bunker was fitted with sophisticated ventilation, and human waste disposal systems. The ground-level outlets and inlets for various equipment were all ingeniously disguised around the outside of the shabby cabin above. For all the preparations that Saffie had made to overpower the guy, she recognized that she'd have had little chance of success if she hadn't arrived on the scene at that precise moment when he was out of his hole, or without the assistance of the bear.

The only thing of interest that they found was a page from a Fairfax County PD notepad with three words and a phone number randomly scribbled on it. *Perry, Lipov, Esteban, 771-456-1357.* She quickly snapped a picture of it, before it disappeared into an evidence bag'.

Saffie and Wolski were finally allowed to leave, after undertaking to send written statements to the Buckhannon Police Department, with copies to the FBI.

It was past midday by the time they drove through the gates of Saffie's home. They'd been too tired to discuss the ramifications of the night's events on the journey and felt no better when they arrived, Wolski disappearing into the spare room to get his head down, although Saffie needed to make some calls, starting with a number from her recent calls list.

"Patsy, I need some more help."

"Tell me what you need?"

"This time it might be a bit more complicated."

"I like a challenge."

"I'm going to give you a number, it's probably a cell, but I not only need to know everything you can find out about it, and any connection to one or more of people called, Perry, Lipov, or Esteban."

"You're right, it will be more complicated. You know what my next question is."

"One or more of them ordered the assassination of my principal client."

"Are you saying that your client is dead?"

"That's right."

"I'll have to make sure I do a good job on this then."

She dictated the number that had been scrawled on the notepaper, then ended the call.

Saffie's next call was to Linda.

"I've been waiting for your call."

"Sorry, but I've been on an op."

"You're a PI now Saffie, you don't go on ops."

"I do now, for as long as it takes to put these bastards in their place."

"I heard about Patryk."

"We need to get together, like we arranged, and soon."

"I don't know how much help I can be now."

"More than you know. Are you still okay for tomorrow?"

"I guess."

"Where, your place or mine?"

"Depends on what you want to do."

"We need to go through what you did with Patryk the other day, so I guess mine would be best."

"That's impossible."

"What do you mean?"

"It was the weirdest security system I've ever encountered. I doubt I could get into it without him."

"Patryk seemed to think otherwise. Would you mind giving it a try? It was one of the last things he asked before he died."

"You were with him?"

"Yes, I was."

"I'll be with you by nine am."

She became very emotional in her call to Mary after she told about Patryk's death. She tried to disguise her feelings by the time the boys came on the line, but Josh picked up on it.

"Are you okay, Mom?"

"I had a bad couple of days. A good friend died."

"Why don't you come to the farm, and we can cheer you up."

"That's sweet, and there's nothing I'd like more, but what I have to do now is more important than ever."

It was true but still wrenchingly difficult to face up to.

174

Chapter Fifteen
Saturday 6:30am - Dunn Loring, Virginia.

Awake and unable to concentrate on anything, Saffie resorted to exercise. It was the one thing she could rely on to chase the fug from her brain and allow her to focus.

After spending an hour, pushing herself in the gym, and following it with a hot shower she had a plan.

Wolski was awake and Cindy had cooked him breakfast.

"Do you want me to cook for you as well, Saffie?"

"No thanks, Cindy. I'll get my own today."

"What's the timetable for today then?" Wolski asked.

"There's a communications specialist coming this morning. We're going to try to hack into Patryk's archive."

"What do you want me to do?"

"Could you ask around among your old contacts and see if you can find a connection between Lipov, and people with the names, Perry, or Esteban. Obviously we know who Lipov is, and Baltimore is a long way off, but anything you can find would be good."

"I've got a buddy I served with in Charlottesville. He transferred to ATF based in Baltimore. He might be able to help."

Linda arrived fifteen minutes early, keen to get stuck in, but with little confidence in the outcome. "Okay, this is probably going to be an expensive waste of time, but I'm ready when you are." Linda's time didn't come cheap.

"Patryk already paid upfront, so we don't need to worry about the cost."

The visiting expert set up shop in the study using what had become Wolski's desk, while Saffie sat at her own.

"How do you propose we go about this then," Linda asked. "Because when Patryk and I worked on it together he didn't give much away. He had a weird set up on his PC just to get him through the portal and a different password for every file."

"Never mind let's just try."

"Two problems; first, we don't have his PC. It was probably stolen when they invaded his home."

"It was, but I don't think that will be a problem, for the same reason that the cameras and keystroke recorder won't have been. We all use two-stage authentication."

"That's all very well, but we don't have his phone, and even if we did, he's not here for us to use his biometrics."

"I've got his phone, and my print, voice, and facial recognition profiles have been added to it.

"What about the weird portal?"

"If it's the same one I use in mine, it only applies to his own PC. Anyone attempting to use it from his PC in a different location would be locked out. Same applies if they tried using any other way in."

"So, how does that help us?"

"Because I understand how the portal works."

"Did he give you his passcodes or something?"

"It doesn't work like that, but once we start we'll only get ten chances before it locks us out. Still, I doubt we'll need that."

"Patryk had an icon to kick-start the process, how do we go about it?"

"Go to *https://opensaysme.com/help* You'll get a pop-up warning saying you have a virus. It won't be your usual one. It will ask if you want to proceed yes or no. Answer yes, and two boxes will appear."

Linda was confident that her own malware protection was strong enough to deal with any threat and went ahead. The two boxes appeared as Saffie had predicted. The first contained a random series of numbers and letters, *pg6-yl5-4xv-u4n-hfb*. The second was an empty dialogue box.

Saffie wheeled her chair to sit at Linda's shoulder. "Okay, now using upper case in the lower box type *P0G96-Y5L55-40X5V-U244N-H2F4B*, Saffie slowly and deliberately dictated.

Linda followed the instructions and clicked where it said *Enter*.

A popup message appeared, telling them they'd entered an incorrect passcode, and they had nine more attempts.

Linda looked at Saffie, "What now?"

"Type the same code but change the second five to a six."

This time the computer pinged, and a pop-up message asked for a biometric response from a phone or PC.

Saffie used Patryk's phone opened an app labelled *Reader* and the screen asked for a fingerprint. After the briefest of touches by her right middle finger on the scanner, the phone screen returned to normal, and seconds later a file manager appeared on the PC screen.

"How the Hell did you do that?"

"I used the numerical time and date alternately to the letters in the code they provided."

"As simple as that?"

"I would have got it right first time, but the minutes changed while you were typing. There's more to it than that of course, that's why they give you ten tries. I was only able to hit on the correct method because I'd already received a prompt on his phone."

"I didn't hear it buzz or vibrate."

"You wouldn't; it's silent and the app only appears when sent the prompt from the website."

"What now though?"

"Let's try one of the files you tried last time. Can you remember which ones?"

"Yes but that won't give me the password and even if it did, there are about a hundred files here, and every password will be different."

"Before he died he told me to remember something, but he was gone before I could clarify it."

"What was it?"

"It sounded like a quote, but I didn't recognize it. Something about not knowing the weight until you've felt freedom."

"It's from The Scarlet Letter. *She had not known the weight until she felt the freedom.* Nathaniel Hawthorne's most famous novel," Linda quoted. "It means, you don't know how much a of a burden something is, until it's taken away."

"Okay how does that help?"

"If we can use that knowledge to generate one correct password, we can probably figure out how to do the rest."

Saffie thought about it, "Let's try one of the files that you restored, as we're pretty sure they won't be what we're looking for."

Fortunately, there were no limits on the number of attempts it allowed to open individual files. The file they looked at first was called *Juanita*, and it took over an hour to find their way in using trial and error. Their numerous attempts finally produced a password that worked, it was *Juan07041804NH*. The first four letters of the file name, followed by Hawthorne's birthdate then his initials. They'd only got that far because Linda recalled the alphanumeric format of the code that Patryk had dictated and remembered the *NH* at the end.

The file was about an operation in Central America involving a drug cartel, *La Familia Rojo*. The operation had been a failure and an undercover CIA agent called Alfredo Garcia had been killed. There was no mention of Perry, Lipov or Esteban. The final entry in the file had been in May 1990.

Then starting at the top of the list and using the same methodology, they made their way through the files. They were about halfway through in order of date created when they came to the second of the restored files. The file, created in 1988 once again featured both *La Familia Rojo* and Agent Gonzalez extensively throughout. There was a single mention of a cartel functionary called Juan Esteban, and an attached jpeg photo of a Latino man in his early twenties.

Moving on through the file list, using the same methodology they'd reached the final file which wasn't called, *Improbable* as they might have expected, but, unimaginatively, *Implausible*. Unfortunately, the password *Impl07041804NH* wouldn't open it as they had expected. The next two hours of using various combinations of upper-case and lower-case letter, and different ways of expressing the date produced nothing.

Cindy knocked on the door and asked them if they wanted lunch, so they decided to take a break.

As they ate, Linda asked, "Cindy, if I asked you to write down the date 4th July eighteen-oh-four, how many ways can you think of to write it?"

Taking her notepad, she began to write. *July 4th, 1804; 4th July 1804; 04 Jul 1804; Jul 04, 1804*. All were ideas that they'd already used. Then she wrote *Independence Day 1804*.

Suddenly the two women looked at each other and simultaneously said, "Independence Day!"

"Cindy, you're a genius. Thank you, thank you, thank you."

Rushing back to the study they went to try getting into the file one more time, only to find that the portal had timed out.

Inevitably the passcode they'd tried before wouldn't work, and the newly generated one wouldn't work using the identical methodology.

After four tries they were scared they'd use all their options without regaining access.

"Will you explain this system to me?" Linda asked.

"It's as I described but using different ways of expressing the date and time."

She pulled a notepad toward her and began scribbling various options.

They'd reached the ninth option before they were back in the archive. Confidently Linda typed *Impl07041776NH* into the dialogue cos and hit the Enter button, only for it to be rejected. Although there were no limits to how many attempts they could make, they'd run out of ideas.

"Shit!" Saffie exclaimed. "What the fuck do we do now?"

"Whose birthday was it on 4th July 1776?" Linda asked, just as the study door opened.

"Uncle Sam," Cindy said. "You forgot your drinks; I brought them through."

Linda turned back to her laptop and typed *Impl07041776US* and the file opened.

"Cindy you just earned a double pay bonus. Fantastic! But I would have expected both of you to know the day we declared Independence."

"We do, but we're so blinded by everything, we couldn't see the wood for the trees."

It took seconds to word search the document to discover that the name Esteban appeared numerous times, as did the name Gonzalez and someone called Ripple. However, there was only a single mention of Perry.

"Can we print this off?" Saffie asked.

"There's no print option although you might be able to copy and paste it into a new pdf file, but are you sure you want to do that?"

"What do you mean?"

"From the little I've read; this is the hottest of hot potatoes. Putting it into an insecure format like pdf could be an offence under the Espionage Act, as could most of what we've already done today for that matter."

"You let me worry about that, you were never here. I don't intend to leave it in a pdf. I'm going to convert it into a double-encrypted document and save it to my own archive. I'll electronically shred the pdf without saving it. I'm concerned that somebody at Langley will shred Patryk's whole archive and we'll lose access to it completely."

"That's a good point. But what would be the purpose?" Linda replied.

"I don't know, but I suspect that somewhere in that file is another name, one that could expose an operation with far-reaching consequences."

"I'm going to leave you to it now. You're on dangerous ground here though Saffie, and you won't make a lot of friends by doing what you're doing.

Saffie thought about Linda's words and knew she was absolutely right, but it wasn't in her nature to back away from a fight. Even if she backed off now, she knew it wouldn't be the end of it. There was more than one side to this, and she was determined that all of the people responsible would receive their just desserts. There were the people who set the Boggs, the Scotts, Blenkhorn and Seymour onto her and her family, which was almost certainly Lipov. He would have been prompted by his failure to provoke Patryk into revealing what he knew about *Project Improbable* and frustrated by Saffie's interference. Then there were the people who sent *Gulliver* and *Handlebar* after Patryk, probably also Lipov. But Lipov was almost certainly being cajoled into his actions by the Russians or someone acting on their behalf. Then lastly there was whoever it was seeking to gain from what they hoped to uncover or conceal.

She hurried back to the study to get there before the portal timed out again, and created the new version of the file, and did the same thing with the *Juanita* file.

Studying the *Implausible* file, it was easy for her to see what all the interest was. Amongst other things, it revealed the existence of a CIA asset within the Kremlin, codenamed *Harbinger*. It didn't disclose exactly who it was, but she suspected that people in the know ought to be able to make an accurate estimation. After reading it through several times, she wasn't clear whether the bad actors in this case were the ones trying to keep it covered up, or the ones trying to expose it. Neither did it give any direct leads to the true identities of Perry, Esteban, or Gonzalez. The lone entry about Perry was where he'd alerted Gonzalez to the potential for *Ripple* to become an asset.

The *Implausible* file had been opened in 1991. At the time Gonzalez had clearly been a junior CIA agent working undercover in Moscow, and the man with the key to everything. *Ripple* had been a junior employee in the State Department.

Gonzalez had discovered a plot to put *Ripple* in place as a minor Russian asset, placing listening devices in State Department vehicles and rooms. Esteban had been the Russian agent who'd exploited *Ripple's* financial vulnerability, a situation created by a sting engineered by Esteban himself.

Discovery of the plot in its infancy by Gonzalez made it easy, using straightforward blackmail, to turn *Ripple*, then control what information went to Moscow and what didn't. So, *Ripple* became a CIA double agent, although initially a relatively low-level one. The beauty of the plot was that due to skillful manipulation, *Ripple's* contribution to US counterintelligence using disinformation became huge, and largely funded by Russia themselves.

In spite of *Ripple's* realistic unsuitability, he found himself maneuvered into positions in the State Department far above his competence and to the bewilderment of his subordinates, yet still not allowed to fail because of his value to the secret services. Benefitting both from his elevated salary and the payments into offshore accounts by the Russian State, *Ripple* became an extremely wealthy man. As far as Saffie could determine, by the time Patrick made his final entry when he retired, *Ripple* was still active. That was something that made Saffie feel very uncomfortable.

By a process of elimination, she was able to assume that Patryk was Garcia, and the reporting of his death was to disguise any link between him and his new ID as Gonzalez. She also assumed that as Gonzalez, Patryk had been *Ripple's* handler up until his retirement, albeit at arm's length. She also assumed that Perry was *Ripple*. The file didn't mention who had become *Ripple's* new handler after Patryk's retirement.

In an effort to locate Perry, Saffie searched a list of State Department employees. It was an enormous department and inevitably there were quite a few people with the name Perry. She was able to eliminate most of them by virtue of age or gender, but there were still five remaining. Using *LinkedIn*, a further three were ruled out, leaving a carpool driver called Wilson Perry, and an Assistant Secretary of State for International Narcotics and Law Enforcement Affairs, Willard Perry-Greene.

Saffie asked herself, 'A limo driver, how the hell could he be an important counterintelligence asset? It must be the other guy.' However, an Assistant Secretary of State was a political appointment. Appointed to the post under Trump, Willard Perry-Greene had been reconfirmed after Biden was elected. To say that it was unusual was an understatement. *Ripple's* career in a variety of posts had spanned six presidents. Could this be how he'd stayed active over that time?

Her thought processes were interrupted by a call. "Hi Patsy, have you got anything for me?"

"Yes, but not much. The number you gave me was a cell, but surprisingly not a burner. It's registered to a guy called Wilson Perry. He lives at 4877 26th Ave, Temple Hills, Maryland, and he's lived there about eighteen years. He's a carpool driver at State Department HQ in Pennsylvania Avenue, and he's been in post for at least twenty years."

"No connections to Esteban or Gonzalez?"

"Not that I could see. The phone is inactive most of the time."

"Thanks Patsy."

'This is weird," she thought, and knowing that Patsy wouldn't want to take her enquiries any further, she called Dexter McDowell.

"Saffie, what can I do for you?"

"I want you to track a cell phone for me."

"Would that be '771-456-1357'?"

"That's right, how did you know?"

"Because I just looked over my sister's shoulder and read her notes."

"For future reference, I'd prefer you didn't share my work product without my permission."

"We wouldn't normally, but we share a workspace so sometimes we learn things unintentionally."

"What do you want to know about the phone?"

"Where it's been, going back as far as possible, where it is now, and where it goes to in the next week."

"Patsy's been listening in, and she says that she omitted to tell you that the phone is now where it's been for as far back as records go, and that's in the State Department building in Pennsylvania Avenue."

"Okay thank you."

She ended the call and looked at her watch. It was four-thirty pm on a Friday. If Perry was working normal office hours, she reckoned she could beat him home.

For most places in the Western world, Friday was POETS day (*Piss Off Early Tomorrow's Saturday*), and Washington DC was no different. The traffic between Dunn Loring and Temple Hill was heavy, particularly on the Capital Beltway and crossing the Wilson Bridge. It was five-twenty by the time she reached Perry's home. There were no cars on the drive of the small single-story house on the well-kept street of mostly similar properties, nor any in the roadway outside.

Taking her lock-picking kit she approached the front door as if making a house call. She knocked on the door. As she'd hoped, there was no reply, and a second knock achieved the same result. It took less than twenty seconds to pick the rudimentary front door lock, and she let herself in, hoping that she hadn't been observed.

The house was clearly a bachelor pad. It was clean and orderly, but there were no frills. The inevitable huge TV, stood in front of a coffee table complete with a tidy pile of soft porn magazines. She didn't have time to conduct a full search, but she did a quick scan of the small five-roomed home, which only produced a small pile of mail. There was a letter from the Comptroller of Maryland with a tax refund check for $107, an invitation to join the local Neighborhood Watch scheme, an unopened letter with the Logo of Heritage4U on the outside and addressed to Perry at the State Department, and a letter from a BMW dealer thanking him for his custom.

The most significant find was an envelope with a Belizean postage stamp and the logo of the Cay Heritage Bank. The envelope had been opened so she read the letter inside. It was from his Account Manager to advise him that his balance of almost BZ$250,000 was nearing the maximum for that type of account, and he should consider transferring some of it to his other account. A quick Google search revealed that the Belizean Dollar was roughly worth 50 US cents.

She was still holding the letter when she heard a car pull onto the drive. A quick glance through the window revealed a small thin man climbing out of a new or nearly new BMW X3 Sport, more than $70,000 worth of vehicle. He was carrying a big bag of groceries.

Saffie didn't replace the letter or try to hide. She just sat in what was clearly Perry's favorite chair and waited, holding the papers in one hand, and her gun in the other.

Perry let himself into his house via the back door, and she could hear him unload his shopping. Then clutching a pack of beers, he appeared in the living room doorway and froze at the sight of Saffie.

"Come in Wilson, don't be shy," she told him, casually slapping the barrel of her gun into the palm of her other hand.

"Who are you? What do you want?"

"Who am I? I'm either your best friend or your worst enemy, that's who. As to what I want, that's simple. I want the answer to a few very simple questions, and your cooperation will determine which of those people I turn out to be."

"What do you mean?"

"Just take a seat and we can have our little chat, and at the end I will either wish you a good evening and leave you to get on with your comfortable life, or I'll call my contact in the FBI to kickstart an investigation into your involvement in an international spy ring. Oh sorry, I'm sitting in your favorite chair."

She stood up, allowing him to see how much taller she was than him, hoping it would increase the intimidating effect. "Make yourself comfortable, it will be so much easier to relieve yourself of your burden of guilt."

"Guilt?" he shuffled to the chair she'd just vacated. "What have I done?"

"Let's just start with all this money you've got stashed away in an offshore bank account," she waved the letter. "I haven't had time to search your whole house, but I'm sure if I did I'd discover evidence of a whole lot more."

"Are you going to take it away from me?"

"Not necessarily, but I need to know where it's coming from because, no offense intended, there's no way you earned it from driving a limo for twenty years. I'm sure the tips are good, but not that good."

"I knew that one day I'd have to give it all up, that's why I haven't spent much of it." He looked almost relieved to unburden himself.

"Fine, but that doesn't explain everything. Start at the beginning."

"I've been in prison."

"Okay, carry on."

"I was caught doing things in the ladies' restroom at the gas station where I worked."

"Doing things? You'll have to do better than that. I'm a big girl you don't need to be coy around me."

"I was looking into the trash bin and doing things."

"You mean you were jerking off into a sanitary disposal bin."

"Y-yes."

"Were there any women present?"

"No, of course not. I wouldn't do that."

"Who caught you?"

"A local deputy."

"And they sent you to prison for that? How long for."

"Ten years."

"Ten years, for that?"

"The deputy said I'd been having sex with a dog. It wasn't true."

"Where was this?"

"Lexington Kentucky."

"So, you did ten years. Then what?"

"I didn't do ten years. After a year, a guy came to see me and told me that if I was prepared to change my name and go to work in Washington as a driver he could have me released right away."

"What else did you have to do?"

"Nothing, just pretend to be this other guy and never tell anybody about it for the rest of my life. They said, if I did I'd have to go back to prison and serve the rest of my sentence."

"Naturally you agreed."

"I hated it in prison. They used to do things to me, and make me do things to them."

"Okay I get it."

"What else happened?"

"They said I'd work as a driver, driving people around in expensive cars, and be given good pay."

"And did they do what they said?"

"Yes, and after a year they said they were so pleased with my work they started paying me a bonus and putting it into the account in Belize."

"And you never spent the money?"

"I spent a bit to buy this house, but nothing else."

"What about the car?"

"I saved for that from my normal salary. I don't have to pay rent and I don't go out much."

"This guy, the one who came to see you. What was his name?"

"He told me his name was Alfredo Gonzalez, but I don't think that was true."

"What makes you say that?"

"I saw his picture in the paper the other day. They said his name was Patrick something or other, and he was murdered."

"This him?" Saffie asked holding up her phone.

"That's him."

"How can you be sure?"

"He saved my life, didn't he? He got me out of prison and got me the best job in the world. I'm not likely to forget him am I? I'm not clever, I'm no good at doing anything, except I'm a good driver. I get to drive all these really important people, in really nice cars, and some of them are really nice to me. Nobody was nice to me before."

"What was your name before you became Wilson Perry?"

"Jed, Jed Nelson. You're not going to make me go back to being him again, are you?"

"It's not my decision to make, but I doubt it. A few more questions. When you went to work in the carpool, did anybody ever ask you what happened to the real Wilson Perry?"

"The others were all told that he'd been promoted, and that I was his cousin and had been given his job. The other Perry was the manager, but I was just a driver. The other guys all used to rib me and call me W2 because I looked so much like the other Wilson."

"Did you ever see the real Wilson Perry."

"A few times. I think he'd had some work done on his face, so he looked a bit different, but I was sure it was him. He got to be real important. I even drove him once, but he never said nothing."

"What about Gonzalez, did you see him again?

"He used to come and visit me every year and tell me what a good job I was doing. He wouldn't ring and tell me he was coming; he'd just turn up. We'd chat for a while; he'd remind me how important it was that I never talk about what we did, he'd give me five-hundred bucks then say goodbye."

She believed she knew the answer, but she asked it anyway, "The old Wilson Perry, do you know what he's called now?"

"He's called Willard Perry-Greene. They said they didn't want there to be any confusion, so they gave him a different name. It didn't make sense to me, but I didn't worry about it."

"One last question. Do you have a cellphone?"

"Yes, doesn't everybody?"

"Where do you keep it?"

"I normally carry it with me, I put it on the kitchen counter when I came in."

"Is that the only one?"

"Why would I need two?"

"Can you remember its number?"

He gave it her; she called it and heard it ring on the kitchen counter.

"Thank you Wilson, or would you prefer Jed?"

"I'm Wilson now. It even says so on my Driver's License and social security card."

"You may get a visit from some other people from the FBI, but I don't think you've got anything to worry about. Good luck."

As she drove back to Dunn Loring, she thought, 'That explains a lot.'

At home she made her nightly call to Mary and the boys, before calling Wolski.

"Hi Saffie, how's your day been?"

"Worthwhile, is the best way to describe it. How about you?"

"I eventually pinned down my buddy, but I can't see him until tomorrow. What have you learned?"

"We managed to do all we set out to do. I've discovered Perry's identity, although it's not straightforward. I won't go into it now though."

"What are your plans for the morning?"

"I'm not sure yet, but I want to go after Bramwell if I can locate him."

"Take care, these assholes on two wheels aren't the sharpest knives in the block, but they can be dangerous."

"I know and I'm grateful for your concern."

Chapter Sixteen
Saturday 5:30am - Dunn Loring, Virginia.

Saffie woke to the sound of her phone vibrating on her nightstand. From the pattern of vibrations, she straightaway recognized that it wasn't a phone call. It was the intruder alarm; someone had crossed the perimeter of her property. On her feet in seconds, and having been sleeping in a lightweight jersey tracksuit, all she had to do was slip into her sneakers, grab her gun and she was ready to go. She called Cindy as she made her way to the alarm console.

"Operation Backstop," she said as soon as the helper answered.

Cindy didn't reply, but Saffie trusted her to respond to the warning, without question.

The intruder alarm app on her phone indicated that the laser beam that stretched across the rear fence had been interrupted twice, indicating that there were probably at least two uninvited people on her property. In theory, she should have called the cops, but if as she suspected it was her friend *Handlebar*, she wanted a crack at him first.

The PIR lights hadn't yet been activated, so she killed the power supply to the outside light, and donned the NV glasses that she hadn't stowed since her trip to West Virginia. Grabbing one of the boys' baseball bats and a taser, she slipped out of the front door, and sidled along the walls of the house to avoid being revealed in the streetlights. There was an area at the side of the house that was never lit from the street, and she used it to cross to the side perimeter hedge. Turning on the NV glasses she immediately spotted two men crossing the big lawn in the direction of the house.

From their build, stance and movement, the one at the front was almost certainly *Handlebar*, but there was no way to identify the other, much taller one.

"She don't even have intruder lights, stupid bitch," *Handlebar* said to his pal as they approached the back door.

"She can't be that stupid if she downed you and killed *Gulliver*."

"Listen, *Crow*, she got lucky is all."

Handlebar didn't get to hear a response from *Crow*, because after the karate blow to his carotid nerve coupled with the immediate application of a taser to his neck, the taller intruder had collapsed to the ground with little more than a grunt. *Handlebar* had no time to assess what was wrong with his pal before a swinging baseball bat hit him in the left knee. Baseball bats for kids are smaller and lighter than those for adults, but when twenty-seven ounces of maple wood travelling at eighty miles per hour hits you on the side of your knee, with all the power of an extremely fit woman behind it, the chances are you will fall over. It was no different this time. *Handlebar's* scream must have woken her neighbors in several directions, but he still had hold of his gun, so she brought the bat down on his right elbow with equal force.

After kicking the gun out of his reach, she knelt by his head. "If you're planning on riding a bike at any time in the future, you need to tell me who sent you to kill Patryk Wilkanowicz. At the moment, you've got shattered knee and elbow joints, and two unaffected limbs. As I still have a baseball bat and haven't yet called for the cops or medics, you need to do the math and decide if you're going to answer my question."

His pal *Crow* began to stir so she zapped him with the taser again.

"Come on *Handlebar*, I've put your pal to sleep again so he'll never know you squealed."

"Fuck off, bitch."

"Fine. Elbow or knee, your choice."

She stood up and tapped his undamaged knee with the bat and braced herself like a golfer preparing to drive off, then lifted it high above her head.

"Knee then. Ready?"

"Okay, okay. It was Alvarez."

"Don't fuck me around or I'll destroy that second knee anyway. Who the fuck is Alvarez?"

"Pedro Alvarez: he gave us ten grand to kill Wilkanowicz."

"What about me? Whose idea was it to come after me?"

"Mine first, because you kept getting in the way, and then because you killed *Gulliver*."

"Where do I find this Alvarez?"

"I don't know. He calls me when he wants to be in contact."

"So, his number is in your phone?"

"Yeah."

She rummaged in his clothes and found two cell phones, did the same with *Crow*, and then called Cindy in the gym.

"You can come out now Cindy. I've caught and detained two intruders. I'll wait in the backyard with them until the cops get here, if you could open the gate for them when they arrive, thanks."

After calling 911, she asked for the cops and paramedics, then called Ramirez."

"You're not doing anything to improve your popularity Saffie. What is it this time?"

"I've caught Bramwell."

"For fucks sake, Saffie, you can't keep doing this."

"Doing what?"

"Catching the bad guys. You almost certainly use illegal means to find them, and sooner or later it's going to catch up with you."

"In the case of Chester Boggs, myself and my colleagues only used investigative techniques available to all law enforcement agencies to locate him, the bear did the rest. As for tonight's episode, I didn't need to locate Bramwell, he came to me. He and his buddy invaded my property armed with suppressed handguns. All I did was subdue them and defend myself. In the process, Bramwell got a little damaged. I didn't break any laws as far as I can see."

"Have you called the cops?"

"Of course, I think I can hear the sirens already."

"Have you questioned him?"

"I tried. but he's having problems articulating at the moment, perhaps you'll have better luck."

She ended the call and said to *Crow*, who was beginning to show signs of consciousness.

"Who's Pedro Alvarez? Tell me now or I'll zap you again."

"He pays us to do jobs for him."

"Where can I find him?"

"I don't know. He doesn't communicate with me, only *Handlebar*."

"Don't you know anything else about him?"

"It's not his real name. I don't know what his real name is."

"Was he there the day you beat up Wilkanowicz?"

"Yeah."

"So, if he wanted this information from Wilkanowicz, and he didn't get it, why send *Handlebar* to kill him?"

"Because the old guy told us how to get into his computer, but we heard the cop, sirens, so we grabbed it and left. Then after we tried to get into it again the hard drive went into self-destruct, so Alvarez told us to kill the guy."

That was when the first cop car arrived.

The next two hours became another tripartite song and dance between the agencies arguing about jurisdiction, but Saffie left them to it, did an hour in the gym, and took some breakfast before Daniels and Ramirez asked if they could do a joint interview. Saffie agreed, but the interview dissolved into a boxing match of duck and weave between them, with her answering their questions completely enough to satisfy their curiosity, but without disclosing information she wasn't ready to divulge. When they got up to leave, she knew they hadn't been completely convinced.

Wolski was in the kitchen with Cindy when she closed the gate behind them.

"Hi there Wolski, I thought you were meeting your ATF pal this morning."

"I was, but he got curious, and we ended up getting together last night instead. Are you going to fill me in about what the Hell went on here earlier?"

"Bramwell and a buddy decided to pay me an early morning visit, I explained to them that they weren't welcome."

"I'd like to have been around for that discussion."

"It didn't last long, not after I pressed my point with a taser, and reinforced it with Ben's baseball bat."

"Did he tell you anything?"

"He revealed the name of the third character who beat Patryk up, or the name he's been using to hire all these small-time crooks; Pedro Alvarez."

"Bingo!" Wolski held his hand up for a high five.

"Why do you say that?" she replied, accommodating his gesture without knowing why.

"Pedro Alvarez is one of the names being used by Juan Esteban. The ATF and DEA have had their eyes on him for years, but they can never join the dots. My pal was interested to know when I mentioned a possible link-up with Lipov."

"How much did you tell him about what we're working on?"

"Just that the name Esteban came up in connection with Lipov in a case we're working on. I didn't mention the first name or the context. It's a common name, and he thought it could be a coincidence, but he said he'll keep an eye out, and speak to his liaison in the DEA."

"Ideally we'd hand this all over to the alphabet spaghetti of federal agencies, but there's a lot at stake here, and we don't know who the moles are or how many."

"What's our next move then?"

"I'd like to corner this Willard Perry-Greene, and see what he's got to say for himself, but he'll probably have protection."

"Not necessarily."

"Why do you say that?"

"Because an Assistant Secretary of State is pretty low down the totem pole. They don't all get 24/7 protection. It'll be mostly when he's on official business."

"Maybe a house call is in order then."

Wolski was doubtful, "Once you open the can of worms with him, there won't be any going back. At the moment we don't know if he's a black hat or a white one. I think it would be better to have everything tied up before you confront him."

"I guess you're right. We have other leads we need to follow. We need to learn a lot more about Esteban for a start."

"And the link-up between him and Lipov."

"That's going to be difficult."

Her phone rang, she picked it up, and after seeing the caller's name, she answered, "Agent Ramirez. How are you?"

"I'm good. More to the point, how are you? You've been put through the mill a bit lately."

"I'm fine, what can I do for you?"

"A quick question about Patryk."

"Go ahead."

"You seem to be the only person left that knew him well enough to comment. We're trying to assess how resilient he might have been to torture."

"I didn't know him when he was a field agent, it was before my time, but like the rest of us he'll have been given SERC training; that's survival, evasion, resistance and escape, like the special ops guys have, but maybe not quite so intense. Why do you ask?"

"After his autopsy, they released his medical records, and when he was admitted they discovered he'd been given a cocktail of drugs including SP-117. We were wondering how well he might have been able to resist telling them what he knew."

"Patryk was a tough bastard, and in normal circumstances I wouldn't bet against him holding out or selling his inquisitors red herrings. The problem is he was aging, suffering from cancer, and it was a long time since he'd been in the field. The other thing to remember, is that no matter how good the training is, nobody knows how well you'll hold out until you're in the situation. It's never happened to me so I'm no expert, but if I had to guess, I'd say that he'd have held out for as long as possible before giving them a morsel to take the pressure off."

"So, he may have given them some of what they wanted to know?"

"Unless they knew precisely what they were looking for, I doubt it would have been much use to them. The passcode and encryption system we use for our archives isn't straightforward. The system requires biometric confirmation and a passcode for entry that changes every attempt you make, and you only get ten opportunities. Even if you succeed in getting through the portal, each file will have a separate password, and every operator uses a different method of generating them, so even if they got into one file, it's doubtful they'd get into any others."

"Okay, thanks a lot. Have you managed to unearth anything else in your enquiries?"

"One or two things, but nothing that's going to put it all to bed yet, and nothing I'm prepared to share until the mole or moles in Langley or the Secret Service have been exposed."

After ending the call, she turned to Wolski who'd been listening in.

"What's SP-117?" he asked.

"I think it's an improved successor to sodium pentothal, a kind of truth drug developed by the Russians."

"Maybe we could try that."

"What do you mean?"

"Well, the Esteban character doesn't sound like the sort of guy who's going to roll over and tell us all we want to know as soon as we threaten to rough him up a bit, and personally I'm not a big fan of waterboarding or slivers of bamboo under the fingernails."

"Fair point. Any idea where we'd get something like that?"

"Not a clue. That's more like spook territory; us cops normally stick to threatening to charge people with crimes they didn't commit, or just simple brutality."

"I may know someone. I haven't spoken to him for years, but he's a former agent who was a colleague of Patryk's back in the day."

"Are you serious? I was only joking."

"Deadly serious. In the heat of the moment, I can be as vicious and uncompromising as anybody, but cold-blooded brutality isn't my thing either."

"Where do we find this guy?"

"I've no idea, I haven't spoken to him for fourteen years," she told him, whilst typing a text. "But in the meantime, I need to cancel the search for Bramwell."

The man she'd been speaking about was Russell Curtiss. Russ had been a field agent for ten years when she was given her first posting alongside

Brett. He'd served in Russia with Patryk, but after his cover was blown, he quit before returning to work as a chemist in the pharmaceutical industry, where he'd earned his degree.

It took her over an hour and about twenty phone calls to run down an address for Curtiss. He lived just outside Lebanon, Pennsylvania. It was two and a half hours away, but she reckoned she'd need to spend some time with him to persuade him to do what she wanted. Without a full understanding of why he was being asked, she doubted he'd be likely to agree to such a request from someone he hadn't seen or spoken to for fourteen years. Assuming he agreed to her request, it was also possible he wouldn't be able to do it overnight.

"Okay Wolski. Here's what I think. I'll leave you here to try and find some way we can get up close and personal to either or both Lipov and Esteban. While I see if I can renew an old acquaintance with Russell Curtiss. I might take a diversion to see the boys on my way back so let's agree to meet back here in a couple of days. Is that okay?"

"Do you ever stop long enough to breathe? You make me feel like I'm just treading water here."

"I'm not normally quite as hyper, but I've got a personal stake in this, but you've been making a great contribution so don't worry about it."

Chapter Seventeen
Saturday 5:30pm - Cleona, Pennsylvania

It was nearly three hours after calling Mary and the boys, when she pulled up outside Russ Curtiss' home in Dogwood Lane. The big, white, faux-timber-clad, two-story house was one of many similar houses in the wide, quiet and well-kept street. It looked too big for a single man, so she immediately assumed he'd now have a family. It was a Saturday so she anticipated that if he was home, then he wouldn't be alone.

Entirely without confidence that the trip would turn out to be worthwhile, she rang the bell. Seconds later a young girl about thirteen years old opened the door.

"Hello, are you Janine? You're very early," the youngster asked.

"No, I'm sorry I'm Saffron Price. I'm here to see Russell, we're former work colleagues."

"Oh, you're here to see Daddy. Okay come in, I'll get him. He's in his workshop. Have a seat."

The girl showed her into a living room and disappeared. A few minutes later a tall man in his mid-fifties came into the room followed by the girl. "Saffron? It is you, my God. What on Earth are you doing here?"

"It's a long story, and I'm hoping for a favor."

"I hope you're going to stay for dinner."

"I don't want to intrude."

"Nonsense. Where have you driven from?"

"I'm in Dunn Loring these days."

"In which case I insist. Where are you staying?"

"I haven't booked anywhere yet. I left in a bit of a hurry."

"Then you can stay the night as well."

"I really couldn't…"

"Rubbish. By the time we've had dinner, told each other what's been happening in our lives since we last met, and I've helped you out with your problem, it will be far too late to drive back. Anyway, the hotels around here are all crap."

"When I tell you what my problem is, you may not want to help."

"Now I'm even more intrigued."

"How do you know my dad?" the young girl asked.

"I'm sorry, I didn't introduce you did I? Saffron, this is my daughter Morgan. Morgan this is Saffron, we once worked together."

"Nice to meet you, Morgan."

"My other daughter Katniss will be home soon; she's been at the movies with her friends.

"Is your wife with her?"

"Sadly, we lost Delia when we gained Katy. What about you, do you have a family? I gathered from the surname that you and Brett must have married. I wasn't surprised. I felt sure there wouldn't be another Saffron."

"That's right, Brett and I married. We had a son we called Ben, then three years ago we adopted Josh, they're both eleven now."

"So, I'm guessing they're at home with Brett."

"No, I lost Brett to Covid last year, the boys are staying with their aunt near Harrisonburg."

"Two lonely souls eh?"

Morgan sniffed. "He's not lonely; he's got a string of desperate females trying to lure him into a church."

"Fat chance of that with you two," he said with a smile. "Every time any of them get close, you terrify them, and they get cold feet."

"So, who's Janine?"

"Janine? Oh bugger, I'd better ring and cancel her. Just a minute," he said as he left the room.

"Janine was supposed to be minding us tonight while Daddy went bowling with his buddies," Morgan explained.

The door burst open, and a slightly smaller version of Morgan came in. "OMG! Tommy Burgin just tried to kiss me… Oh hello, are you Janine?" she added, spotting Saffie.

"This is Saffron, she's an old friend of Daddy's," Morgan explained.

"Are you minding us tonight?"

"I don't think Daddy's going out tonight now; he's just cancelling Janine."

"You must be Katy, and please just call me Saffie."

"Hi, it's nice to meet you. Do you like Indian food, curry and stuff?"

"Yes, what about you?"

"We love it, but most of the minders won't eat it, they say it makes their breath smell. I think it's because they all want to sleep with Daddy."

"I'm not a minder, and I'm not looking for a sleeping partner. Not that there's anything wrong with your daddy of course."

"Saffie's got two sons," Morgan told her sister.

"Really, how old are they?"

"Eleven they'll be twelve later this year."

"Twins?"

"No, one of them is adopted."

"Isn't that unusual? To adopt a child the same age as one of your own?" Morgan suggested.

"Probably. It's a long story."

Morgan whispered in her sister's ear loud enough for Saffie to hear, "Saffie's a widow."

"That's sad. Have you got photos of your sons?"

She took out her phone and showed them a picture of the boys on one of Mary's tractors.

"They're very good looking," Katy asked. "Are you a farmer?"

"No, that's my friend's farm. They're staying with her at the moment."

Morgan wanted to know what she did for a living.

"I'm a private investigator."

"Wow! That sounds exciting!" Morgan enthused.

"It has its moments."

"Are you two pestering Saffron? Give her a chance. I bet you haven't even offered her a coffee."

"Sorry Daddy." They rushed out of the room.

"What a lovely couple of girls, it must have been a challenge bringing them up by yourself."

"It wasn't without its difficulties, but we muddled through. But enough of that, tell me what your problem is so I can decide how best to help you out."

The girls brought in a tray of coffee and cookies, and Saffie began by bringing him up to speed with her domestic and employment situation.

"So, you're no longer with the agency?"

"Without going into too much detail, Brett and I got royally screwed by a crooked agent near the top of the tree, and we decided it was time to move on."

"So, if this isn't agency stuff, how can I help?"

"That's the trouble, it is agency stuff, even though I'm acting kinda freelance. It's pretty sensitive and quite shocking so probably best if we talk about it when the girls aren't around. I'm sorry girls."

"Aww," Katy complained. "I wanted to learn more about what Saffie does for a job."

"I'm sure you'll get plenty of time to interrogate her over dinner. Why don't you go and choose our evening meal." They got up to leave. "And no listening at the door," he told them. "I'm sorry if they were being too nosey."

She smiled, "For a few minutes, it did feel like I was being interviewed for the post of the next Mrs. Curtiss."

"They do that to any eligible female that comes through the door. They're desperate to marry me off, but I doubt if a woman that meets their exacting standards exists. Tell me your tale."

Saffie began by asking how well he'd known Patryk.

"I did a spell in Moscow for a while. He was my controller during that time. I liked and trusted him."

"Patryk's been murdered."

"Dear God. Are you trying to find the killer?"

"We know who the killer is, and he's been caught. What we don't yet understand is why he was killed. At the moment there are two, maybe three key players who can give us the answer. Just pulling them in and questioning using official channels may end up doing more harm than good. So, I want to go about it in a less conspicuous way."

"How can I help? I've been out of the game so long, I doubt anything or anyone I know could be of use to anybody?"

"It's not your agency expertise I'm after."

"Tell me then."

"If I remember correctly your degree was in biochemistry."

"That's right."

"When I get these guys in front of me, I don't want to resort to torture to get the information that I need - not that it would do any good with people like these. They're career criminals who live a life of extreme violence. They kill and maim without a second thought. What I want to do is chemically subdue them so that they answer my questions with as little resistance as possible."

"You want me to provide you with a truth serum, as some like to call them?"

"Well, yes and no."

"You do know that sodium pentothal or rather its successor Propofol, if that's what you're after, is readily available? You could have found a dispensing drug store that wasn't too careful with their records. You didn't need to drive all this way."

"Look Russell what I'm about to say is a big ask, so I'll understand if you're uncomfortable with it."

"Tell me why it's you that's doing this rather than the traditional enforcement agencies."

Saffie's explanation of events was as complete as she could make it without revealing vital national secrets.

"So, you're saying that the USA have a high-placed double agent passing misinformation to the Russians and this is all part of a plot to expose him?"

"That or this is subterfuge to prevent him from being exposed, or that even he's been turned and is now handing over the stuff he's supposed to be keeping hidden. We're pretty sure there's a mole as well."

"And you say you can't trust the FBI, Professional Standards at Langley, or the Secret Service to wheedle the mole out?"

"I'm not convinced that there isn't more than one mole."

"Jesus, and I thought things were Machiavellian enough when I was in the agency. Okay, tell me what it is that you want. I can't guarantee I'll be able to help though."

"From all I've read so far these drugs are short-acting in that they take effect quickly but are also not very long-lasting. What I'm looking for is something that will not only act quickly but will last long enough for me to extract all the information I need, but without leaving lasting effects."

"Is that all?"

"I'm sorry, I know it's a lot to ask."

"No, I mean, is that really all you need?"

"Yes, why?"

"Because I can sort that out for you without resorting to Frankenstein's laboratory as the girls call my workshop."

"You'll need to wait until tomorrow though, it would raise a few eyebrows if I went into work at this time on a Saturday evening."

"Are you saying that there's already something like this on the market?"

"It's not exactly on the market yet, but it's in the final stages of clinical trials. It's called Pentapropathal, although when it is on the market, it will probably have a different name. After a first correct dose is administered, the patient can be expected to be awake and responsive to gentle questioning for between two to three hours. If that's too long then there's a counter agent that will bring him or her round in five to ten minutes. It's not recommended for children or pregnant women for the time being, but the only significant side effects are, like most anesthetics, the possibility of hypotension, apnea, and post-treatment headache, so you might need to keep a close eye on him while he's under."

"And you can get me some of this by tomorrow?"

"How much do you need?"

"There are three potential patients, if that's what we're going to call them."

"I'll get you four doses of it and the same of the counteragent. It will have a shelf-life of approximately four weeks, and you'll need to keep it refrigerated."

"If you can do that, I wouldn't be able to thank you enough Russell."

"I won't be able to make a habit of this you know."

"I hope to God that I'll never need it again. You won't get into trouble for this will you?"

"I'm head of department, so I shouldn't think so, but the company is being taken over and I've been offered a severance package that was too generous to refuse, so I'll be leaving in the next two months."

"This is going to make my next moves so much less problematic, thank you," she told him. "What's the legitimate purpose of this drug?"

"It's a low-level anesthetic, for simple surgery."

He called to his daughters, "Okay girls you can come in now,".

The door opened without a moment's pause; they'd obviously been listening outside.

"I thought I said no listening."

"We know but it all sounded so exciting. We won't tell anyone, we promise," Morgan pleaded.

"It's really important that you don't girls. People could die if the wrong other people were to learn about some of that stuff, and Saffie or I could go to prison."

Katy made a zip sign across her mouth.

"Are you a spy then, like our daddy used to be?" Morgan asked.

"Some people used to call us that. I preferred to call myself an intelligence expert, but like your daddy I'm not anymore."

"All that stuff about truth serums sounded like spy stuff to me. Have you had to kill people? Daddy said he didn't."

"Most of the time, being an intelligence agent is less like James Bond or Lara Croft, and a lot more like being a nosy neighbor."

"You didn't say if you'd killed people."

"I am not, nor have I ever have been, an assassin. I have no license to kill, and I don't want one. When the need arises, I defend myself, as do most people, and I'm subject to the same laws as everybody else."

Russell stepped in to her rescue. "Enough with the questions girls, have you decided what we're going to eat tonight?"

"We ordered already. It should be here in twenty minutes," Katy told him.

"How did you pay?" he asked.

"Morgan took your card out of your wallet; you left it on the kitchen table."

"I sometimes think I'm surplus to requirements in this house, just here to provide money and cab rides to your after-school activities."

"We didn't want to waste time choosing the food, so we just ordered the set menu for four."

"Where did you order from?"

"The Khana Bistro. We like their stuff."

"We'd better set the table then."

The food arrived and it was obvious that the three of them had a routine for setting the table, but Saffie pitched in.

"Have we got to give thanks?" Morgan asked before they started to eat.

"It's up to you Saffie, we don't usually observe that ritual."

"We don't in our house either."

"That's how Morgan scares off a lot of the old biddies that Daddy invites to dinner. If they insist on saying grace, she tells them she's an atheist and wants to be a witch when she grows up," Katy explained.

"See what I mean," Russ said.

Saffie laughed.

Halfway through the meal Katy asked, "Are you one of Daddy's ex-girlfriends."

"Saffron was far too sensible to get mixed up with me, and she was already spoken for when I came on the scene."

"Daddy's not seeing anyone at the moment, Saffie," Katy suggested.

"Whoa, just one minute you two. Who elected you matchmakers? Saffie's twenty years younger than me, and quite capable of finding a partner on her own."

"I was just saying."

"Do I get a say in this?" Saffie asked. "The facts that your daddy is free, and twenty years older than me are both immaterial. Russell would be a fine catch for anyone looking for a partner and whoever they were would be lucky to get him, especially when he comes complete with two such lovely girls. But we live 150 miles apart and we each have two fantastic kids to look after and that trumps romance every time."

Eventually, Russell sent the two girls off to bed, and the two adults finished the wine as they reminisced.

"So, has there been anyone else?"

"Since Brett you mean?"

"Yes."

"Not had the time nor inclination, how about you?"

"A couple of dalliances; none that really stood any chance of sticking, and definitely none that would pass Morgan and Katy's cross-examination. Did you bring a bag?"

"Yes."

"Why don't you fetch it while I turn down the bed in the spare room."

"Don't bother, I'm only here for one night, it seems a shame to dirty a clean set of bed linen."

"Are you sure?"

"Why not?" she replied.

Chapter Eighteen
Sunday 08:00am - Cleona, Pennsylvania

When she joined the family in the kitchen as Russell made pancakes, the two girls were at the breakfast table wearing grins as wide as watermelon slices.

"Would you like bacon with your pancakes, Saffie?" Russell asked.

"Yes please," she said, as she poured herself a cup of coffee, while trying to ignore the scrutiny of Katy and Morgan.

"Apparently the curry making your breath smell thing, isn't quite such a big turn off after all," Morgan remarked to Katy, who instantly dissolved into giggles.

"What are you two laughing about?" Russell asked as he placed a plate of pancakes on the table.

"Nothing Daddy," Katy tried to say.

Morgan explained. "We were just discussing the merits of Asian cuisine as a medium for controlling fresh breath."

At this point, Katy got up and rushed out shouting, "Gotta pee."

"I think we got found out, Russ," Saffie said, unable to stop herself laughing.

"Nosy pair of tykes."

"What's the schedule for this morning?" she asked.

"I'll finish eating, then drive into the plant. I'll come straight back, but it'll take about an hour. Then I'll let you get away. I can't let you come into the plant with me, I'm afraid. That'd definitely get people asking questions."

"That's okay. I'll stay here with the girls."

She helped them clear away before calling Mary and the boys.

"Are those girls I can hear talking?" Ben asked.

"Yes, I stayed over at my friend's home in Pennsylvania. Those are his daughters."

"Okay," he said, sounding unsure."

"Why don't you hang up, go and get your iPad, and call me back on mine then you can all say hello on *Facetime*."

A few minutes later, after couple of minutes awkwardly introducing themselves, Morgan said, "Hey your mom's real cool isn't she?"

"Yeah, we think so."

"Our dad used to be a spy like your mom and dad were, but he gave it up when I was born."

"Mom's not a spy anymore…"

Saffie left them chatting and called Mary on her cellphone.

"Hi Mary, how are you and Rusty holding out?"

"Pretty good. We've got into a routine now. They're so well behaved and fun to have around, but they're missing you."

"I'm just waiting for my friend to come back, then I'll be leaving and coming straight to you. I'll stay over, but will it be okay to leave the boys with you another few days. I think we're reaching the end game now and it's difficult to tell how it will play out?"

"That'll be okay. Like I say, they're always welcome here, but Josh needs constant reassurance that you're safe."

"I get it. I promise not to make a habit of this. I'll see you later."

Her call to Wolski was intended to be more out of courtesy than anything, but it turned out to be a deal more functional than that.

"I'm glad you called; I think I can say I've made some headway."

"Oh yeah? Tell me more."

"Those two characters are meeting up the day after tomorrow, and I think it might be an opportunity to get them both at the same time."

"Even better then, because that stuff you were talking about - I think I've managed get hold of some."

"You spooks make strange acquaintances. The guy we found in the woods the other day; do you think it would be possible to have a little chat with him sometime? I think it would be good to know what else he has to say."

"It's worth asking but I'm not optimistic. Listen I'm staying over at Mary's again tonight, but I'll be back as early as I can tomorrow. We can make some proper plans then."

"Okay then."

She rejoined the girls in the kitchen just as they were signing off.

"Your boys are cute," Morgan assured her, "and fun."

"Yeah they are, aren't they.?"

"I like Josh but he's very shy isn't he?" Katy told her. "He's the first boy who recognized where my name comes from."

"Josh is a big reader, and a bit of an artist. Here, look at the picture he drew of my husband." She showed them her photo of the drawing.

"Josh did that and he's only eleven? Wow?"

"He had a real rough time before we adopted him, he doesn't like to talk about it, but it's probably why he's so shy."

"They told us how you shot two men who were holding them up with a gun."

"Yes well, thankfully it's not something that happens very often."

"Ben said you did it once before, when he was eight."

"I'm kinda hoping it won't happen again."

Russ returned with an insulated cool box and handed it to her. "There are four adult doses in there and four of the counteragent. It's a very efficient cool box and there are freezer blocks in there which should keep them cool enough until tonight. I'd swap them over when you go to bed and again in the morning. If you maintain them at approximately domestic cooler temperature until an hour or two before you use them they'll be okay for about a month. Instructions for administration and calculating doses are in there, as are a pack of ten syringes."

"I don't know how to thank you Russ, this is going to make all the difference."

"No thanks necessary. Perhaps when it's all over you can bring the boys to meet the girls in person and we can have a cookout."

"I'd like that."

Under the watchful eyes of the two girls, she kissed his cheek, and she climbed into her car with the cool box, he handed her bag to her, and she drove away.

At one-thirty, she pulled into the yard at the farm. Gwen the dog greeted her with her usual friendliness, and the two boys ran from the house to hug her. For reasons she couldn't explain she felt more emotional at this reunion than usual. "I've missed you boys so much," she told them, choking back the tears."

"We waited lunch until you got here," Mary told her, affectionately watching their interaction.

They hurried her through to the kitchen where Mary had prepared a meal fit for visiting royalty.

"This is a bit over the top isn't it?"

"The boys wanted to prepare something a bit special because you'd been upset, so we went to town."

"We made the sandwiches, Mom, and helped Mary make the cake," Josh told her.

It became clear that Ben was anxious to move the conversation on when he said, "Morgan and Katy are really nice, aren't they?"

"Did you like them?"

"Morgan is really hot!"

"Hot?"

"You know what I mean," he said, realizing he'd mis-chosen his words.

"I think you meant pretty. Yes she is; so is Katy," Saffie smiled, "And for what it's worth, they both thought you two were cute."

"They did?"

The boys were grinning from ear to ear.

The conversation moved on until Josh asked, "Are you going to have a baby now?"

"What makes you ask that?"

"Katy said you slept with their dad."

Mary was struggling to keep a straight face.

"As it happens, we did sleep together, but that doesn't necessarily imply that we made love, and even if it did, it wouldn't mean I would have a baby. I thought you understood all that now."

"We do, but if you're not on the pill you could get pregnant and…"

"We're in the home of a close family friend, in the middle of lunch, do you really think this is the right time or place for me to be discussing my sex-life with two eleven-year-old boys?"

"Sorry, Mom."

"It's okay, but just to put the record straight. I slept with an old friend once, I did not get pregnant, and we have no immediate plans to develop the relationship further. Although in other news, there was mention of a bi-family cookout later in the year."

"What's in that cool box you brought in with you, Mom?" Ben asked.

"Something really special and very important. Which reminds me, Mary. Have you got a couple of freezer blocks I can swap with mine overnight?"

"No problem."

"Can we go find Rusty now, Mom? He's using GPS to plough a field. He said we could watch how he does it."

"Sure; don't get in his way." They went rushing off.

As soon as they were out of earshot, Mary turned to her, "So, are you going to tell me or what?"

"What do you mean?"

"Listen, missy, you go away for a few nights, sleep with a man you've made no mention of in the past, and then arrive here with a face that says, 'I just got laid and I loved it'. What the Hell do you think I mean?"

"It was nice."

"And…?"

"He's a guy that was around at about the same time Brett and I first got together, an agent just like us. He had a couple of bad breaks and quit."

"So, what brings him back into your life now?"

"He's a biochemist, and I needed somebody with that sort of expertise."

"That's not some sort of biological warfare shit you're planning on putting in my cooler I hope."

"Nothing like that; it's medical."

"Prospects…?"

"Very few. There might be the occasional hook-up, but he's twenty years older than me, he's got two kids, and so have I. Mixed families are a recipe for disaster, especially when they're all nearly the same age, and with the raging hormones of preteen pubescence on the horizon. Apart from that we live 150 miles apart."

"Oh well no harm in asking I suppose. How's your investigation going?"

"I think we're on the edge of a breakthrough and I hope to tie it up by the end of the week. This isn't like anything I've done before and I can't be certain that we've identified all the players yet, but I'm hoping the plan we're developing will expose the remaining bad actors."

"You're a gutsy broad and no question, Saffie, but this is so dangerous I get scared for you and for the boys."

"I don't intend to make a habit of this. I only became involved for Patryk's sake, but once I was in, I wasn't given a lot of choice but to see it through.

Three hours later Rusty returned from the field.

"Where are the boys?" Saffie asked.

"I don't know," he replied shrugging his shoulders.

"I thought they were with you."

"They were for a while, but they got bored when they realized that ploughing a field using GPS tractor guidance just means sitting in the cab and making sure you don't run anything over. They went to find something more interesting to do."

"Call them," Mary suggested.

Saffie tried that, but both went to voicemail. "Where the Hell are they?"

"Why not try locating their phones?" Rusty asked.

"I've told them to leave their locations turned off while all this business is going on," she explained. "After those assholes found their way here."

"They must be around here somewhere," Rusty said. "You look around here, I'll go see if they're over in the old Sanders' place."

They scattered and regathered twenty minutes later without any idea where they were.

"Have any of the hands seen them?" Mary asked.

"Abe said he saw them jump down from the tractor and run off in this direction. One of them was on the phone."

Saffie was getting frantic by this time. "Oh God, do you think they could have been taken?"

"There's been no sign of any vehicles, and none of the hands have seen anything unusual."

"Shall I call the cops?"

"I should give it another hour or so. You know what kids that age are like," Rusty said.

"They could be anywhere in an hour; we don't even know what time they could have been taken. I think I should…" That was when a ringtone sounded from the phone in her hand.

"Ben. Where the Hell are you? … Upstairs? What are you doing upstairs? We've been searching all over for you. … Oh, okay, sorry. … What? I don't know, I'll ask."

Wearing an embarrassed expression, Saffie turned to the other two, "They're in their rooms talking to the two girls. They want to know what time's dinner."

The others laughed.

"In another hour, if they can tear themselves away from their girlfriends."

"Did you hear that?" she asked her son. "He says they're not their girlfriends just girls who're fun to talk to."

"I wonder what they find to talk about."

"Star Wars, movies, soccer, sex. What did you talk about when you were that age?" Rusty asked.

"Sex! They're eleven for God's sake."

"In the abstract of course. They won't be discussing actually doing it, but you can bet your life they'll be talking about which celebrities they fancy; who's hot and who's not, that sort of thing."

"You weren't much older than the boys when I caught you kissing Jake Perkins in the barn," Mary pointed out.

"Were you kissing boys when you were our age, Mom?" Ben asked as he joined them in the kitchen,

"I'm not ready for a session of true confessions, so maybe the less said about that the better. Let it be enough for me to say I didn't rush back to repeat the experience," Saffie said, before changing the subject. "What did you find to talk about with the girls?"

"Katy called Josh and asked if he'd do a drawing of her if she sent him a picture. He said yes, so she's been watching him do it on the iPad. Morgan and I were just talking about stuff, but my battery was low, so we said goodbye. That's alright isn't it?"

"Of course. We just didn't know where you were is all. I'm pleased you made some friends your own age, you don't get to meet many other kids being home tutored."

"Katy and Morgan are home-schooled as well."

Josh joined them in the kitchen after his iPad needed recharging. "When can we go and meet them properly, Mom?" he asked.

"In the summer break I expect."

Chapter Nineteen
Monday 9:40am - Dunn Loring, Virginia

Somehow, knowing that the boys had made some friends made her feel better about leaving them again, and the drive home hadn't been such a chore. Ten minutes after she drove through the gates, Wolski arrived. They grabbed a cup of coffee each and got right down to it.

"Okay, so what's this opportunity to get Lipov and Esteban in the same room, and where did it come from?"

"Didn't I ever tell you about my cousin Aleksy? He's a communications engineer working in Baltimore?"

"No, I don't think so."

"That's probably because he doesn't exist, but if he did, he'd look just like I do but with red hair."

"What are you getting at?"

"I got together with Dexter, and together we devised a plan."

"Explain."

"It turns out that there's a lot more to him than meets the eye. He's developed a piece of kit that can listen to what's happening in its immediate surroundings and transmit what it picks up via Wi-Fi so it can't be picked up by conventional bug detectors."

"That's all very well, but how do you intend to plant it?"

"It's already done."

"How the Hell…?"

"Obviously I didn't want to endanger young Dexter, so we came up with a way to go about it so it wouldn't be necessary."

"Have you made some sort of entry into The Vault."

"Kinda."

"How did you achieve that?"

"Dexter temporarily killed the broadband to the club and the building either side, so the company had to come out to fix the fault. The building on one side is a cryptocurrency exchange so there was no way they were going to allow the fault to persist. Within an hour the area was swarming with communications engineers, including Cousin Aleksy, who narrowed the fault to somewhere within the nightclub."

"How did you get into the building without ID?"

"I followed one of the company teams in. It turned out that Lipov has a dedicated broadband cable. I watched while the cable guys ran their tests, memorized the company Wi-Fi passkey, and entered it into Dexter's piece of kit. As they were clearing up to leave I stuck it to the back of the router, then Dexter restored the service. I've been recording everything that's said in his office ever since."

"Jesus that's clever. How does that help us get Lipov and Esteban in the same room though?"

"That would have been a problem, but my pal in ATF let it slip, that after years of listening to heavy metal and the crap they play in those nightclubs, Lipov is as deaf as a post, and whenever he speaks on the phone he always puts it on speaker."

"And…?"

"One of the first things I recorded, was him arranging a meeting with Esteban for eight o'clock tonight in his Hotel room. I checked and found Esteban booked in at the Anchorage Hotel under the name Pedro Alvarez. Apparently he always stays there when he's in town."

"What's the purpose of the meeting?"

"Lipov is pissed off with being ordered to do things without being told the reason why, and without being paid. He says he's losing too many men, and his foot soldiers are getting restless."

"Won't they have minders?"

"From what the ATF guy tells me. In the past, Lipov occasionally brings one of his meatheads with him, but Esteban never does. Neither of them let anyone near them when they're in the room, apart from room service, and then only long enough to deliver their food."

"No chance of putting one of Dexter's gadgets in there then."

"I doubt it, and if we do this right, there won't be any need. It wouldn't work anyway because the broadband cable won't be anywhere near the room. It'll be Wi-Fi connection only in there."

"So how do you suggest we go about this?"

"This is the bit you might not like."

"Why is that?"

"These meetings are a regular thing, and apparently they eat while they talk. So, at some point early in the evening the kitchen will send up a trolley. We need to waylay the girl, give her a handful of cash for you to take over from her. Enough to make it worth her looking for a job somewhere else if necessary."

"What if it's a guy?"

"Unlikely from what I hear, but it wouldn't matter anyway, would it? I'm not suggesting you impersonate anyone, just replace them."

"That makes sense. What happens once I'm in the room?"

"This is the bit when the plan relies on you doing one of your Superwoman acts and overpowering two violent criminals long enough for me to get in there to back you up."

"Where will you be?"

"Waiting on another floor for word from you that everything went okay." He waited for her reaction. "Well, what do you think?"

"I was quite enjoying it, until the last bit."

"Does that mean you're not going to do it?"

"Of course not. I just want to see if we can find a way to shorten the odds in my favor, when I get to be alone in the room with those two assholes."

"I've been thinking about that, but I haven't come up with anything?"

"What are these trolleys like, the ones they use to take the meals up?"

"I haven't seen them."

"No possibility of hiding you in the bottom then?"

"This isn't a reenactment of the Pink Panther, and I'm not Peter Sellars."

She laughed, "Maybe not then. So, unless something else comes up we'll go with Plan A. But I'm confused about one thing."

"What's that?"

"That neither of these people have any sort of bodyguard."

"As I understand it Esteban never has a minder anywhere, but as I said, in the past Lipov has occasionally used one of his tame gorillas as his backup.

"So where is he likely to be while we're abusing his boss?"

"My guess he'll be waiting outside the door. But I can't be sure."

"A minor detail you omitted to mention."

"I thought I could distract him."

"What are you going to do, stand by the elevator, lift the leg of your pants and show him a shapely ankle?"

Wolski looked hurt. "I hadn't decided yet."

"If we're going down the distraction route, it will need to be subtle enough not to alert the two targets but serious enough to demand the attention of the minder."

They thought silently for a few minutes, until eventually she said, "What we need is a master key."

"Where are we going to get one of those?"

"The house keeping staff would have one."

"We could use the trolley girl's."

"If she's kitchen staff she might not have one. Anyway, that would be too late, I need one this afternoon."

"Why?"

"Because we need to start this operation now. Grab everything we're likely to need, while I see if I can get us a room in the same hotel. What floor is Esteban on?"

"The fifth. Room 521."

An hour later they were in her car fitted with false plates and on their way to Baltimore.

"Did you get a room?" he asked.

"Yeah, not sure what floor it's on yet."

It was a ninety-minute drive to Baltimore, and on the journey she explained her plan. It was nearly two o'clock when they checked in as Mr. and Mrs. Hanrahan and were given a room on the sixth floor.

The first thing she did after opening the door was go to the minibar and help herself to a Mars bar, take a single bite, and smear the end on the bedcover.

Wolski looked at her as if she were crazy, but she ignored him, picked up the house phone and complained about soiled bed linen. Ten minutes later two housekeeping staff arrived to rectify the problem.

"What's your name, do you speak English?" she asked the girl who appeared to be in charge, as they quickly removed the dirtied cover.

"I am Maria, and I am very sorry Senora; it is not my fault; I do not do this floor today."

"Don't worry about it Maria, it's not a problem. Do you like working here?"

"Please don't make me lose my job Senora, I need the money."

"You misunderstand me. I just wanted to know if you like it here."

"It the same as everywhere; hard work very little pay."

"How would you like it if I gave you ten thousand dollars to work somewhere else?"

"You want give me a new job?"

"No that's not right either. I want you to give me your master keycard. I was guessing they would let you go if you lost it."

"They not let me go; they just make me new one."

"So, if you were to give me your card and not tell anyone until tomorrow you could keep your job and the ten thousand dollars, is that right?"

"Ten thousand dollars for me to give you keycard, is that all you want?"

"Mostly, yes."

"What about Consuella?"

"Does she understand what we're saying?"

"No."

"Then, how about if I make it twelve thousand, and you decide how you divide it up?"

"I think it good deal."

"Okay then, let's do it.

Saffie went to her bag and took out two bundles of fifty-dollar bills and a bundle of twenties. Consuella's eyes opened as wide as saucers.

Maria handed her the keycard, but when she reached for the bundles of notes, Saffie snatched them away.

"One more thing, I need you to get me a kitchen staff overall, one that a room service maid would wear. Can you do that?" the maid nodded enthusiastically. "And we need to be clear, you mustn't mention this to anybody, either of you."

"We do not tell boss; she would make us give her money."

Saffie handed it over and the two girls left, grinning from ear to ear.

"There, that was easy wasn't it?" she said to Wolski.

"Expensive though."

"Patryk already paid. Let's just hope the same strategy works with the kitchen girl."

"What now?"

"Ideally we need to see if we can swap rooms with someone on the fifth floor."

"How are we going to do that?"

"I'm not sure yet. Let me ring Dexter."

Calling the young tech, she waited, hoping he'd pick up straightaway, she was disappointed when it went to voicemail.

"Dexter, I've got a quick job for you. If you have time, can you get back to me ASAP?" She ended the call.

"What now?" Wolski asked.

"Grab something to eat from the minibar or just wait I guess."

"I'll wait. I'm pre-diabetic and chocolate is definitely off the menu at the moment."

"You should spend more time in the gym. You could use ours, if you want."

"I'll think about it."

Maria returned with the overall just as her phone rang. She took it from her with a smile. "Dexter, thanks for getting back to me so quickly. … It's a small job, and I'm not sure it's inside your work boundaries or not. If it isn't something you'd want to do, just say. … I need someone to hack into the Baltimore Anchorage Hotel's system. I need to find a room on the fifth floor as close as possible to room 521, booked for one night only, and preferably with a single occupier, for tonight I mean."

"This is a new one for me. You'll need to give me half an hour or so. Do you also need to know who the reservation is for?"

"Yes please, and whether or not they've already checked in."

"No promises. I'll get back to you."

Ten minutes later her phone rang again, she put it on speaker. "Dexter, what have you got?"

"Room 522, reserved for James White. He hasn't checked in yet, but he's arriving at BWI on Southwest Flight 3193 from Houston, it landed about 5 minutes ago."

"That's fantastic Dexter, couldn't be more perfect."

"You're running up quite a bill now. Any chance of a down payment?"

"Of course, sorry. Email me your account details and the total so far. I'll pay over the top, that way you can hold some on account for next time."

"I won't argue with that. Do you want me to use the same reference number as before?"

"Perfect."

"I'm guessing you're going to try and do a room swap with the guy as he arrives," Wolski said.

"That's the plan. I was kinda hoping to persuade you to pose as hotel security or something and speak to him as he goes to his door."

"I won't know what he looks like. It'll look pretty suspicious if I just hang around the fifth floor waiting for someone to go to Room 522."

"I'll loiter around the check-in desk and see if I can pick him out for you. Then you can follow him up to the room."

They proceeded as planned, and in the end, didn't have long to wait. It was Wolski who spotted the first potential candidate. He nodded toward a lone traveler wheeling a small case across the concourse toward the check in desk.

Saffie wandered over to stand nearby, browsed tourist brochures, and listened whilst the man went through the ritual of identifying himself and offering his card.

"Thank you Senor Rodriguez, how was Denver?"

"Good thanks," he replied, taking the offered room cards in their little wallet.

"You're in Room 211 this time, I hope that's okay."

"Fine thank you."

Saffie shook her head to Wolski, who went back to pretending to read a newspaper.

It was only minutes before another single man arrived and began the same check-in routine.

"Have you stayed with us before, Mr. White?" she overheard the desk clerk ask.

"No, this is my first time in Baltimore."

"Business?"

"Family business."

"You're in Room 522, Mr. White."

Saffie nodded to Wolski who tagged on behind their mark as he made his way to the elevator. She took the same elevator car but stayed in it when the others got out. As the doors closed she heard Wolski say, "Mr. White, may I have a brief word?"

It took only moments for her to gather the cool box with her and Wolski's bags and walk back to the elevator lobby and wait until White emerged, still pulling his case.

She knocked on the door to 522. Wolski answered immediately.

"How did it go?"

"Simple, I offered him a thousand bucks. He couldn't take the deal fast enough."

She laughed. "Did you have to give him a story?"

"I told him I was a P.I. working on an attempted blackmail case. He wasn't interested, especially after I told him he could use what he wanted from the minibar, because it would be charged to us.

"We're all set then."

"One last thing. As I was letting myself in the room, Esteban arrived and let himself in across the hall. I don't know if he's seen a picture of us, or if he got a good enough look to recognize me. but we need to be aware that it's a possibility."

"Recognizing you would have one of two effects. They'd either call off the meeting or bring in some heavies to sort us out."

"We don't want this to end up in a shootout, because whatever way it ended, we'd be the losers," Wolski observed.

"I've no intention of taking a gun in there, but a taser. I'll definitely have one of those."

"I've brought one as well. I saw the one you've got and bought one the same."

"We need to keep a watch through the spyhole to see if anyone else goes inside."

"That's going to be fun," he ironically remarked.

"I'll take first shift if you can go get us something to eat."

"If one of us leaving the room coincides with him leaving his, the likelihood is we'd be figured out."

"Fair point. If you're hungry there's some energy bars in my bag, and I spotted one or two in the minibar."

After the first hour they gave up watching through the spyhole except when they heard someone in the hall, or they heard the elevator stop at their floor."

"How are you going to be sure of catching the kitchen girl on the way to the room?"

"I was planning on loitering near the service elevator."

"There isn't one, they just use the one nearest the window, it's the only one that goes to the basement," he told her.

"In that case, I'll need to loiter in the elevator lobby on the floor below."

"Safer to ride it up and down until she gets on, in my opinion."

"You're probably right."

Chapter Twenty
Monday 7:45pm - Hotel, Baltimore, Maryland

"I guess I'd better make a move. Are you ready to go?" she asked.

"I'm ready when you are. As soon as you've taken over from the kitchen girl, call my phone and put yours on mute so I can hear what's happening."

"Okay, got it."

She let herself out of the room dressed in the kitchen overall that Maria had provided, hurried to the elevator lobby, and pressed the call button. Fortunately, the first to arrive, on a downward journey, was the one she planned on riding until the room service girl got on board, but just as the doors opened, the one next door stopped there as well on its upward trip.

She was certain that she hadn't been seen, but when the elevator discharged its passengers she spotted Lipov with someone who could only have been his minder. The doors had barely closed, before she was calling Wolski.

"Lipov is here, and he's got a bodyguard. About forty years old, five ten, 220 pounds, shaven head."

"Okay, are you going ahead?"

"Yes."

"Just leave the line open now."

"Okay."

Saffie rode the elevator for more than half an hour, getting strange looks from people who saw her in the same place more than once. Then a girl with a trolley got on at basement level.

Putting a foot against the door to prevent it from closing, Saffie asked, "Is that for Room 521?"

"Yes, who are you?"

"Never mind that for a minute. Would you like to earn a lot of money right now?"

"What do you mean?"

"I mean, if you let me take the trolley up in your place, I'll give you ten thousand dollars, then you can finish your shift or go home, whatever you want, and say no more about it."

"Is this illegal?"

"What, me paying you to do some of your work? No, I shouldn't think so. But nobody's going to get hurt, and you'll be a lot richer, so I don't see why it should be a problem."

"How much?"

"Ten thousand dollars."

"Okay, but I want the money now."

"Sensible girl." She pulled the bundles of notes from the pocket of the overall and handed them over. "No mention of this to anybody, okay?"

"Okay," the girl said, snatching the money away before Saffie could change her mind. She stepped out of the elevator, leaving Saffie alone.

As she pressed the button for the fifth floor, Saffie's heart was already thumping. Then when a man wearing a jacket with the hotel logo got in at the first floor and looked her up and down she began to worry that it was all about to go wrong.

"You're new aren't you?"

"Yes, sir, first day."

"Name?"

"Cissy, sir."

"Is that for Mr. Alvarez in 521?"

"That's right."

"Don't hang about then, he's a regular guest."

"No, sir."

The man got out at the second floor, and it didn't stop again until it got to the fifth.

Wheeling the cart along the hall, there was no sign of anything untoward, so she knocked, and called, "Room service."

Instead of the door to Room 521 opening, the door to 523 opened and the minder said with a Russian accent, "I need check that."

She stood back and watched as the oaf lifted the cloth that covered the food. He was presumably looking for weapons searched the trolley. Then grinning he said, "Now I search you."

He mauled her about then pressed his hand into her crotch, "You have weapon hidden in here?"

"Fuck off, you piece of shit."

He laughed, knocked on the door to 521 and said, "It okay boss."

The door opened and the thug turned back toward his room."

There followed a rapid sequence of events. First the door closed behind her, and at the same time in the hall, Wolski pressed his taser to the neck of the bodyguard who collapsed before being dragged into his own room, where he was immobilized and gagged with duct tape but, as Saffie pushed the cart further into the room, Esteban jumped out of the bathroom and grabbed her around the neck. Lipov stepped in front of her, aiming a vicious punch at her lower stomach and was thwarted only Saffie's quick twisting movement to plunge the needle of the hypodermic syringe in her left hand into Esteban's thigh. The blow merely glanced off her hip and Esteban released her, staggering away.

Saffie lifted the taser in her right hand and caught Lipov on the upper arm before he'd recovered from his mistimed punch. The overweight Russian cried out and fell to the floor. She stood over them holding her hip, while she waited for Wolski to finish disposing of the other Russian thug.

The door opened. "Are you okay?" Wolski asked.

"I guess, nothing permanent anyway. Help me get these assholes on the beds then you can fetch the rest of our stuff from across the hall."

It took the best part of half an hour to get each of the men on a bed, stripped to his underwear, and restrained. Then she drugged Lipov with Pentapropathal as she had Esteban. It was another fifteen minutes before Esteban was awake enough to respond to questions.

"Good evening, Pedro. How are you feeling?" The man groaned. "It is Pedro isn't it, or would you prefer Juan. I heard that you sometimes like to be called Juan."

"Juan, my name is Juan," he sleepily replied.

"Juan it is then. My name is Cecily, we haven't met before but I'm really glad we've got this chance to get to know each other. I've been hearing so much about you lately. For instance, I heard that you wanted to kill my friend, Patryk Wilkanowicz, and I didn't understand why."

"Enemy, old enemy."

"I didn't know that. Where from?"

"Bogotá."

"Yes of course, I'd forgotten he was in South America. It's a long time to wait to take your revenge though."

"Zykov wanted Wilkanowicz bastard to say who is *Ripple* before I kill him."

"Remind me again who Zykov is."

"FSB agent on Capitol Hill."

"Of course, I'd forgotten about him. What's his other name? Can you remember?"

"Woman Senator, Shelley somebody."

"Don't you know any more about her?"

"Sits on committee."

"Which one?"

"I can't remember."

"Did you find out who *Ripple* is?"

"No, *Handlebar* killed Polish bastard before we found out."

"I heard that you're an agent for the FSB, is that right?"

"I do work for them, but only as sideline."

"Do you have a code name?"

"They call me *Black Wattle*."

"Who do you send it to, the information that *Ripple* has gathered I mean?"

"My contact in Moscow, called *Harbinger*."

"If you work for the FSB, why do you use such poor support, like Lipov's bikers?"

"Zykov won't authorize use of FSB assets, because I'm not Russian."

"Was it Zykov that ordered the actions that started all this?"

"No, me, I was getting suspicious about *Ripple*. He was my project, and I didn't want to be discovered."

"Thank you so much, Juan. You've been very helpful so far, so I'm going to let you have a nice rest in a minute, but first I want you to tell me how you know about *Ripple*?"

"Zykov found out from *Missionary*."

"Who is *Missionary*?"

"Only Zykov knows. He's in the CIA."

"Okay then Juan, you can rest for a while now," she told him, and put earplugs in his ears.

Grinning at Wolski she stepped over to the other bed and removed the earplugs from Lipov's ears and the tape from his mouth. "So sorry to keep you waiting Sergei. Is it okay if I just call you Serge?"

"Okay," he lethargically agreed.

"My name's Cecily."

He shook his head. "Saffron Price."

"Okay then Serge, if it helps you to think that. Tell me how you know Chester Boggs."

"Zykov thinks his father is *Ripple*."

"Why does she think that?"

"DNA test."

"How did they do that?"

"*Missionary* found sample of *Ripple's* DNA in CIA files."

"How does that connect to Chester Boggs?"

"Because Boggs also sent sample to genetic history site."

"And the site found a match did they?"

"Father was somebody at the State Department."

"How come they still don't know who *Ripple* is?"

"Because the man who's DNA they found is halfwit, not clever enough to be double agent."

"There must be a mistake in the CIA database."

"That what I say, but *Missionary* say no, history site make mistake."

"Why did you kill Felix Carter?"

"Alvarez say he had to die so *Missionary* wouldn't be uncovered."

"One thing I don't understand though, Serge. How did you get involved in all this spy stuff?"

"I handle all Russian trafficking through Alvarez, and he needed muscle to handle everything with this Wilkanowicz business."

"What sort of trafficking?"

"Cocaine, cannabis, heroin, women." He yawned.

"Yes this must be tiring, Serge. Never mind; we're nearly finished now. If you could just tell me the names of your senior drug and people traffickers and the addresses of your distribution warehouses, then we can call it a day."

It took twenty minutes and quite a number of prompts for him to dictate the details she'd asked for. Then, after asking him to tell her his passwords and passkeys to his laptop and phone, she used his fingerprint to authorize adding her own to his phone. She repeated the exercise with Esteban.

Finally, she asked Esteban, "Tell me everything you know about *Missionary* and Zykov.

In the event, Esteban was able to tell them very little more than Lipov about either of the two new characters, except that Zykov was considered the head of the network.

Saffie turned to Wolski, "Our last job is to arrange a little photo shoot for two aspiring porno stars, but before we get to that, I need to take the cool box down to the ice maker and fill up every available space to keep things cool. It looks as though we might need those spare doses."

"I'll do that. You're limping."

"Thanks, that asshole Lipov caught me with a punch on my hip."

After stripping both hostages naked, they shifted the barely conscious Esteban onto the same bed as Lipov and spent the next hour posing the two of them in explicit positions and photographing them.

"What are we going to do with the guy next door?" he asked.

"I've been thinking about that. Do you think we could quickly drag him in here to join these two, without being seen?"

"It's past one o'clock in the morning. We should be okay if we're quick and didn't make too much noise, but he won't come quietly."

"I've been thinking about that too. Grab me a few of those bottles of vodka from the minibar will you.

When they went next door, the man had given up his struggle to escape the very effective duct tape bonds that Wolski had created, but when he saw them he became reanimated.

"Hush, hush, Ivan, or whatever your name is. You've had a very uncomfortable evening I know. To compensate you for that I'm going to give you a few tots of your favorite tipple. If you'll just hold still, it won't take long."

She turned to Wolski. "Ivan here is quite a big lad, and no doubt an accomplished drinker. How many shots do you think it will take to mellow him down a bit. Six enough do you think?"

"I'd go for eight, seeing as we're in such a generous mood."

One by one between them they filled and refilled the two used syringes with vodka and injected the contents into his arms until they could see that the guy's eyes were swimming. Then they quickly dragged him into Room 521, succeeding only moments before the doors to the elevator lobby opened. They stripped him as naked as his pals and left him semi-conscious on the floor.

"Are we done now?" Wolski asked.

"Not yet. Have you got another pair of nitrile gloves?"

"Sure," he went to his bag and handed them to her. He'd been wearing his own throughout.

If you could help me wipe prints from everything I could conceivably have touched, that would help. I didn't go into the bathroom so you can leave that out."

After cleaning the prints, they moved their things across the hall to room 522, where Saffie asked Wolski to call the desk and complain about loud noises coming from Room 521. While he was doing that she went back to Ivan, stood between his legs and kicked him in the balls as hard as she could. In spite of his highly intoxicated condition, he screamed and writhed in pain, but she wasn't finished. Taking Lipov's gun from the jacket hanging on a chair, she removed all except three bullets, put it in Ivan's hand and ran from the room. He'd haphazardly fired all three shots in her direction and collapsed on the floor, before she was out of his sight and safely in the room with Wolski.

"Ring the desk and report the shooting, if you can get through."

Once he'd done that, they waited until the first cops arrived, before making their escape. The hotel was crawling with police by the time they drove out of the car park, and it was four o'clock by the time they drove through the gates at Dunn Loring.

Chapter Twenty-One
Tuesday 8:45am - Dunn Loring

Wolski was at the breakfast table with Cindy when Saffie joined them, still rubbing her neck with a towel. "Have you been in the gym?" he asked.

"Couldn't sleep. Too much going on in my mind."

"That was some bat-shit crazy stuff you played last night."

"What do you mean?"

"With the gun. What the Hell did you put it in his hand for?"

"Because I needed the three of them to be treated like perps not victims. I needed the gun to be run through ballistics to check if it had any outstanding crimes against it and hopefully incriminate them further. They all need to be out of the way now that asshole Lipov recognized me even under the influence of the drug."

"He'll get bail and still come after you."

"Not if he's got his gang after him as well."

"What do you mean?"

"Biker gangs aren't normally the most LGBT friendly people, so when they see those photos, he'll be persona non grata."

"How will they see the photos?"

"Because I posted a few select examples on their website last night and sent them to all the local papers."

"They'll know they were set up."

"Will they? Some might believe that, but there will be enough with doubt in their minds.

"The papers won't be able to print anything that graphic."

"With the judicious use of pixels, they'll be able to show enough to convince most people."

"It's already on the web pages of most of the Baltimore papers," Cindy remarked. "The Maryland Banner's headline is, *Baltimore Nightclub Owner Arrested After Hotel Gay Orgy Ends in Shooting*, and they're all saying much the same thing."

"Is it always going to be like this, working with you?"

"Don't you like it? I'm not twisting your arm."

"It beats sitting around filling in forms all day."

"That's good, because I think we make a good team."

"Seeing as you don't want to rest after being up all night like normal people, what's on the program for today, Boss?"

"At some point today, I think we can expect a visit from Ramirez and Daniels, but I also want to get Dexter involved with trawling those laptops and phones for useful info, if he's free."

Wolski nodded. "What do you know about this senator, Shelley?"

"Nothing at the moment. I took a brief look at the list of Senators and there are three called Shelley. First up is a Shelley Scott-Collins, a Virginian Democrat, first time senator at the last election, surprise appointment to the Armed Services Committee. A real firebrand when she talks."

"I like her," Cindy said. "She's really hot on women's issues."

"There are two others. Shelley Smith, Republican for Nebraska, three-time re-elected, sits on the Budget Committee, and Shelley Blackburn, Republican for Oregon, two-time re-elected, sits on the Intelligence Committee."

"How are we going to narrow that down?"

"I don't know yet," she replied. "Some sort of sting I guess."

"How are we going to get up close and personal with them? And what about Willard Perry."

"I'm less concerned about Perry now, because it looks pretty certain that he's *Ripple*. If that's the case, if we're not careful we could risk exposing him."

"He must have sent his DNA off to try to find out about his heritage. Given his circumstances that was pretty stupid."

"From the file, I think we can be clear that he's not the sharpest knife in the block."

Wolski changed the subject. "Why does Boggs think Patryk betrayed him and his father?"

"I haven't figured that out yet. We need to speak to both Perrys to be sure. When I went to Wilson Perry's home, there was an unopened letter from Heritage4U. it was addressed to *Wilson Perry at the State Department*."

Wolski thought about what she'd said. "So, we're saying the Russians have been given *Ripple's* DNA profile and have been using it to keep watch for a familial match. When Chester Boggs sent in his DNA they would have dismissed him by virtue of age. But they would have known that if a paternal match came up they'd be on the home straight, so why wouldn't they have picked up Willard?"

"We don't know when Willard sent in his sample, do we?"

"How are we going to ID *Missionary*?"

"I think the only chance will be by going back into Patryk's archive."

"Surely if Patryk had known who he was, he'd have raised the alarm before now."

"If he'd been looking maybe, but perhaps there's a clue in the archive that wasn't obvious at the time."

She called Dexter McDowell. "Dexter, hi. Are you busy?"

"Nothing pressing. What can I do for you?"

"I was hoping to spend some of that advance I sent you."

"Sure. What do you need?"

"Something different this time."

"Everything you give me is different. Give me a clue."

"I've a couple of phones and a couple of laptops that I've confiscated, and I need to trawl through them for useful information. It might be better if you can work here with Wolski; he'll be better qualified to recognize something relevant. Also it would mean that I would be on hand for a second opinion."

"When do you want to do this?"

"As soon as possible."

"If I come now, would that be too soon? Only I've got a big job coming up on Thursday and I need to clear the decks."

"That would be perfect."

Her call to Mary and the boys revealed that they had been Facetiming the two girls a lot, and Josh's drawing of Katy was causing quite a stir, but generally they seemed quite content to stay for another few days.

Dexter arrived with a laptop bag and a case full of gadgetry. In anticipation of Ramirez and Daniels' arrival, she had them set up shop in the dining room but just as she was about to try getting back into Patryk's Archive the gate bell rang and Cindy announced the arrival of the two federal agents. After greeting them at the door, she showed them through to the study.

"A lot of cars here this morning, Ms. Price. You must be busy," Daniels remarked.

"Just a couple of associates doing some work for me."

"I recognize Mr. Wolski's car, but the other one is new."

"If you're that interested to know who I work with, I'm sure when you check his license plate, you'll find out soon enough, but as it's none of your business I don't feel obliged to tell you. Is there something I can help you with, or is this just a social call?"

"I don't understand your hostility, Ms. Price."

"And right back at you, Agent Daniels."

"I'm not hostile. I just like to maintain professional boundaries."

Ramirez stepped in, "Can we just get on with why we came?"

"I wait breath abated, Agent Ramirez."

"Where were you yesterday, Ms. Price," Daniels asked.

"Why do you want to know?"

"Are you refusing to say?"

"Am I suspected of a crime?"

"Not at the moment."

"Then I'm not obliged to tell you."

"Can we just stop this charade you two?" Ramirez said. "Angela, can you reel your neck in and let's just try to work with Ms. Price and not against her. Saffie, you were filmed at the Anchorage Hotel yesterday, so we know you were there, and we know you checked in under a false name. I'm quite certain that you'll be aware that there was a shooting incident overnight. We want to be sure that you weren't involved in that."

"Have you recovered the weapon?"

"Yes."

"Do you have a suspect in custody?"

"Yes."

"Is ballistic and forensic evidence consistent with the suspect firing the weapon?"

"Yes."

"Is there any evidence that I was in any way involved in the incident?"

"No."

"Then I don't understand."

"You haven't answered my question."

"You haven't asked one. You just said you wanted to be sure I wasn't involved. There must have been several hundred other people in that hotel. Are you going to be visiting all of them."

"For fucks sake, Ms. Price, stop skating around this. There were two prime persons of interest in the Wilkanowicz affair involved in that incident last night, both of whom appear to have been drugged. Were you, or were you not involved with that."

"There's no need to lose your temper, Agent Daniels. If it helps you to understand my presence there, I can tell you that I had received information that Juan Esteban and Sergei Lipov would be present at the hotel. I booked a room in the hope that they would agree to answer a few questions."

"And did they?"

"They were reluctant at first, even a little hostile, but after a little persuasion from me they agreed to be helpful, and both provided me with some useful tips that will help guide my future investigations."

"Did you use drugs?"

"I'm a private investigator not a drug dealer."

"Not that sort of drug, a truth serum."

"I would have done, Agent Daniels, but Walgreens was all out of truth serum last time I asked."

"You could have used Retinol or Fentanyl."

"Really? You seem to know a lot about this sort of thing. Is that what they do in the agency these days? My, how things have moved on."

Ramirez interrupted again, "Did you learn anything to move your investigation forward?"

"Yes, but nothing I'm prepared to reveal yet. The most important thing I learned was that the Russians have at least two highly placed assets. One in the CIA and another in the senate."

"Do you know who they are?"

"One of them yes."

"Why won't you tell us?" Daniels asked.

"For all I know you could be the one in the agency."

"Don't be ridiculous. What if something happens to you?"

"If subpoenaed by a court, my lawyer will grant access to my journals, after my death."

"How do we know we can trust you?"

"If you didn't trust me to some extent then I'd already be under arrest. But if you're finished wasting my time, I've a lot of work to do. Before you go though you can help me with a couple of things."

"What are they?"

"There are two people I need discreet access to, but as things stand it isn't possible. They aren't suspects, just people who probably hold information that may help me join a few dots."

"Who are they?

"The first is Chester Boggs, who I believe is still in hospital."

"He is, and he's refusing to speak to anyone."

"Has he asked for a lawyer?

"Not yet."

"He may speak to me. I saved his life."

"Okay we'll see what we can do. Who's the other one?"

"Assistant Secretary of State for International Narcotics and Law Enforcement Affairs, Willard Perry-Greene."

Daniels looked apoplectic. "What!"

"Are you suggesting that Perry-Greene is a Russian asset?" Ramirez asked.

"No, I don't believe he is, but like I say, he's in a position to provide information to help further my enquiries."

"I doubt he'll agree."

"Just tell him that I don't want to make life any more difficult for him than it already is by making too many wavelets. It might change his mind. But, and I can't stress this enough, nobody, nobody at all must know about the meeting before or after it has taken place."

"Wavelets? What's that supposed to mean?"

"To you, nothing, but to him, quite a lot."

"I'll see what I can do."

"I'm happy to comply with any conditions he wants to set."

"Is that all you're prepared to tell us?"

"Agent Daniels, I could have walked away from this two weeks ago. If I had, by now you'd have learned the precise sum of fuck all. And if I had told you all I've learnt so far, the chances are that you'd have effectively silenced the key witnesses by arresting them. That being the case, you'd know nothing at all about the existence of two highly-placed Russian assets or possibly alarmed them enough to send them running. Not only that, but you could very well have exposed a vital existing asset of our own."

"That's very patronizing."

"Maybe so, but I'm so deep into this, if I stepped back now, me and my family would continue to be at risk, so if you're unhappy with the situation, tough. Don't let the door hit you in the ass on your way out."

"Can we take it from what you've said that you're making progress?" Ramirez asked.

"Yes, and if you can get me together with those two people, there's a good chance I can wrap it up in a few days. But after that, all I'll be able to do is, tell you the story. It will be up to you to put these people behind bars."

The two agents left not much wiser than when they arrived, and she joined the other two in the dining room. "Anything of note yet?"

Wolski looked up, "So far we've only looked at the phones, but we've got a whole lot of interesting numbers and text messages. We're just about to look at the first laptop. Lipov's."

"That's great I'm going to take another look at Patryk's archive. Let me know if something striking turns up."

It took five attempts to open the portal this time, and with no idea where else to begin, she arranged the files in *date created* order and started with the earliest. It was time consuming and tedious work, made worse because she had no idea what she was looking for.

In the early files it was revealed that Patryk was using the cover name Alfredo Garcia, and he'd made numerous mentions of Esteban, first as an ambitious but low-level falcon – a street spy - and occasional mule. Then, as time wore on he was given more and more responsibility, eventually achieving promotion to lieutenant, a *teniente*.

Patryk had spent a lot of time learning about Esteban, insisting that he was a rising star, and could one day become important. For over a year he'd been trying to identify a Tomas Xandru, somebody who Esteban had mentioned several times in his communications. Eventually Patryk was asked to drop it because there were other things that demanded his attention. Not long after that, Patryk's cover was blown, and he was transferred to Langley. After that there were no mentions of Esteban until Moscow 1991, when Patryk had spotted his meeting with Wilson

Perry, a low-level State Department employee. The successful operation that followed, resulted in developing Perry as a double agent operating under an unnamed codename. That was where the file ended.

Saffie read on. The next file covered Patryk's appointment as head of the Russian section at Langley. One of his roles was to oversee the handling of a double agent codenamed *Ripple*. The controller was an agent named Alfredo Gonzalez who Saffie now assumed to be Patryk himself. Nonetheless the entries were always made in the third person. The files formed a detailed journal of Patryk's activities throughout his career, and, in this respect, were very similar to how her own had been when she was an agent, and still were.

She didn't stop for lunch, because she didn't want to lose the thread, and it wasn't until halfway through the afternoon when she sat back sipping the latest in the long succession of coffees that Cindy had been providing when she realized that something was missing. Why had nobody followed up on why Esteban had been in Moscow? Or perhaps somebody had, but if so, who was it, and why wasn't it Patryk? Maybe that task had been given to Felix Carter.

She picked up her phone. "Agent Daniels, I need help."

"If I can, I'll see what I can do."

"Juan Esteban had been a person of interest on the agency's radar for years. I need to know who's running his file."

"You're not cleared for that level of information, and probably wouldn't have been even if you were still an agent."

"Then you need to get me that clearance and quickly. Because it may be the difference between the success of this operation, and catastrophic failure."

"I can't risk passing on that sort of information, Ms. Price."

"Fine," she said, ended the call, and immediately called Ramirez.

"Saffie. What's happening?"

"I'm onto something and I think it's huge, I need information. but I'm being stonewalled by Daniels."

"What is it you need?"

Without giving a detailed reason of why she needed to know, she explained what she wanted.

"Are you saying you've identified the agency mole?"

"At this stage, all I'm saying is that I've identified someone who's a key part of the investigation, a major person of interest, and at this stage all I need is an ID. I've no need to confront them."

"I'll need to take this right to the top, so don't expect an answer straight away. But while we're on this call, Chester Boggs has agreed to see you, but you'll need to get your skates on because he's likely to be discharged from hospital tomorrow or the day after. If he's arraigned he'll get bail, and if I'm any judge, the chances are he'll skip and disappear."

"Which hospital?"

"Warren Memorial in Front Royal. I've arranged clearance for you."

"Front Royal is a long way from Wildcat?"

"He was originally taken to Davis Medical Center in Elkins, but his insurance had him moved."

"Suits me, it's one Hell of a lot closer. I'm leaving now."

With almost no sleep for thirty-six hours, she knew that she shouldn't be driving but she was high on caffeine and adrenalin. She didn't want to miss the opportunity of speaking to Boggs while he was still willing to help.

At gone five o'clock she pulled into the hospital car park, and hurried to reception who directed her to Room 235 on the second floor. There were two Front Row PD patrol officers stationed outside the door, neither looked pleased to be there, nor to see her when she explained why she was there.

"Mr. Boggs is currently under arrest, and isn't allowed visitors at present ma'am," PO 1 told her.

"Officer, I don't want to make your life difficult, but if you care to check up the line, I think you'll find that I've been given clearance."

"You're just a P.I. Why would you get special treatment?"

"It doesn't matter to you why, only that I have. But if it helps to move this thing along, let me explain. Boggs is a police officer just like you. One of the charges against him is conducting illegal surveillance of me. Also, I'm a witness in the other charges against him. I've withdrawn my statement on condition that I get to have this conversation with him. People way up the chain from you, are happy with that, as I'm sure Mr. Boggs will be. I'm sure you'd want to help out a fellow officer if you could, wouldn't you?"

PO1 turned to PO2. "Check this out will you, Stanford?"

Saffie waited while Stanford moved away to speak into his radio seeking clearance from his sergeant to admit her. She hadn't withdrawn her statement, but if the interview went the way she hoped, she fully intended to. Finally, Stanford nodded, and she was allowed inside.

She found Boggs sitting up in bed, and it was clear that his injuries must have been far more severe than she'd been able to see by torchlight that night in the forest.

"Good afternoon, Mr. Boggs. How are you feeling now?"

"You that Price bitch?" he said, his speech severely slurred by his facial injuries.

"If you can't talk to me with respect then any chance you ever had of getting the charges against you dropped will evaporate. Are we clear?"

"You can do that?"

"If I've a mind, and if you can give me some truthful answers to my questions."

"Why did you save me, after what Blink and Seymour tried to do with your kid?"

251

"Two reasons. First, if it had been you who'd tried to do it to my child, I'd have gladly sat and watched you bleed to death. But it wasn't and I'm not a psychopath. Second, I needed to know what the fuck your problem was."

"I didn't want to get involved in any of that shit, but Blink said he weren't gonna lose his job cos some private eye bitch didn't know her place. I overheard him threaten to kill your boy and I knew what a crazy sum bitch he was. I didn't want anything to do with it and stayed out of the way."

"But you didn't do anything to stop him."

"I was going to, but I saw you going in there, and then it was all over before I knew what was happening."

"Was that the only reason you were at the farm that day; because of your suspension?"

"Crazy now I think about it."

"How did you get involved in the first place?"

"This guy came to see me about my search for my father."

"Who was he?"

"A beaner; called himself Pedro Alvarez; said he was a lawyer. Told me that he knew that I'd sent my DNA sample into Heritage4U, and they thought that it was possible I was related to his client, a rich guy from Tennessee. Not my father but a second or third cousin and he wanted to get in touch with whoever I found. He told me that if I got an answer from them, they'd pay me a thousand bucks to tell them about anybody they identified."

"And did you get an answer?"

"Yeah, but it was a fraud. They gave me an email address to contact a guy they said was my father. His name was Wilson Perry. When I contacted him he was real shocked to hear from me because he said he'd never sent any DNA to a genetic history company. We agreed to meet up anyway and he told me that he wasn't the real Wilson Perry. He was just using his name because the real one was hiding from an international hitman."

"That doesn't make sense."

"I know, but the guy was an airhead, the real guy could have told him anything and he would have believed him. Thank fuck I'm not related to him; he was dumb as shit."

"So, who was the real Wilson Perry; the one who was really your father?"

"He told me it was a guy called Alfredo Gonzalez, but he didn't know how to contact him."

"Did you ever tell the lawyer that?"

"Yeah he told me that that wasn't his real name. He was really called Patryk Wilkanowicz."

"So, you think that Patryk Wilkanowicz was your father?"

"Yeah, piece of shit. Betrayed my mom, betrayed me."

"What were your plans for him once you'd found out?"

"I was just going to knock him about a bit, but Alvarez said if I helped him, we could really fuck with his head."

"And he got you to have my car tracked?"

"I didn't know whose car it was. It was supposed to be any car that he told me to track. He had someone watching across the street. I didn't want to be filmed putting a tracker on a car, so I paid Clay Scott to do it."

"Who killed Clay Scott and his son?"

"I guess it must have been Alvarez."

"I suppose by this time you must have worked out that he wasn't a lawyer."

"Yeah, I didn't want any more to do with him. But he never contacted me again anyway."

"Okay then, Chester. You've been real helpful so here's how it goes from here on. I'm going to do what I can to get the charges against you dropped. It's not entirely within my gift, but I think I can persuade the right people. In return, I want you never to speak about my involvement in this to anybody, ever again."

"Thanks. Sorry about the bitch thing."

"Forget it. You need to know that Patryk Wilkanowicz was not your father. I know who your birth father was, and I can assure you that you wouldn't be any more impressed with him than you were with Wilson Perry. As for your dad betraying your mom, it was her who walked out on him, not the other way around. If you'll take my advice, your best bet now is to forget about genealogy and get on with your life."

"How do you know about my dad?"

"I know a lot more than that, and a lot of it I'm sure you'd prefer not to know."

Returning to her car she sat in the driving seat and thought about all she'd learned that day. The next thing she knew was the sound of someone knocking on the driver's window. She woke with a start, to find a security guy standing by the car.

"Are you okay ma'am?"

"Sure, I was just really tired and dropped off for a while."

"You've been there for more than three hours, so it was more than a while. You can't stay here all night; you need to go home and get some sleep."

"You're right, I'm sorry."

Her head was muzzy from the lack of sleep and the sudden wakening. How she managed to drive home without an accident, she wasn't sure. She operated the gates and drove through, foregoing the discipline of garaging the car. Wolski's car was still there but Dexter had left.

The light was still on in the kitchen, and her associate was nursing a cup of coffee.

"You give up answering your phone, did you?"

She lifted it and realized that she'd left it on silent since arriving at the hospital and it was now past midnight.

"Oh God, I'm sorry."

"Your kids were tearing their hair out, so I sent out a search party and was able to reassure them."

"Search party?"

"I tracked your phone, saw where you were, and called the security guys at the hospital. He called me back an hour ago."

"Tracked my phone, I've got my location turned off, how did you do that?"

"I'm a detective, I'll tell you in the morning. Go and get some sleep.

Chapter Twenty-Two
Wednesday 8:15am - Dunn Loring

"Listen to me young lady," Cindy admonished, as she stepped into the kitchen, "You've got too many people relying on you these days for you to go killing yourself."

"I'm sorry, but everything is happening at the same time and it's difficult to keep up."

"I appreciate that, but a brief text or a phone call can save an awful lot of unnecessary worry. Do you want me to cook you a breakfast?"

"More than anything in the world right now. I haven't eaten since this time yesterday."

"How did you get on with Boggs?" Wolski asked.

"Better than I could have imagined. He managed to answer so many outstanding questions. What about you and Dexter?"

"We, or rather Dexter, uncovered mountains of information. How much will be any use to us is another question. If the DEA or ATF knew you had those laptops, they'd tear your doors off their hinges to get at them. Dexter's left them so that we can easily get back in if we need to."

When they got together in the study, she explained everything that she'd learnt from the files the day before, and what Boggs had explained.

"So, you're planning on letting that asshole off the hook?"

"He didn't have to tell me anything last night, but I think that the fact that he did, demonstrates a little remorse. I don't believe that he instigated what went on at the farm; he was being exploited by people with real malign intent right from the start."

"If you say so."

"If you'd seen the state he was in, you might be more sympathetic. Show me what you found."

They started with Lipov's computer, and Wolski was right about the mountain of information, and worse still, there was no order to it. Neither of the laptops' owners had any idea about discipline in PC management.

"Where the fuck do we start with this?"

"Dexter installed a little utility on them that might help if we know what we're looking for. We can do global searches for any documents, files or emails containing more than one phrase without specifying file type throughout the computer. For example, if we were to search for Patryk Wilkanowicz and Saffron Price it would only return items that included both of those things. Not just documents, but emails, images, Internet searches, anything including deleted items. You can also get it to exclude files containing words or phrases."

Saffie tried it using the search criteria he'd suggested. It returned three items, an email from Alvarez to Lipov telling him to ensure that Patryk was isolated, and everyone should be discouraged from helping him out, particularly her. A lot of her personal information was included; address, date of birth, car license plate, known telephone numbers, names of her children and their phone numbers. As well as similar information about Cindy and Wolski."

"Shit!" he said, "that's scary."

That was exactly how Saffie felt. "He's got help. One of those numbers is only supposed to be known by Langley."

The second and third items were from his Internet search history where he'd recovered news items relating to the Bannerman affair. When they removed Patryk from the enquiry two more items appeared, one a newspaper article which included a poor photo, the second a Wikipedia page dedicated to her that she hadn't even known existed.

"How about we work side by side, and we run the same searches on both computers at the same time? That way we can be sure we don't miss anything out."

"Great idea. Where did the power cords come from?"

"Dexter brought a selection with him. He said he'd bill you."

Working together and using the notes that she'd made whilst trawling through the files they came up with a few things that required a second look but nothing that rang alarm bells, except the name Tom Alexander appeared on both computers while looking at other things.

The last name on her list was Tomas Xandru. They both ran it with zero returns. "That was a disappointing result from two hours work," she remarked.

They were silent for a minute or two, wondering what to do next.

"Isn't T.O.M.A.S. the Spanish way to spell Thomas?" Wolski said.

"I guess. But how does that help?"

"What about Xandru? That's a new one on me. Where does it come from?"

After a quick Google search, they got their answer. "Xandru is another Spanish name for Alexander. Tomas Xandru was the name of a person with connections to Esteban that Patryk had been trying to pin down in Columbia, thirty years ago. It's too big a coincidence for my taste."

"What do we do with the information?"

"Let's wait and see if Ramirez or Daniels get back to me with what I asked them for. Until then, I think we earned a break."

Saffie used the next hours tying up the loose ends in her journal then called the farm to apologize for missing them the day before.

Wolski went home for a change of clothes.

Toward the end of the afternoon her phone rang. It was Ramirez.

"Why did you ask for the name of *Ripple's* current controller?"

"Because it's vital to putting the final few pieces of the puzzle together. Is there a problem, other than the usual ones, I mean?"

"Yes, he's gone missing."

"How long?"

"About three weeks."

"About?"

"He's undercover, and not answering calls."

"Is there now any reason I can't know his name? If he's been missing three weeks it's a top-level agent lost emergency. Which country?"

"Belarus."

"What! He's handling a home-based asset from Belarus while there's a war going on! This stinks. What's the DDO have to say about this?"

"They're not saying."

"You need to get me the information I need, and quickly. Either this guy has gone rogue, or he's been silenced, and what's worse it looks as though our asset is exposed."

"How bad could this be?"

"If our asset is turned again, and he's as highly positioned as I believe he might be, it could hardly be any worse."

"I'll do what I can."

Over an hour went by before Daniels called.

"I've been ordered to give you our Belarus agent's name. It's Cameron Archer and his codename is Tenor. But I'll tell you this now, Price, if he gets hurt as a result of your maverick behavior, I won't rest until I see you sentenced for crimes under the Espionage Act."

"Agent Daniels, there are three likely scenarios as to why Tenor is not responding to calls, and they are that he's already dead, he's gone on the run to avoid arrest, or he's gone into hiding because he believes he's about to be exposed. If you can think of a way I can possibly make this situation worse by exposing high-level Russian assets operating in your organization and the government please tell me."

"If you have evidence of any of that you have to tell me, and I mean now."

"Unless you already know about the people I suspect, then you could end up bringing about the one thing you say you're trying to avoid.

"What are you going to do now?"

"I'm going back to my evidence source to try and find what links Cameron Archer to the other names that figure high on my suspect list. But you can help by giving me the name of the current head of the Russian section."

"I'm surprised you don't know already; you seem to know everything else."

"Just tell me and stop fucking around."

"It's Thomas Alexander."

'Bingo!' she thought. "Thank you."

"Does it help for you to know that?"

"It might. You need to put a discreet watch on him right away."

"Are you saying that Alexander is a Russian asset?"

"Let's just say that I wouldn't rule it out. I still need to get face to face with Willard Perry-Greene."-

"Do you suspect him as well?"

"Not so much, but I believe he knowingly or unknowingly has information that can help tie this up. You need to make it clear to him that he will not be putting himself at risk by speaking to me."

"But Perry isn't the Russian agent in government?"

"I don't believe so."

"Does that mean you've identified who is."

"I have a strong lead but proving it might be another matter."

"I'll do what I can."

Saffie decided to go back to Esteban's phone and computer and see what she could learn from something other than running simple word searches. She began by looking at his phone histories, Dexter had printed them out, making them much easier to follow. There had been a lot of texts and call traffic between Esteban and a character called Kovzky. The texts were in Russian but thankfully not in Cyrillic Script. Saffie could read the Slavic alphabet, but it took her much longer. There was no indication whether Kovzky was male or female, but it was clear they were disguising the true meaning of their words by the phraseology they employed. It would have been almost impossible to determine the subject of the exchanges without knowledge beforehand. Then, near the end of Esteban's text history, he'd received a message from Kovzky. *My influential friends are saying that it would be a shame if the Polish wolf were to be extinct before we learned the cause of the wavelets.*

It didn't take a codebreaker from Bletchley to know that that translated to, *Don't kill Wilkanowicz without learning the identity of Ripple.* Neither was it a giant leap from there to assume the Kovzky was Zykov. If she was right, and she could identify Zykov, she would have answered most of her outstanding questions.

Dexter was going to be busy, so Saffie called his sister.

"Patsy, are you busy?"

"I'm at work, but the shop is quiet at the moment."

"I've got another commission for you. I've sent you the numbers of two cellphones, I need to know everything you can tell me about them. They belong to two Russian agents; my target is a third one. Between them, they're responsible for multiple deaths. I've left them turned on and fully charged."

"No problem with that. It's my afternoon off, I can take a look at it then."

"I'd be really grateful, thanks."

She and Cindy were sharing lunch when Ramirez called. "Willard Perry has agreed to meet you."

"Fantastic! Where? When?"

"There's a small independent movie house in Fairfax. They show classic movies back-to-back. This afternoon at four o'clock they're showing Shane. Go there buy a ticket, the seats aren't allocated so just take a seat in the back row. There won't be a problem - they rarely sell more than twenty tickets for daytime shows. Perry-Greene will come in and take the seat in front of you. After about five minutes, he'll leave by the fire exit. Follow him."

"Is this your plan or his?"

"Mine, he's not going to be challenging for a place in Mensa anytime soon, but he isn't stupid. What he is though, is very, very scared."

"I'm no threat to him."

"It's not you he's frightened of."

She checked the time and saw that she had another hour before she needed to leave to meet Perry-Greene, so she went back to checking Esteban's PC, starting by doing a word search for Cameron Archer and got nothing. Then she ran a search for Bowman, and immediately got a hit in a brief email from Kovzky, *Bowman is the key, but he seems to be difficult to locate at the moment. Perhaps after we've located him, we can persuade him to explain.*

'Maybe Tenor has gone into hiding, because he doesn't trust his support team,' she thought. 'The problem with people in the intelligence community is that they can never say anything like it is.' So, searching for any hidden meaning behind the name Tenor, if there was one would be a difficult and time-consuming business. That was the whole point of course. By the time she had to leave for the cinema, she'd exhausted all the synonyms for the word that she could think, as well as musical references and come up with nothing.

The drive to the movie theatre was over in minutes. She parked in the street only yards from the ancient single-screen film house. It didn't look like it had been upgraded since the days it was built in the 1930s and the ticket kiosk was staffed by a man who looked old enough to have been one of its first customers.

She stood at the kiosk waiting for him to acknowledge her presence until she was forced to ask, "How much are the seats?"

"The seats ain't for sale, but you can buy a ticket," he coughed, laughing at his own joke. "Can't you read?" he pointed at a faded and torn piece of paper stuck to the glass that read, *$10*. "An eagle, ten-spot, dixie, sawbuck, tenner. Been that for twenty years."

She handed him a twenty and told him to keep the change. Then as she pushed her way through the poorly fitting double-swing doors into the theatre, she suddenly realized. *Tenner, not Tenor!*

The dark and dusty building smelled of tobacco and sweat; she understood why it wasn't over-patronized. She took a seat in the back row close to the square hole through which the movies were projected and waited. Tiny flecks of dust floated in the flickering beams of the advert for an ambulance-chasing lawyer that was currently showing. The other five moviegoers seemed to be entranced by the *No win, no fee* claims of Clayton C. Glaser, Attorney at Law currently offering his services.

As the Paramount Pictures Logo appeared on the screen, and introductory music sounded through tinny speakers, one of the two entrance doors opened. A short overweight man in an expensive suit entered, quickly glanced at her and took the seat in front.

The first scene introducing Alan Ladd as the eponymous Shane had barely begun when Perry stood and walked toward the fire exit next to the screen. Saffie stood and followed. Outside she watched him walk nervously toward a late model Audi Q4. He climbed in the driving seat and waited. Taking the passenger seat, she waited for him to speak.

"What do you want?" he eventually asked.

"Believe it or not, I'm here to help."

"Help with what?

"With the jam you find yourself in since the death of Patryk Wilkanowicz or Alfredo Gonzalez as you knew him."

"I don't know what you're talking about."

"Willard, you wouldn't be here if you didn't know what I was talking about, so let's cut to the chase. I'll tell you what I think I know, and you can let me know where I go wrong.

"At some time in 1991, an FSB operative called Juan Esteban lured you into becoming an agent for the Russians by use of an elaborate sting. Unfortunately for him, the plot was discovered in its very early stages, and you were caught in yet another con by the CIA. You were then cajoled into becoming a double agent against the Russian State. The Russians thought they were recruiting you to plant listening devices in State Department vehicles and offices to overhear or record conversations between senior Department officials and/or visiting foreign dignitaries. Unfortunately for them, because their scheme had been uncovered by Wilkanowicz before it had even begun, you ended up becoming a conduit for whatever information the US secret services wanted passed to the Kremlin.

"Over the following years you've been promoted through echelons of importance in your day job until now, where you find yourself Assistant Secretary of State for International Narcotics and Law Enforcement Affairs. I think even you would agree that's barely believable, given your limited talents. However, I suppose it would give the information you pass on a level of believability that wouldn't otherwise be credible. That's if the Russians were ever to discover that it were you that was the source rather than the sucker who was given your name. Of course, over the years you've personally benefitted from this not only by the status you've gained and the salary you've earned, but also from the very generous stipend that the Russians have been depositing in your account in Belize. You'll never need to worry about money again.

"Things were going beautifully until two things happened. The first was when Patryk Wilkanowicz resigned, so could no longer be your controller. A new one was appointed. His name was Cameron Archer, codename Tenner. Now it's your turn."

"How do you know all this?"

"It doesn't matter how I know. What matters is you believe me when I tell you that I am no threat to you, none at all, but there are others that are. Personally, I think you're a treacherous asshole, who was prepared to sell out your country for a few bucks. I think this went way beyond anything you envisaged, and I think you've been exploited by the state, by Wilkanowicz, and by the Russians. Wilkanowicz should have pulled the plug on this years ago. Now though, things have changed. The Ruskies have twigged that's something's not right. They now suspect that it might be you that's been the Deep Throat all these years and not the man using your identity, and that you may have been feeding them a line in bullshit that's cost them money, prestige, and secrets. Am I right?"

"Yes, I'm terrified. But who are you? What can you do about it?"

"Don't worry about who I am for the minute, just know that it's in yours, mine and the country's interest to put a stop to this bullshit before anybody else gets hurt."

"Hurt?"

"Wilkanowicz was murdered, some people held my eleven-year-old son at gun-point and threatened to kill him, and at least eight other people are dead because of this shit."

"Oh God."

"I take it you don't want to continue being a spy."

"No, definitely not."

"Then you need me to help you dig yourself out of the hole you're in. Tell me everything that you know, but I should tell you right now that part of the reason that this kicked off, is because you sent your DNA off to a genealogy site and the Ruskies had sent in a sample of their own."

Perry looked deflated. "When Gonzalez had me change IDs, he sent me for reconstructive surgery, so I no longer looked much like the guy who took my place. Then it started small, placing listening devices in cars, offices and meeting rooms, most of the time I didn't even have to do it myself. Gonzalez would come to me with a list of where they'd been planted or with taped recordings I was alleged to have made."

"But you knew all along it was Wilkanowicz, right?"

"Yes, of course. After they caught me taking money from the Russians, they didn't give me any choice but to cooperate, that's when Patryk revealed that he was in the CIA. At first I was really angry, but after a while I thought he'd done me a big favor. I was making so much money, and the State Department work was interesting even if it was other people doing most of it for me."

"How did you pass on the information you had allegedly ascertained?"

"There was a system of dead letter drops, and dead letter emails. Once the system was up and running I never saw Esteban again, and everything went smoothly. Mostly they would send me instructions of what rooms they wanted bugged, leaving the equipment in a dead letter drop. Sometimes they'd get me to plant incriminating evidence against people who were causing them difficulties. Occasionally Gonzalez would provide me with something to pass on to them that they hadn't asked for. The guy they put in my place was almost my double."

"How did you learn how to conceal the bugs?"

"Esteban arranged for me to attend a short course of lessons. Gonzalez made me tell him everything I'd been taught. He gave me some lessons of his own in what he called tradecraft, he even said I'd become quite good at it."

"So, you began to enjoy the life as a spy?"

"It was exciting, although I didn't think I was in any danger. After a while though, I started to feel guilty that I had a son somewhere and he'd had to make his way in the world without his real dad, so I thought I'd try and find him."

"You did find him, but fortunately for you, you'd decided to use your birth name on the forms, and they sent the results to your replacement, and his details to your son. Thankfully neither play with a full deck and both were too dumb to put two and two together, or you'd be dead by now.

"I managed to intercept most of the mail from Heritage4U, but I think I missed some."

"What made you suspect that something wasn't right?"

"My controller, the one appointed by Patryk before he retired, was transferred to Belarus, and the following week a man came to me and told me that Cameron was being replaced and that he was going to be my new handler. But both Patryk and Cameron had warned me what to do if something like that were ever to happen. I was to expect any approach to include a prearranged codeword. If it didn't, I was to deny all knowledge of what they were talking about."

"Who was this man?"

"He said his name was Greg Sanders. He said he'd leave me alone for a day or two, to give me time to consider."

"So, as far as you know, no-one other than me and Cameron Archer know for certain that you're *Ripple*?"

"Oh God you know my codename."

"At present, as far as I know, I'm the only one that can connect you with that name for certain, other than Archer, if he's still alive."

"What happens now?" the man pleaded.

"If I have anything to do with it, within the next forty-eight hours, you'll no longer be a secret agent, nor an Assistant Secretary of State. You'll have been moved to another part of the country and given a new identity. I don't have any control over that, but I'm optimistic that I won't have left them any choice. In the meantime, take some sick leave, go home and don't answer the phone or the door to anyone without speaking to me first. Here's my card."

"What about my money?"

"Seriously? That's what you're worried about?" She returned to her own car, leaving him to fret about his future.

At home she found an email from Patsy with an attached report of the activity associated with Esteban's phone, and a promise to finish Lipov's as soon as possible. Just a glance at the printed report, and experience had taught her that it would take all her attention and some time to absorb the contents and analyze what it all meant to her investigation but she was determined to tie it up by the end of the week, if only so she could get back to some normal existence with her children.

She called Mary for a catch up and found that they were all in one of the cattle sheds watching a difficult birth being assisted by a veterinarian. She told them not to worry. She'd speak to them the following day.

There were at least two more things that she wanted to do before she turned the investigation over to Ramirez and Daniels.

At present, Esteban was in custody, and it was likely that he'd employ every legal trick in the book to be released on bail, enabling him to skip the country. Saffie couldn't allow that to happen. Neither could she allow the man responsible for Patryk's murder to negotiate some sort of leniency on the promise of some witness protection deal in exchange for information. She needed him to become a target in jail.

The second thing was to positively identify which of the Shelleys in the Senate was Zykov. She hoped that Patsy's phone reports would help her do that.

She'd been forming the beginnings of plans which would achieve both these things.

In the event, Patsy's first report was surprisingly succinct. She'd tracked Esteban's phone activity back two months. In that time he'd only used it to make calls 38 times, some to Lipov, whose number she recognized, but a surprising number to the same phone, another cellphone, always located inside the United States Senate Office, in Constitution Avenue, DC. That other number had fallen silent the day before. In other words, after Esteban had been placed under arrest.

Patsy had highlighted one interesting incoming call; it had lasted only seconds and had come from a different number but from the exact same location as the others. Seconds later, another incoming call had come from the first number in the same location and lasted two minutes. Both numbers were unregistered so there was no way of being sure who they were owned by, but Patsy had given a possible explanation that could connect the two calls.

Working on the assumption that at least one of those numbers belonged to Zykov, Saffie had her own theory about the calls and how she could use it to prove which Shelley had been the caller. She called Ramirez.

"Saffie. Good news I hope."

"I thought I was close to tying things up, but earlier, while I was talking to WPG, a new name came to light that needs pinning down, and there's one more key player I need to positively identify before I can say we've got them all."

"Are you going to give me a clue?"

"We can talk about that when we're not on the phone.

"I'll come over right away."

"Okay, but just you. Leave Daniels out of this for the time being."

"You're making life very difficult for me again, Saffie."

"You'll understand why when I tell you."

It was forty minutes before Ramirez arrived from her home in Clinton, Maryland, and she started talking before the door closed behind her. "Right, tell me who these suspects are," she demanded.

"You can call them suspects if you want, but at least two of them are as verifiably guilty as OJ. The main character is a female US Senator, but I won't say more than that at present. To be absolutely certain I need to set up a sting that involves me being in the room with all the key players alongside you or Daniels, or preferably both."

"I don't know how I can arrange that if you won't tell me who they are."

"I'll come to that."

"Who's the new name?"

"Greg Sanders.

"Sanders? How's he involved?

"You know who he is then?"

"Yes, he's CIA Assistant Director of Intelligence for Russia and Europe, he's only been in post for a about a month."

"What did he do before?"

"He was CIA Assistant Director of Support Services for a while."

"Doesn't Professional Standards come under that these days?"

"I'm not agency remember, but yes, as far as I recall. Before that he was the Vice President's Deputy Chief of Staff."

"Are you kidding me; a senior executive in the White House?!"

"How is he involved in all this?"

"At the moment, he's just a name, so I can't be sure that he's involved, or whether it's someone using his name. The key to this whole thing is Willard Perry-Greene, although he doesn't know it.

"What do you suggest we do next then?"

"If it were me, I'd have Perry-Green taken into protective custody as soon as possible, before he goes in the wind. I don't believe he's one of the bad guys, but he's a key witness, and he's in danger."

"I think I can swing that. Anything else?"

"Get the agency to throw everything they've got into finding Cameron Archer, the missing agent. I don't believe he's dead. I think he's in hiding."

"Why do you think that now, after all you said about him being out of touch for three weeks?"

"I've since heard evidence that the other side are looking for him as well. That would indicate that he's gone underground."

"Saffie, we've got to bring this to an end as soon as possible, but we've got to be careful how we go about it. I'm going to need to take this to Andrea Torres." Torres was Deputy Director of the FBI.

"I think that's the right move, but I don't think you should include Daniels in the conversation."

"Don't tell me that you think she's tied up in this as well."

"No, but I'm concerned that she might have divided loyalties, and she might inadvertently let something out that alerts someone in time for them to make a run for it."

"I think I understand."

She turned to leave but Saffie stopped her. "In the meantime, I need you to get me everything you can on Greg Sanders."

"If there were anything that obvious he would never have been appointed."

"Maybe, but when cross-referenced with Patryk's archive it could throw something up."

"I'll try to get Torres to release Sanders file to you. Will that be enough?"

"I hope so."

After Ramirez had gone, Saffie set about completing her plan to foil any attempt by Esteban to avoid punishment for what he'd done. She picked up her phone, selected a number and waited for an answer.

"What do you want?"

"Mr. Newgate, I find myself in the unusual situation where we could do each other a favor."

"Is this some kind of joke?"

"No, it isn't, I'm deadly serious. I'm offering you a world exclusive on a story that will break in the next seventy-two hours. A story that involves a network of Russian spies that has been operating in our intelligence services for decades and involves a senior politician."

"How come I get to be the beneficiary of this exclusive?"

"Because I need a news reporter who can get this story in the media as soon as I give them the go ahead, and I don't have time to foster relations with someone new. The offer is only open until the end of this phone call, so if you want to take advantage of it you need to say yes now and come immediately to my house."

"Okay, but this had better not be a hoax."

Chapter Twenty-Three
Thursday 7:30am - Dunn Loring

Responding to a late-night text from Saffie the night before, Wolski was waiting for her in the kitchen when she finished her exercise routine. "Is this D-Day then?"

"We'll see. I want to run it all past you first and see if you think I've missed anything."

"What did you manage to uncover yesterday that I know nothing about?"

"Not a great deal, but I managed to confirm a lot that we suspected. However, another name came into the frame that throws a lot of what we thought we knew into a new light."

"Who's that?"

She explained how Greg Sanders turned up in her investigation.

"Is that normal in the CIA, for someone without and intelligence background to be placed in such a prominent position?"

"Not in my experience, but he was moved sideways to ADI from Support Services."

"They're pulling that sort of crap in police departments these days, making accountants and property lawyers into police commissioners. In other words, bean counters and pen pushers with no idea what it's like on the streets," he said with disgust.

Saffie set about explaining her summary of the whole sequence of events to Wolski as if he knew nothing at the start, because that was what she expected she'd have to do for Angela Torres.

"In the late 1980s, Patryk had been a career field agent operating in Central and South America. His operations concentrated on the war on drugs using the cover name Alfredo Garcia. One of his principal adversaries was Juan Esteban. When Esteban discovered Patryk's identity after an operation went disastrously wrong, Langley pulled him out, running a cover story that he'd been killed. Patryk was transferred back to Langley and placed in Russian Section. After a year, Patryk was transferred to Moscow as a junior field agent under the cover name Alfredo Gonzalez. Quite by chance, whilst engaged in the day-to-day activities of his cover identity, Patryk observed a meeting between Wilson Perry, a man he knew to be a junior employee of the State Department, and his old adversary Esteban. Perry was in the midst of being recruited by the FSB as a low-level asset. The agency used their early discovery of that meeting, to engage Perry as a double agent, initially to relay misinformation to the Kremlin.

"Over the coming years Perry was given the codename *Ripple*, and the new identity Willard Perry-Greene. In order to explain his ability to provide such high value intelligence, should his new ID be uncovered, the secret services developed Perry by promoting him, thus, providing him with credibility. However, his cover ID was never discovered, probably because his controller, Esteban, wasn't FSB, but a stringer operating with a profit motive. Nonetheless, the information he was providing made him appear invaluable to the FSB. What they didn't know was that what they were getting was just an assortment of misinformation and low-level or harmless accurate data.

"In 2020, when Patryk was forced to retire, his position as controller was taken by Cameron Archer, and things carried on much as before. Then, in the early months of 2024, Greg Sanders was appointed DDI, and somehow he arranged for Thomas Alexander, a Russian mole, to be made head of Russian Section. Once in position, Alexander posted Archer to Belarus, using that as an excuse to attempt taking control of *Ripple*. Because of Alexander's complete disregard of established protocols, Archer, suspecting that something wasn't right, disappeared to avoid *Ripple's* exposure. Until this time the FSB had been obliged to accept that *Ripple's* true identity had to remain a secret, that would probably have remained the case except three things happened at about the same time.

"First, *Ripple* had developed a conscience, and decided to send off his DNA to a bio-genealogy company with a view to identifying his son, so he could send him some money. Foolishly, he gave the name and work address of the man who had adopted his true identity; confident that he would be able to intercept any mail to his stand in. That confidence proved to be unjustified.

"Second, Perry's natural son (now known as Chester Boggs sends his own DNA sample to the same company hoping to identify his father, because he'd grown to hate him so much that he wanted to hurt him.

"Third: The FSB somehow acquired a sample of *Ripple's* DNA, possibly via a mole within the CIA. Armed with that sample, they'd been keeping watch on bio-genealogy company websites. When *Ripple's* sample arrived, they got a double match. They dismiss Boggs because of age and concentrated on Wilson Perry as the paternal match. However, after observing Perry, they rule him out from being *Ripple*, not least because his work profile wouldn't give access to the sort of information he'd been providing, and probably also because he was intellectually incapable of the task. At this point we can only speculate that the FSB and the mole assume that *Ripple's* controller, Gonzalez had been too clever for them. They decide that the only people who can identify *Ripple*, are his handler Cameron Archer, and Patryk Wilkanowicz who had been DDO for much of the time that *Ripple* had been active. Approaches to Archer result in him going into hiding, so they decide to up the ante and instruct Esteban to begin his campaign against Patryk."

Wolski interrupted her flow, "If the Russians thought that everything they were getting from *Ripple* was bullshit, why not just drop him?"

"Several reasons, the most important was they still weren't certain that his product was false, second they would hope to turn him again, and third because if he were proven to have been giving misleading information all that time, then they'd want to kill him."

"I get it."

She continued:

"Patryk had become somewhat isolated after his retirement, because many inside Langley blamed him for the whole Bannerman affair and the consequential loss of three field agents. Esteban or the FSB must have decided that that his isolation was beneficial and figured that I was the only person likely to help Patryk. That was why they tried to warn me off. Meanwhile, Boggs had contacted Wilson Perry. In their meeting,

Wilson confessed part of the story about his change of ID and indicated that his real father was Alfredo Gonzalez. Boggs didn't know how to find Gonzalez and would probably have given up, but two things happened. First, $10,000 was deposited in his bank account as an anonymous gift from his birth father. Boggs took it as an insult, and it incensed him so much it rekindled his determination to take some sort of revenge for what he saw as his abandonment. Then, when he was approached by Esteban and told that Patryk was Gonzalez, he agreed to become involved in efforts to destroy his life.

"Up to that point Esteban had been using street criminals as his foot soldiers. Then after the ambush of Patryk at Burke Lake Park failed to produce the results they wanted, he decided to bring in heavier hitters and involved Lipov and his gorillas. The crazy decision to try beating information out of Rupert Golightly was destined to fail from the start, but it was an indicator that their sources within the agency weren't operationally experienced. There is no way Golightly would have the first idea how to get into the files in Patryk's archive. They did succeed in coercing him into providing access to the portal. However, the fact that they even knew the name of the *Improbable* operation revealed that their source within the agency was extremely well-informed.

"The raid on the Harrisonburg farm was entirely unrelated to the plot against Patryk. It was instigated by Blenkhorn and Seymour in an effort to persuade me to drop charges against them and save their careers. Boggs hadn't wanted to be involved but didn't have the balls to refuse. They weren't aware that it was Patryk that had made the complaint not me. The attempt to beat information out of Patryk was equally doomed to failure. He was a lifelong professional in the intelligence community, but his adversaries were mere crooks. Patryk would have died before giving them what they were after. In the end, he outwitted them by giving them access to a relatively innocuous file. He convinced them that he'd provided them enough information that if they escaped with his computer, they'd be able to do the rest by themselves. So, when I inadvertently interrupted them giving Patryk a brutal beating, they grabbed the computer and made a run for it. Of course, his security arrangements had precluded a successful hack by those means. That they chose not to kill him at that stage is still a mystery."

"How do you know how Patryk outwitted them?" Wolski asked.

"Because I listened to the recording made by the microphone in his smoke detector."

"How did you get hold of that?"

"I had my British friend hack into Data-Fort's system."

"Is that why you didn't have it shut down as soon as you found it?"

"Not specifically, I needed to know how much of what I'd said had been recorded, as well as what Patryk had been doing."

"Didn't you trust Patryk either?"

"In this business, you learn not to trust anyone completely, but in this case I just wanted to be sure that he wasn't holding anything back."

She continued with her summary. "I'd made an early decision to exclude the agency from my investigations, because it was obvious that it had been penetrated, and I didn't know how deep that went. The mutual cooperation between the agency and the bureau made me distrust the FBI as well, not because I thought they'd been compromised, but because I felt that the information flow between them might be damaging. Out on a limb, I was obliged to use unconventional and sometimes illegal means to gather information. I won't be revealing my sources, so if anybody is intending to bring charges they need to consider the damage it would do the agency.

"It was clear to me that Esteban had not been acting on his own initiative, and I was determined to discover who it was that was pulling the strings. In the last minutes before he died, Patryk authorized me to use his phone and gave me vital clues how to access his archive and open the individual files.

"The information I gained from interviewing Esteban and Lipov was pivotal in providing a clue to the identity of a highly placed Russian agent in our government. Then, using their confiscated phones and laptops, in conjunction with other things I've learned, I have been able to deduce that there are at least three black hat players in highly influential positions. One is now acting head of Russian Section codename *Missionary*; another is a Deputy Departmental Director in the George

Bush Center, codename currently unknown; and third is a US Senator with a seat on an important committee, codenamed *Zykov*.

"Jesus, Saffie that's gonna set the world on fire, but who are you going to tell it to?"

"Angela Torres, Deputy Director of the FBI, I hope."

They weren't given the opportunity to take the break they'd promised themselves, before the gate bell rang. It was Ramirez.

Chapter Twenty-Four
Thursday 2:30pm - Dunn Loring

When Saffie let the Special Agent in Charge inside, she looked flustered.

"I've just been with Torres, she says she's allowed you all the slack she's prepared to, and she's given you and me until the end of the day to bring an end to this or she's sending a team into the George Bush Center herself."

"You and me?"

"Yes. As of now, you're no longer a free agent. If you're not happy to agree to that she'll send a team of agents in here and place you under arrest."

"Just in case there's any doubt, and for the record, if I'm arrested for anything that I've done while attempting to get the country out of the shit it put itself in, then a full account of my actions will be given to the New York Times and the Washington Post within twenty-four hours. Are we clear?"

"I did tell her that's what I thought you'd say…"

Saffie held up her hand. "But as it happens, that's what I was going to suggest anyway. Did you get the information I asked for?"

"Greg Sanders full personal file is on this thumb drive. It's password-protected, and it can only be viewed by using my laptop." She held up a tiny USB flash drive.

"Perfect, bring it through to the dining room then we can get all three laptops working at the same time."

"Three?"

"Yours, mine, and Wolski's."

"I don't know if Wolski should be included in this. He doesn't have clearance."

"Neither do half the Russian State and the FSB, but they seem to have been running riot through the country's intelligence community for thirty years."

"Fair point. Let's get on with it."

Saffie started by giving Ramirez the summary that she'd given Wolski earlier in the day.

"Well, I know who the Head of Russian section is: Callum Peterson, but what about the other two?"

"Wait, what? Callum Peterson is Head of Russia Section? Since when?"

"I think Daniels told me that he replaced Tom Alexander about a month ago."

"Shit. That's one theory blown up. So why didn't Daniels tell me that this morning? Do you know why he was replaced?"

"She said it was one of a number of changes happening as part of a shake-up."

"Whose idea?"

"Greg Sanders."

"Ah, theory partially restored."

"What do we know about Callum Peterson? Also do we know where Tom Alexander has gone?"

"Let me have a minute." Ramirez picked up the phone.

"Excuse me Ma'am, we need some information; urgently. … What's known about Callum Peterson, and where has Tom Alexander been moved to. … Thank you Ma'am." She turned back to the others. "We'll have the information within the hour."

Saffie was looking harassed. "I hope so. Next, no prizes for guessing that the compromised Department Director is Greg Sanders, but we need to confirm that using the information in Patryk's archive."

"And the senator?"

"The biggest maggot in the apple is one of three US senators all with the Christian name Shelley. They are, Shelley Scott-Collins, Shelley Smith, and Shelley Blackburn."

"Great, how do we eliminate the two not guilty ones?"

"I have a plan, and it involves Angela Torres pulling rank, twisting arms, calling in favors, or whatever other metaphor you can think for putting pressure on people to do something that they'd prefer not to."

After describing her plan to her two astonished listeners, they looked at her as if she was mad. "That is either the smartest move I ever heard or the dumbest," Ramirez said.

"What do you think, Wolski?"

"You're gambling on a piece of information based entirely on intuition. If you're right you'll be the hero of the hour; if not, the most important part of the investigation goes down the toilet. Are you planning on telling Torres about this in advance?"

"I don't anticipate being given the choice."

"In that case, I want to be there?" Wolski said.

"That'll be up to Torres," Ramirez told him.

Anxious to get on, Saffie said, "Okay, let's see what we can use to nail Sanders."

Ramirez set her laptop on the dining table, pressed the flash drive into the USB port, and entered her password. "What now?"

Saffie explained how she and Wolski went about it before. Ramirez wouldn't need the utility that Dexter had installed on the other computers because she would only be searching a single open file.

It took a while for Saffie's first search of Patryk's archive to produce just one mention of Sanders, Wolski's search of Esteban's laptop produced none.

"What does it say?" Ramirez asked.

Saffie reopened the file and discovered a record of a meeting in December 2023 between Patryk, Tom Alexander, and Rory Stewart, the then DDI. As the proposed incoming departmental head, Greg Sanders had been invited into the meeting as a courtesy. The subject of *Ripple* had been raised by Stewart, but quickly closed down by Patryk, saying that it was a subject for discussion in a different meeting.

"Is that it?"

"No, that's only the start, but it's an indicator that something could have been said that flagged *Ripple* up to Sanders. Is there a record of that meeting on Sanders' file?"

"None. What do we do next?

"Next, you need to read through his file and flag up anything that indicates if he's used an alias or codename at any time in the past."

"That'll take forever. There are reams of it."

"On your first trawl, you'll find that a lot can be dismissed at first glance. If you're happy for me to look over your shoulder, I might be able to help."

"Have you got a spare monitor we can connect to my laptop? It'll save you getting a crick in your neck."

"Great idea." Saffie hurried to the office and returned with her spare monitor and as the two women began their trawl through Sanders file. Wolski disappeared to make them coffee.

First searches revealed no mentions of Esteban or Alvarez. "What about Moscow, Bogota, or Colombia?"

Ramirez ran the searches. "Nothing."

"Try Vladivostok or Yekaterinburg."

"Okay, but why?"

"Just a guess I suppose. That's where there are US consulates in Russia."

Vladivostok brought up nothing, but Yekaterinburg returned an entry in the very basic part of his personal information. Sanders' mother was part Kazakhstani, and the family had spent some summers in Kostanay, a city in the North of the country and close to the border with Russia. During their stays they would sometimes visit her family in Yekaterinburg just across the border, where he was given the affectionate nickname, Grischa, a short form for the name Gregory or Grigorij in Russia.

"It can't be that easy, can it?" Ramirez asked.

"We'll see. Let me run it through Patryk's archive, while you see if there are other utterances of it in Sanders' file."

The dual searches brought up nothing, but after Wolski returned with the coffees and tried in Esteban's computer the name Grischa brought up over thirty entries. The first was in an email to gmayerislost@gmail.com from two years earlier, it read, *Grischa, good to hear you're still in the game. We'll be able to settle some scores together, even though we're on a different playing field.*

Without context, their exchanges were mostly bland and meaningless, but the connection had been established.

"What about Esteban's phone calls?" Ramirez asked.

Wolski searched the digital record of his texts and found only two with the word Grischa spelled correctly, but several using the spelling *Grisha*. They were all to the same number.

"Okay, let me see what I can find out about that number, and the email address. She called Patsy but it went to voicemail, and Dexter's number did the same.

Finally, she called Digits. Minerva picked up on the second ring.

"Minerva, I hope you're not really busy, I need help urgently. I'm in the room with my associate and an FBI Special Agent in Charge."

"I understand. How can I help?"

"I need everything I can get on the ownership and locations of an email address and cell phone. It's critical to an investigation I'm working on that I need to finalize by the end of the day, and it has national security implications. I've emailed you the details."

"I'll get onto it immediately and feed you what I discover as I go."

Saffie thanked her and ended the call.

"Who was that?" Ramirez asked.

"Someone who wouldn't want to be identified to you. She's British, and Minerva isn't her real name."

"She sounds very young."

"She probably is. Never mind her for the minute. Let's summarize what we've already learned. What was Sanders' mother's birth name?"

Ramirez checked, "It was Mayer."

"So, we have an email that appears to be owned by someone using the name Mayer, which is Sanders' Mom's maiden name. He spent summers in Kazakhstan, and visited Russia while he was there and where he was given the nickname Grischa. Esteban writes to the email owner using Grischa as his introduction, and he uses the same name in a number of texts."

"Looks like you've nailed him," Wolski remarked.

Ramirez wrinkled her nose. "I'll wait until I see what your Minerva has to say before I make any commitment, but you're right it looks pretty sure at first glance."

"What I'd really like to look at right now are the email records of the three Shelleys, but I know that's never going to happen."

"I take it that this Minerva knows that what she's doing is a felony."

"As you're never likely to know who she is and she's in another country the point is moot."

They didn't have to wait long for the first reply from Minerva. It was an email:

Saffie, Email address gmayerislost@gmail.com has been used from numerous locations, but most frequently from 7231 30th Street North, Arlington, VA. That address is also the most frequent location of +1 (202) 906 3725, the cell phone number you gave me. For interest the phone is currently located at 1000 Colonial Farm Road, Langley, VA. Call log attached. Let me know if you need more. Minerva.

"Jesus that was quick! It'd take our techies two or three hours to come up with that."

"Now we know that the phone owner is currently inside Langley HQ. What's Sanders home address?"

Ramirez went to his personal file, "7231 30th Street North."

"If that isn't enough for a warrant, I don't know what is," Wolski proclaimed.

"If warrants were what we were after, I agree. But we can't afford to rely on coordination of multiple suspects, especially when three of them are prominent politicians, two of whom are innocent. The reputational damage could be huge."

"What do we do now then?"

"We wait until I've reported this to Torres. That's what," Ramirez told them. "I'm going to step out of the room now and report back to her."

Once she'd gone, Wolski turned to Saffie, "This is the bit where all your work gets swept up in the Fed's vacuum cleaner, before reemerging with their name it on a few days later."

"Normally maybe, but they still haven't got what we've got, a way to separate the rogue senator from the other two."

"They'll find a way to take the credit. It's what they do."

"To be honest, I'm not interested in the credit, only that the traitors responsible for Patrick's death and trying to screw our country get put away."

Ramirez came back into the room. "The Director says to thank you for your services and to tell you that the Bureau will take over the investigation from now on. We'll be in touch if we need your assistance in the future."

"Fucking feds. I knew it," Wolski said. "Will it be you or someone else that I see on TV, standing on the steps of the Federal Courthouse boasting about the tireless efforts of courageous FBI agents bringing about the arrest of dangerous foreign agents?"

"I'm sorry, Saffie. Nobody understands better than me how hard you've worked and the risks you've taken to bring this about."

"Forget it. I need to see my kids, so you're welcome to it."

Ramirez gathered the laptop and made for the door. When she'd gone, Wolski turned to Saffie. "I could have put money on them doing that. They're all the same.

"Don't let it worry you. Go home have yourself a few tots of JD, or whatever's your poison and relax in the knowledge you just earned the biggest bonus you're ever likely to get. If you're still up for it, I'll see you on Monday and we can talk about that associate appointment.

Within the hour, she'd said goodbye to Cindy and was on the road to the farm.

Chapter Twenty-Five
Friday 7:45am - Mary's farm

The sound of a cockerel crowing woke her. When she checked the time on her phone, she knew it wouldn't have been its first of the day; she hadn't slept this late for years. Hurrying out of bed and into the shower she decided to skip her exercise routine, which was something else that rarely happened.

Appearing at the kitchen door, Mary looked up from her laptop where she'd been studying the farm accounts. "I heard you moving around so I started to prepare you something to eat. The bacon's ready, eggs or pancakes to go with it? You can have both if you like."

"I'm so hungry, I could eat a horse and its rider. Could I go for both?"

"No problem. Sit down. I'll pour you a coffee."

It had been past eleven at night when she'd finally arrived at the farm. The boys were in bed of course, but Mary and Rusty had waited up. They could see how drained she appeared and didn't press her for details, just allowing her to climb almost wordlessly into bed.

Now as she sipped the steaming hot coffee and smelled the first pancakes on the griddle she felt more relaxed than she had since the original call from Patryk. She didn't know if she'd given the Feds enough to make the killer blow, but she'd done all she could.

"Is it over now?" Mary asked.

"I think so, but I won't be certain until I see the arraignments."

"Will they pay you for sorting out the government's business. They damn well ought to."

"Patryk paid me well before he died. Which reminds me, I need to pay Wolski." She lifted her phone and by the use of a few taps, and her fingerprint she transferred some money into her associate's account. "Where are the boys? They should be getting ready for their schoolwork."

"They're out collecting eggs, but it's Memorial Day weekend. Their teacher has given them an extra day because she's going away."

"That's fantastic news. We finally get to spend some time together."

The boys arrived at the kitchen door, each carrying a basket of eggs.

"Mom, are you here to stay?" Ben asked.

"If it's okay with Mary, I'd love to stay over for a couple more nights, yes."

They both cheered and hugged her just as her phone began to ring - an unknown Washington number. She put it on speaker and hushed her children. "Hello?"

"Mrs. Price?"

"That's right. Who's speaking?"

"My name is Meera Desai, I am personal secretary to Francis McKeegan, First Presiding Officer of the House of Representatives."

"What can I do for you?"

"You are invited to meet with Mr. McKeegan and a small private gathering of Senators at two pm today to thank you for your services to the nation."

Everyone in the room had gone quiet.

"Is this a joke?"

"Mrs. Price, I've never been more serious."

"I don't want to be thanked; I just want to spend some time with my children."

"Of course, I should have mentioned that your children are also invited."

"I'm still not convinced that this isn't a hoax. So, if you would, please thank Mr. McKeegan for me but I'm busy."

"But..."

"Have a good day Ms. Desai." She ended the call.

"Did you just hang up on a call from the House of Representatives?"

"I think it was some asshole trying to lure me into a trap. I'm done with that shit."

"But what if it wasn't?" Josh asked.

"I don't care. I'm not interested in listening to some politician spouting insincere bull, when I could be spending some time with you people."

"Finish your breakfast, Saffie. Your eggs will get cold."

Unable to resist the draw of the food, she began to tuck in as she answered questions from the boys. She'd nearly finished eating when her phone rang again.

"Ramirez, I thought we were done."

"What the Hell is wrong with you? You need to be there."

"Do you mean that Capitol Hill thing wasn't a pile of bullshit?"

"I'm not saying there won't be bullshit involved, but I'd have thought you'd have been able to read between the lines. This was the only way that Torres could think of to get all those senators in the same place at the same time. They didn't want to know at first, but when she told them there'd be cameras, they couldn't agree fast enough, especially after it was mentioned your boys would be there. They do love to have their photos taken with kids."

"Will you be there?"

"Yes, so will Daniels. Wolski has been invited too. Surely you want to be there for the grand finale, you're the one with the final piece of the puzzle."

"I guess, but I don't want this turning into the denouement at the end of an Agatha Christie play."

"That might be hard to avoid."

"Get someone to send me the details, will you?"

"They should already be in your inbox."

When she checked her email, she saw the latest was from Meera Desai, it included all the necessary instructions and a wish that the boys would be there.

"What do you think then boys, do you fancy spending the afternoon in an office trying to be polite to a bunch of politicians, or shall we stay here on the farm?"

"What if they don't catch the right person because you're not there though, Mom?" Josh asked.

Ben agreed, "Yeah, Mom; don't let them ruin all the hard work you did."

"Okay then, but we'll need to get a move on, because I need to collect some things from home, and we need to get you looking like you're not a pair of hillbilly kids."

"Can we come back here after?" Ben asked.

"Would that be okay, Mary?"

"I'd be hurt if you didn't."

At one-twenty she parked her car at Union Station, where she'd been recommended was best. They caught a cab to the Capitol Building. Security was bound to be tight after the January Sixth insurrection, and she hadn't been there before, so she didn't know what to expect. However, when she presented the email with the invitation along with her ID, they were admitted and escorted to Francis McKeegan's outer office. Meera Desai stood to greet them.

"Mrs. Price, I'm so pleased you agreed to come. Mr. McKeegan's office is too small to accommodate the number of people, so we've commandeered a meeting room for us today. I'll take you along, just as soon as I get the word that everyone is here."

The boys had been in awe of their surroundings and hadn't spoken since they'd set foot inside the building.

"I need the toilet, Mom," Josh told her.

"There are rest rooms across the hall Mrs. Price," the secretary told her.

She watched the two boys into the gents' washroom and went to use the ladies' herself. She was washing her hands when she heard a man's voice behind her say, "For a woman with two young children, you take an awful lot of risks, Ms. Price."

She looked up into the mirror to see a man who she'd only before ever seen in photographs; Tom Alexander. Her reaction was swift and unforgiving. She spun and punched him hard on the point of his nose, grabbed his wrist in both of hers, and swung beneath their arms. In moments, she had him pressed over a washbasin with blood dripping from his nose and his arm twisted between his shoulders, one of which was now badly misshapen. He cried out in pain.

"If that was meant to be some sort of threat or warning about my children, you came to the wrong woman. I know who you are Tomas Xandru, do you understand me?"

"Yes," he struggled to reply.

"Good, now fuck off." She opened the door for him and as he passed, she shoved him in the back, and sent him staggering into the hall clutching his dislocated shoulder.

A nearby officer of the Capitol Police turned to see what was happening, "What's going on?"

"Mr. Alexander found himself in the wrong restroom and as I helped him to leave, he lost his footing on the slippery floor, banged his nose on a wash basin, and twisted his arm. Are you okay Mr. Alexander?"

"Yes."

"Officer, I think you should find somewhere for Mr. Alexander to rest. I believe that he has an appointment with Mr. McKeegan and the FBI very shortly, and I know that the Presiding Officer would be very disappointed if he weren't there."

The boys came out of the Men's room and Saffie led them back to Ms. Desai's office where they found Wolski waiting.

"You made it then," he redundantly observed.

"Yeah, I hope this isn't just going to be an ego-massaging exercise for politicians."

As she spoke a phone on Ms. Desai's desk rang. She picked it up and listened, before turning to the others. "They're ready for you now. I'll take you along."

"I'll just take a moment to speak to Mr. Wolski, if that's alright."

"Of course, I'll wait outside."

When they were alone, Saffie asked, "Are you here voluntarily, or were you ordered?"

"It was more like an invitation it wasn't in my best interests to refuse."

"I get it. Look, I have no idea what the Feebies have got planned, but I have no faith in their ability to do this on their own. You know what I've got that they haven't, so you need to be ready for me to do something to make it go down if I see their plan going tits up. Okay?"

"I got you."

Desai led them along the hall and opened a door. They went through a small antechamber and into a large room laid out as if for a lecture. About twenty people were seated facing the front, but six people at the front were seated facing them. A man in the center of the group stood and began to clap, and the rest of the room joined in. In the front rows, amongst those who rose to applaud, were the CIA Deputy Director of Operations Saul Bernstein, Greg Sanders Deputy Director of Intelligence, Ramirez, Daniels, and Angela Torres.

When the applause had died down, the man in the middle spoke. She recognized him from his photo on the Internet as Frank McKeegan. "Ms. Price, please join us with your family, and you too Mr. Wolski."

Saffie was already pissed off. She detested this kind of ritual. McKeegan stepped forward and introduced himself as did the other dignitaries, each maneuvering to claim pride of place in front of the inevitable cameras as they flashed away. Included in the array of great and good, as they saw themselves, were the three senators she'd expected, plus two others she vaguely recognized all of whom wasted no time making themselves known to Saffie and the boys, whilst ensuring they presented their best sides to the group of five photographers.

Finally, she and the boys were allowed to take seats in the front row alongside Wolski. The senators eventually took seats facing the audience behind McKeegan, who was still standing front and center. Nobody had yet spoken to Wolski.

"Ladies and gentlemen, we all know why we're here today," McKeegan said. "It's to recognize the services of an extraordinary woman. A woman who at great risk and personal sacrifice to herself, and without thought of reward has uncovered a plot that has put the country's intelligence services at great risk.

"I'm not allowed to tell you the fine detail of how she accomplished this remarkable feat, and to be truthful, I'm not even allowed to know most of it myself." He paused for a laugh that struggled to materialize and then droned on for another ten minutes before saying, "The nature of this work, is so confidential that this small gathering, is being held out of the public eye. Nonetheless that does not diminish the importance of the occasion. So, you'll understand, when I tell you that in recognition of her work, the President has authorized the award of the National Intelligence Cross to Saffron Price. Saffron, please join me."

The applause began again, and she stepped forward. McKeegan shook her hand and reached up to pin the medal to her jacket and whispered, "Ms Torres tells me that you know what to do next." He shook her hand again, stepped away and joined the applause. "Perhaps you'd like to say a few words."

Momentarily stunned, she turned to the audience. After a lifetime of remaining under the radar for a living, public speaking wasn't something she had any experience of. She wasn't nervous, just unsure of what she should say, so she paused to gather her thoughts.

"Um…I didn't get involved in this because I wanted recognition. I responded to a call for help from a man who I loved and respected.

Patryk Wilkanowicz was someone who spent a lifetime in the service of his country, and if there was to be an award ceremony today it would have been more fitting if it had been for him rather than me. Patryk was my mentor, confidante, and friend. He remained so until his death, apart from a brief hiatus caused more by those around him than himself. That he should have had to come to me for help says more about the organisation he'd worked for than it does about me.

"As an agent, in order to come to the conclusions that I have about who was responsible for the attack on Patryk's integrity and the country's intelligence community, I would have had access to a wealth of resources and a team of professionals. However, without those, I've been obliged to step outside the constraints of procedure and sometimes even the law. I make no apologies for that. That I've succeeded in uncovering a network of foreign agents operating within our intelligence service is a testament as much to those that assisted me as anything. I include in that my associate, Jan Wolski, who has remained scrupulously within the law throughout.

"Most of you will be aware that many arrests have already taken place, what you won't know is that there are number of offenders that remain at large because they haven't yet been identified. You'll be pleased to hear that I now have the means to identify them, and you'll be surprised to learn that at least two of them are in the room with us today. My problem is that whilst I believe I know which of you they are, I haven't yet had the opportunity to prove my suspicions."

She paused to allow the hubbub of remarks among the audience to settle. Then she nodded to Torres, who typed something into her phone. As six men wearing FBI over jackets silently filed in and lined up at the back of the room, Saffie continued. "Fortunately, I believe I may now have that opportunity." She took a cellphone from her pocket. "This is a phone I took from Juan Esteban, a Russian agent with the codename *Black Wattle*, who has been operating unhindered in the country for at least thirty years. I've had it analyzed and learned a great deal from the results. I'm hoping for your indulgence while I conduct a little experiment. I'm going to use it to call some numbers, and we'll see if anything happens. In the meantime, please don't interfere with phones in your pockets or bags. The first number belongs to an agent I've identified as having the codename *Grischa*. Can I ask you all to be silent for a few moments.

Saffie sensed that all in the room were holding their breath until they heard the faint sound of a phone vibrating. People looked around attempting to identify the source. "Mr. Sanders, I believe that's your phone, isn't it?"

"It's my office trying to contact me," he stuttered.

"If you'll just hand it to the FBI agent at your side, we can verify that."

He could see that he had little choice and the agent took the device.

"Who does the phone say is calling?" she asked the agent. "Is it his office?"

The agent took the phone and told her it was someone called Alvarez.

"Answer it for me, would you?"

The move established that it was Saffie calling.

Torres stood and ordered two of the agents to arrest him. They cuffed him and led him from the room.

"Thank you, Ms. Torres. If it's okay with everyone I'll continue now."

Before she could speak again, one of the women behind her spoke, "I'm sorry, Mr. McKeegan. I'm too busy for parlor games. You'll have to excuse me."

"I have no need to detain you for more than a few more seconds, Senator. Please bear with me."

A phone in the senator's bag began playing the Mission Impossible theme tune. Saffie smiled, "Are you going to get that, Senator Scott-Collins. or am I? Maybe you'd prefer me to call you by your codename *Zykov*, or perhaps *Kovzky*?"

McKeegan snatched the bag from the senator's hand, removed a phone and announced, "*Black Wattle*."

Two more agents did the honors and led Shelley Scott-Collins protesting out of the room.

"Dear God, I never thought I'd see the day a US senator was arrested in The Capitol for treason. Is it over now?" McKeegan said.

The room was now in turmoil with many people standing and talking animatedly among themselves.

"Possibly," she replied, and turned to the room. "Ladies and gentlemen, please forgive me for turning what should have been a dignified ceremony of gratitude into a floor show, which wasn't my intention, but if I could ask for your patience for just a few more minutes, I would be very grateful. I want to try one more number. It doesn't relate to a particular codename, nor to any specific illegal act, but I believe it might indicate suspicious activity."

The room fell silent. Saffie selected a number from the phone, and the voice of Steve Holy singing *Good Morning Beautiful* sounded from April Daniels' purse. The woman exploded out of her seat, scattering nearby audience members and knocking chairs over as she made for Saffie. "Fuck you bitch!" she yelled.

She was less than ten feet from her intended victim and clutching a vicious-looking black knife when Wolski thrust out a foot and tripped the charging woman, sending her sprawling at Saffie's feet. Wolski was on her before she could move. He restrained her until the remaining FBI agents could take over. She didn't go quietly. She fought, and shouted expletives until a pair of Capitol PD officers arrived to help out.

Turning to McKeegan, she said. 'I think it's over now, sir. Sorry for all the trouble. I wasn't expecting that reaction." She gathered her sons, "Are you boys okay?"

"We're okay, Mom," Ben assured her, "I thought it was going to be boring, but it was brilliant."

"It was a bit scary at the end," Josh admitted.

Saul Bernstein, the DDO came up beside her, "Can you spare me a minute, Ms. Price?"

"Sure, what can I do for you?"

"I'm sure you found that all very entertaining, but you humiliated the agency with that little cabaret act. All that could have been discreetly achieved by using traditional investigative methods. The agency has a long memory. We won't forget that in a hurry."

"Those traditional methods you speak of, would they have been supervised by a mole in the agency appointed by you to Head the Russian Section, or supervised by another mole such as the Deputy Director of Intelligence, and maybe overseen by yet another compromised officer in Professional Standards. Yeah maybe if I'd handed over the evidence I had to the FBI a day or two ago, the same result could have been achieved, and waited for them to come to the same conclusions using traditional methods, maybe not. In the meantime, God knows how much more damage could have been done, and how many of them would have gone on the run? At the moment you've got an agent in hiding in a war zone, because your agency couldn't protect him. Why not concentrate on finding him rather than trying to place the blame for the agency's failings on someone who just spent two and a half weeks trying to rescue it?"

"I don't approve of your methods, Ms. Price."

"Like I give a fuck. Piss off. I need to get on with my life."

The pompous Bernstein walked away without further comment, and McKeegan, who'd been watching nearby approached.

"I had hoped there'd be a short reception where we could learn a little more about you and what you did, but I sense that it would be inappropriate now."

"You're right, sir. I doubt anybody's ready for polite conversation after that. I'm not allowed to talk about most of it anyway. You've been used to enable this charade to take place today. It wasn't my idea, and had I been asked I'd have found another way to go about it. I apologize."

"No matter, it livened up what would have otherwise been a tedious end to the week. Don't leave without the box for your medal, it's on the table over there."

297

They shook hands and Ramirez joined them, Saffie noted that most of the attendees had already left, including Torres and the remaining senators.

"There will need to be a full debrief about this, Saffie. You know that don't you?"

"Of course."

"You'll need to hand over all the evidence you've retained."

"I know that too, and I'll be happy to do it, except I won't be explaining how to get into Patryk's archive."

"They'll probably try and fight you over that."

"That's as maybe, but the result will be the same. What's more, I won't be answering any questions until Tuesday. It's Memorial weekend, and I need to spend time with my family."

"Before you go, can you just explain how you figured out Daniels. That phone number you called her on wasn't one that we had."

"It wasn't in Esteban's phone either, until I put it there, but I found the number in Scott-Collins' phone log. Analysis indicated the predominant location that its calls were made from, coincided with those frequently made by Daniels in her calls to me and others."

"It wouldn't have been an indication of wrongdoing though?"

"I know that, and I have no evidence that she's directly involved, and until today none that she had been in a relationship with a now proven Russian agent. However, I think her reaction this afternoon speaks volumes on its own."

"Did you know that it was Scott-Collins beforehand?"

"I strongly suspected, but I couldn't be certain."

"Why suspect her in particular?"

"We'd found an incident, where two consecutive calls to Esteban's phone came from different numbers in the same location, moments apart. The first of the calls only lasted three seconds, the next one, three minutes. My supposition was that they were from the same caller, and that they'd inadvertently used the wrong phone to make the first call and ended it immediately when they realized what they'd done."

"How did that help eliminate any of the three 'Shelleys'?"

"Because I'd compared the call history of the other phone with all three Senators' diaries, and on one occasion, Senator Blackburn was out of the country. Senator Smith's diary was recorded as attending a meeting in the White House, but the minutes of the meeting said she had cried off because her son had been taken ill."

Ramirez smiled and shook her head in admiration, "If you've downloaded Daniels' call logs, does that mean you did mine as well?"

"Yes."

"You weren't kidding when you said you'd broken the law, were you?"

"I assure you, that if those in the tall seats decide they want to do something about that, it won't turn out to have been in their best interests."

"You're a dangerous woman, Ms. Price."

"You'd better believe it, Agent Ramirez, as I've told you before."

Before they left she caught Wolski to thank him for his timely intervention.

"No problem, I didn't want anyone making holes in my new boss before I even started work."

"How did she even get that knife through security?"

"It was ceramic; wouldn't be picked up by a metal detector."

"It will have to be Wednesday before we have our tete-a-tete. Are you still okay with that?"

"What, after you just gave me a million bucks? You bet your life I am. Anyway, where else am I gonna get this sort of entertainment and get paid. What do you do for an encore?"

Saffie laughed, "I can't guarantee that it will always be this active."

She and the boys were escorted from the building. When they returned to the car she tossed the medal on the back seat where Joss grabbed it and reverently placed it in the box that he'd rescued before they left.

They were back at the farm by six pm where the boys excitedly related the afternoon's events to Mary and Rusty.

"I didn't understand a lot of it, but it looked as if Mom made them all look stupid," Josh told them.

"And she told the head of the CIA to piss off," Ben added.

Epilogue

The following day a report credited to Brian Newgate of the Mclean Register was syndicated to all the major press and media outlets.

A whistleblower from within the George Bush Center for Intelligence disclosed the successful conclusion of an operation to break a ring of spies. Senator Scott-Collins, along with CIA Agents Sanders, Alexander, and Daniels were named among those arrested on suspicion of being part of a group of Russian agents that had been operating in the country's intelligence community for many years.

The arrest of the traitors had only been possible because of the efforts of FBI agents, together with a CIA agent codenamed Lemon Tree who exposed the FSB agent at the head of the nest. On the promise of a new identity and US citizenship, Lemon Tree had persuaded the spy, who used, among others the cover name Black Wattle, to reveal the names and activities of other network members.

Enquiries are continuing to ensure every member of the network has been caught.

*****

The debrief by two agents Saffie hadn't met before, took place in the FBI 4th Street offices and took most of the day. She'd been accompanied by her lawyer, Franklyn Cohen, and he had effectively stamped on every attempt they'd made to get her to incriminate herself. She voluntarily handed over all the cell phones and laptop computers she'd acquired in the course of her investigation, except for Patryk's. She provided them with printouts she'd made of the call logs, to help explain how she'd come to some of her conclusions.

The agents had tried hard to persuade her to reveal who she'd used to gather electronic data, even going so far as to threaten her with a subpoena. Nevertheless, Saffie continued to steadfastly refuse to give up her sources. In the end she told them that if they persisted, she'd withdraw her cooperation altogether.

When she left, she knew that the way she'd conducted her investigation wasn't compliant with court requirements, so they'd still struggle to get all the convictions they wanted, and they'd have to use those 'traditional methods' to get more evidence if they needed it but Saffie was comfortable in the knowledge that she'd done her best to expose a complete network of spies operating within the intelligence services.

The meeting to agree terms for Wolski to work alongside her went well, and the publicity surrounding the scandal would doubtless allow them to pick and choose which cases they decided to take next.

The following week, the media was full of reports of how a joint operation between agents of the FBI, ATF and DEA, in a series of coordinated raids had recovered hundreds of firearms, seized tons of marijuana and cocaine, and arrested dozens of gang members.

In mid-June Saffie read a small article in *The Mclean Register* reporting the murder in the Pennington Gap Federal penitentiary of a prisoner awaiting trial. She scanned the piece to assure herself that the name of the prisoner was Pedro Alvarez.

Printed in Great Britain
by Amazon